THE EXORCISM OF WINCHESTER HOUSE

THE EXORCISM OF WINCHESTER HOUSE

DOUGLAS WYNNE

Trade Paperback Edition © 2023

The newspaper clippings that appear in several locations throughout this book are reproduced from actual news archives from the era in which the story takes place, were originally published before 1926, and are in the public domain. Courtesy of the California Digital Newspaper Collection, Center for Bibliographic Studies and Research, University of California, Riverside, http://cdnc.ucr.edu More information here: https://cbsr.ucr.edu/CDNC

Editor and Publisher, Joe Morey

Interior by Cyrusfiction Productions

ISBN: 978-1-957121-44-4

Weird House Press
Central Point, OR 97502
www.weirdhousepress.com

This book is dedicated to the victims of gun violence

SHOT IN THE BACK.

Cowardly Murder of a Resident of Sisson.

A Case of Hard Feeling Settled With a Winchester Rifle.

Arrest of a Man Partly Answering the Description of Pete Olsen, the Napa County Murderer.

Special Dispatches to THE MORNING CALL.

SISSON, Sept. 24.—At 4 o'clock this afternoon Nate Defreese was shot by Frank Cochran at the La Grande Hotel. Defreese was sitting in the office of the hotel when Cochran rode up on horseback with a Winchester rifle in his hands. Defreese, seeing the gun, ran, followed by Cochran, who had dismounted. Cochran fired two shots, one of which struck Defreese in the back, passing out at the left breast. Cochran, after the shooting, mounted his horse and rode off to the woods, pursued by Constable Green. At a late hour he had not been captured. The shooting was the outcome of hard feelings existing for several days. Defreese died at 7 o'clock.

LAD NINE YEARS OLD KILLS HIS COUSIN.

Shoots a Young Girl Who Tried to Prevent Him Getting a Rifle.

SEATTLE, April 7.—Details have been received here of an awful calamity which occurred yesterday at Castle Rock, in the southern part of Washington. Roy Hayward, a lad of 9 summers, killed his cousin, Gertrude Davis, a girl of 12. The children were at the Davis home alone, and the boy insisted on having a Winchester rifle which was hanging in a room upstairs. The girl refused to allow him to have it, but the boy, running upstairs, got the gun and turned it upon his cousin and shot her through the head. Death resulted instantly. The parents of both children are nearly distracted.

HORRIBLE SELF-SLAUGHTER.

The Ghastly Work of a Winchester Rifle Bullet.

A wonderful instance of human vitality occurred shortly before noon yesterday, when Frederick Rentschler blew nearly half his head off with a Winchester rifle, and did not die for fully twenty minutes afterward. Rentschler was the Vice-President and General Manager of the Indianapolis Manufacturing Company, and has been despondent for some time over financial matters and trouble with his business associates. Monday evening he carried home a new Winchester rifle, fully loaded, and yesterday morning he did not leave the house at the usual hour. He was alone in his bedroom all the morning, and the first heard of him was the report of the rifle. W. H. Ward, a friend of the family, was sitting in an adjoining apartment, and rushed in just in time to save Rentschler from falling to the floor from his seat on the edge of the bed. From all appearances the suicide had rested the butt of the gun on the floor, placed the muzzle to his mouth and pulled the trigger with his toe. The heavy bullet ranged upward, carrying away two thirds of the teeth of the upper jaw, the nose and a number of fragments of the skull, besides scattering the brains over the wall behind him. Strange to say, Rentschler was still breathing, and after Ward laid him on the bed, it was, as above stated, twenty minutes before his death struggles ceased and a final convulsion gave the signal of death. The mutilation was most frightful, and Deputy Coroner Lane spent half an hour in gathering up the scattered portions of the face and head. The corpse was not removed, in accordance with a wish of the widow, and the inquest will be held in the residence, at No. 625 Ivy avenue. The deceased was a German by birth, 38 years of age, and leaves a widow and three children.

TWO BROTHERS FIGHT TO THE VERY DEATH.

CORDELE, Ga., March 3.—In the public road near here the dead bodies of Thomas and Shepard Wood, brothers, well known and well connected, were found this morning. By the body of one was a Winchester rifle and by the other a revolver. Both men were killed by a Winchester rifle, however, and it is thought they engaged in a fight and that one was killed and the other committed suicide.

This theory is so conclusive that the Coroner's jury has returned a verdict accordingly. These brothers were the best of friends and were almost constant companions. They were rich and prominent in business and social affairs. They owned properties jointly, and were commonly referred to as the "Wood brothers," and were never known to have had a dispute among themselves. They were last seen at Seville yesterday afternoon. There they attended to business matters and left for their home shortly before night. They seldom went armed, and why both of them should have carried arms on this occasion is yet a mystery. Where the bodies were found a horse and buggy also stood, and it is believed that the two men disputed while riding and agreed to stop and fight it out.

FINE ECLIPSE OF THE MOON

The total eclipse of the moon this evening is creating much more than ordinary interest in astronomical circles from the fact that it is the most thorough eclipse of the kind in many years, and that the last total eclipse four years ago, visible in this country, came on a cloudy night and was witnessed but by a few in favored localities. This eclipse will last 5 hours and 46 minutes, the moon passing through the very center of the shadow, a distance of over ten thousand miles.

She moon will enter the penumbra or light shadow at 8:54, enter the umbra or dark shadow at 9:57, the total eclipse beginning at 10:58. The total eclipse will end at 12:36, the moon will emerge from the dark shadow at 1:37 and from the light shadow, closing the eclipse at 2:40 tomorrow morning. The size of the eclipse will be 19.57 digits, the moon's apparent diameter being estimated at 12 digits, and the diameter of the earth's shadow at point of contact being 10,000 miles.

The actual eclipse is generally considered when the moon enters the dark shadow at 9:57 and ends when the moon leaves the dark shadow at 1:37 a. m., a period of 3 hours and 40 minutes.

STRANGESTRUCTURE

The Winchester Mansion Is Still Uncompleted.

ADDITIONS STILL BEING MADE.

Out on the Saratoga road about six miles west of San Jose, the workmen are again sawing and hammering in the work of building another addition to and constructing more turrets on the Winchester mansion and placing in position a large metallic American eagle with wings outstretched, which is to add its share in beautifying the strange structure, so pleasantly situated on a pretty fruit farm of 100 acres. This elegant piece of architecture is the home of Mrs. S. L. Winchester, the widow of the inventor of the world-famed Winchester rifle.

Ten or a dozen years ago the handsome residence was apparently ready for occupancy and the consequent dismissal of the builders, but improvements and additions are constantly being made, for the reason, it is said, that the belief exists when work of construction ends disaster will result, and it is rumored among the neighbors that this superstition has resulted in the construction of domes, turrets, cupolas and towers covering territory enough for a castle' Although no part of the structure is over two stories high, the house is large enough to shelter an army.

LIKE A GERMAN CASTLE.

The house stands in the midst of a large and extremely beautiful lawn. Fountains throw their sprays over figures that seem almost human. Beautiful flowers grow everywhere. Roses, lilies, trees, vines, pampas grass and the rarest of plants of every description help to make a magnificent setting for the buildings which resemble an old German castle with its surrounding strongholds.

There are many buildings besides the house, and they, too, show the effects of the owner's odd belief. Summer-houses and conservatories are made with the most picturesque of pinnacles and there are many unexpected niches where groups of statuary are hidden. Even the barns and the granaries are built with the same prevailing idea and they are full of L's and T's which suggest that they were made in parts and are ready at any time for a resumption of the work of improvement.

The first view of the house fills one with surprise. You mechanically rub your eyes to assure yourself that the number of turrets is not an illusion, because they are so fantastic and dreamlike. And as you approach nearer, others and many others are still revealed in a bewildering spectacle. How it is possible to build on an already apparently finished house and preserve its artistic appearance through so many changes, is a query that no one can answer, but the fact remains that it continues to be done.

PROLOGUE

February 8, 1906

Joe Colton looked up at the Winchester mansion and tried to tell himself the voices he heard on the wind were all in his head. He stood outside his cottage at the western edge of the property watching tattered clouds scudding past the blood moon above the turrets and gables. It was almost midnight, and most of the windows of the house were dark. A few gas lamps burned through the night in the usual locations, but it was the seventh floor tower that drew his eye. Strange lights shimmered and shifted behind the curtains in that room. He believed the scream that woke him had come from that room as well, and the elusive voices now reaching him on the wind.

Mrs. Winchester had locked her daughter Annie's ghost in that tower, supposedly to keep her safe at times when infernal influences surged in the house. Tonight's blood moon eclipse was undoubtedly one of those times, but Joe didn't believe the girl's spirit was more protected in the tower than any of the other poor souls that walked the halls of Winchester House.

He'd worked all over the house as a carpenter in the daylight hours but had sworn to his fellows that their rich employer couldn't pay him enough to sleep within its walls. Fortunately, Mrs. Winchester provided housing on the grounds for senior workers, and the modest cottage suited Joe just fine. The cottage had never felt haunted like the house itself. Now, staring up at the cursed thing under the dark moon, he was struck with two ironies: He was considering approaching the most haunted room of all on the night of an eclipse. And if he could summon the courage to do so, it would be for the sake of a girl who had been dead for decades.

The carpenter still didn't quite comprehend how it had happened, but the fact was, he'd befriended the ghost of Annie Winchester over the course of the few years he'd been employed at the house. Like anything that becomes familiar, he was no longer afraid of her, even if her voice and visage did still make the hair on the nape of his neck stand up with each encounter. It had been some time since the last of these. Ever since Mrs. Winchester had locked her daughter in the tower, Joe's conversations with Annie had been limited to furtive exchanges via the speaking tubes the lady of the house used to call for servants.

Annie's voice was as thin as an onion skin in person, even more so projected through a pipe, so it seemed absurd that she could have woken him with a scream tonight, even from the tallest tower. No one else was responding to the call—no new lamps lighting in the windows, no commotion among the servants. Only the din of shifting voices that he felt certain must belong to other ghosts taking shelter with Annie while the ravenous beast walked the labyrinthine corridors, sniffing at the cracks under the doors.

Had he heard her cry of distress in a dream? There was no denying the connection they'd forged since that fateful day in the grand ballroom when Annie had placed her trust in him. And why should her voice be limited to travel only on the air and not on the winds of her mind? She was, after all, dead.

"What exactly are you thinking of doing here?" he asked himself aloud.

It was a primal impulse, the desire to comfort a frightened child. But Annie was no child. She had died as an infant and grown up in the Winchester house. Technically, she was older than him. *What a strange fact!* But their conversations had revealed that she still possessed the mind of a child. And who could say how the dead aged?

Joe had no wife or children of his own, but he'd come to feel protective of Annie. Sarah believed she could keep the girl safe, but Joe didn't believe that for a minute. *She's a sorceress, though. She's forgotten more about spirits than a hammer monkey like you will ever know. What could you possibly do to protect Annie from what's on the prowl?*

The fact was, he didn't know, and he might get caught sneaking around if he tried. On the other hand, he *had* defended Annie from the thing once before…

At the very least, he could enter the house and listen to the tower speaking tube. Maybe Annie wasn't in distress and it really was all in his head. The voices. The paranoia. He did wonder lately if his sanity was fraying from exposure to the house. Most workers found excuses to leave after a year or so. The money was good, but how well did a man have to be paid to sacrifice his mind? Or his soul?

The wind had changed direction while he stood frozen on the spot contemplating the tower. He saw it tossing the palm trees on the south side of the gardens. If there were voices in the night, he could no longer hear them.

Call it all a bad dream and go back to bed?

Like a fucking coward?

Joe made the sign of the cross and stomped across the dewy grass toward the crescent hedge and the nearest entrance.

The house felt like a ghost ship, the dark wood corridors dead empty. He supposed silence was to be expected close to midnight, and having never set foot in the place after dark before, he couldn't say what was normal. But he couldn't shake the feeling that the servants and secretary, perhaps even the lady herself, lay awake and listened with bated breath for the sounds of strange visitors. Would he hear those sounds as he ascended to the upper floors? Would he hear the cries of distress from the locked tower room that he'd imagined reaching him on the wind? Or would he hear the snuffling and scraping of the roving predator first? And would those be the last sounds he ever heard?

Joe had entered with clear purpose—to make his way to the speaking tube, try to contact Annie, and decide on any further course of action based on what, if anything, she told him. But now, imagining what he might encounter on his way, he found his feet carrying him to the grand ballroom. There were two things he might need on this excursion. It would be best to take them both before climbing the stairs.

He passed other rooms with fireplaces where he could have obtained the first item, but he felt a superstitious attachment to the one he'd used at his last encounter with the beast. There was something ceremonial about the grand ballroom. It had the air of a temple with its stained glass windows flanking the hearth, an aura that also lent power to the rack of fire tending tools. When he stepped into the regal space with its pipe organ and red velvet curtains, he breathed a sigh of relief to find the room unoccupied, his weapon of choice resting in its rightful place.

He drew the iron poker from the rack and turned to go, but there was that second item still beckoning to him, if he dared take it. Indecision held him in place again until he reasoned with himself that taking it didn't necessarily mean using it. Better to be prepared than wanting, if he climbed all the way to the seventh floor.

He found a box of matches on the mantle and struck a flame. The shadows of ivory statuettes nestled among the bookshelves stretched and danced in the wavering light. The crystals of the darkened chandelier glimmered like diamonds in a cave. He didn't dare switch the light on but used the flame to get his bearings and locate the book before the match burned down to his fingers.

There. A red leather spine with raised bands and gold foil. *The Collected Works of William Shakespeare.*

Joe tilted the book off the shelf just as the flame reached his thumb, shook the match out, and tossed it into the fire grate. Then, working almost entirely by touch and what little veiled moonlight reached the ballroom from the nearest windows, he opened the heavy tome to the location of a silk ribbon bookmark. He didn't require light to read by. The text of this particular page might have some significance to Mrs. Winchester, but right now that was no concern of his. What mattered was the silver key tied to the ribbon. It was right where Annie had said it would be.

He fiddled with the knot, anxious to be on his way but not impatient enough to damage the book. When it finally came loose, he slipped the key into his pocket, returned the book to the shelf, took up the iron rod, and hurried to the nearest staircase.

He slowed his step when he reached the third floor, treading lightly on the stairs to evade detection. But he found the servants' call room empty at this desolate hour. If Mrs. Winchester needed anything in the night, she would press a button in her bedroom, which would ring a bell here, rousing the head housekeeper who slept in an adjacent room.

Joe slipped into the office and closed the door behind him.

A network of speaking tubes ran throughout the house. There were rows of holes in the tiled walls of the kitchens so that the lady could call for food from various locations in the sprawling mansion. Other tubes, paired with call buttons for bells were situated on stair landings and places where servants gathered. The carpenters and plumbers were always rerouting the pipes as the architecture changed according to Mrs. Winchester's whims. He knew the port for the tube that ran to the tallest tower well, and now he crouched beside it, his ear cocked for sounds of distress.

Joe had listened at this port on previous occasions when Annie's mother had confined her to the tower. The two of them had conducted surreptitious conversations at odd hours when the office was left unattended. The tube system could be fickle, and if questioned Joe could always fall back on the excuse that he was talking to a coworker in the basement where all of the pipes converged under the house, troubleshooting the network. But his luck had held out, and these opportunities for dialog had gone undetected. Tonight was riskier. There would be no talking his way out of it if he were caught here at midnight. Reluctant to speak into the port, he listened for Annie's voice, but all that came back was a faint and desolate howling of empty air, like the sound from a conch shell.

"Hello?" he said. "Annie? It's me. Are you all right?"

"Joe? It's really you?"

"Yes. I thought I heard you cry out."

"You shouldn't be in the house, Joe. It isn't safe. Not tonight. You should go."

"Only if I know you're okay."

"The beast is on the prowl. It hungers for the dead, but that doesn't mean it can't hurt the living…"

He heard other voices behind hers. A man who sounded agitated, distressed. A woman moaning…a child crying?

"Is someone else there with you?"

"They begged for shelter, so I let them in. But they're *awful.*"

"*Who* is? Who's with you?"

"It doesn't matter. Just go home, Joe. Leave until the shadow passes. You need to–"

A male voice overwhelmed Annie's. *"Why isn't it over?"* he wailed. "It should have ended everything! But it's not *over*. It's *never* over!" The voice was garbled in a way that didn't sound like a byproduct of the speaking tube's weird acoustics. It sounded as if the man spoke through a burbling layer of viscous fluid, and Joe couldn't help imagining shattered teeth in the wreckage of a face. He recoiled from the hole in the wall and tightened his grip on the fire poker. His nightshirt was damp with sweat from running and climbing, but also from fear. It prickled with an electric current over his clammy flesh.

He couldn't leave Annie at the mercy of the demon, and iron had held it at bay once before. If he stood guard at the tower entrance until the blood moon passed, he just might protect her from it again.

But what's locked in the room with her? Can you protect her from that?

He thought he might know who she was sheltering. Not their names, but their nature. He hoped they would leave when the danger passed, move on and find peace. For now, it would have to be enough to put himself between the demon and the door.

The house was a maze, but he'd built enough of it to keep the layout clear in his mind, even in the dark. He bounded down winding passages and clambered up narrow, twisting stairs until he reached the last landing before the final flight to the tower. The air smelled like an abattoir, thick with a miasma of suffering. And something else—black powder.

The silence from the door at the top of the stairs was unnerving.

Clenching the fire poker tightly, he crept up the last flight and put his ear to the door, but the only sounds he heard came from below: a mechanical ratcheting of gears approaching from the last corridor he'd traversed before climbing.

Something heavy thudded against the door making it shake in its frame. The doorknob, engraved with an elaborate Celtic knot, rattled.

"Let me out!" The same garbled male voice he'd heard through the pipe. "I just want it to end! Dear God, let it *end!"*

There were murmurs of protest, a muffled argument beyond the heavy wood. Then again, the man spoke: "Let it eat me, then, if it'll be the end! I just want it to stop!"

The knob rattled frantically on its shaft.

The mechanical noises from below grew louder as their source approached the bottom of the stairs, but gazing down the flight Joe could no longer see the landing. A pool of thick black smoke had gathered there, shifting languidly, sending up wisps and tendrils.

"Annie?" Joe called through the door. "I'm here, Annie. Are are you all right?"

The commotion of voices in the tower room ceased, as if he'd startled the occupants to silence. He imagined them listening for his next move as he listened for theirs.

Joe shoved his sweaty hand into the pocket of his canvas trousers and struggled to free the silver key from the fabric. He slotted it into the keyhole and struggled to make it catch in the lock.

There were sigils drawn on the door in chalk. How had he not noticed them before? They glowed aquamarine in the murk.

"Joe…don't," Annie whispered.

"I just need to know you're okay. Who's in there with you? Did they hurt you?"

"You shouldn't have come," she said. "He's here, isn't he? On the stairs. I can smell him through the door."

He could smell it, too. Something musky, bloody, and burned. Something foul and rancid.

Orange fire kindled in the oily cloud coiled in the stairwell. In its protean light, shapes took form: horns streaming up, a tongue stretching down, eyes smeared wide. A sound like a hoof or a hammer blow struck the bottom stair. The beast snorted, and a nauseating stench overwhelmed him. He gagged and retched, his bile rising with the hairs on his arms. Everything about the presence repulsed him and filled him with a primal urge to flee.

He dropped the fire poker and fumbled with the key in the lock.

Someone was shouting. Maybe more than one voice. He couldn't make out the words. His unraveling mind didn't have room for anything but the imperative: *FLEE!*

At last the latch turned and the door swung inward. The predator bounded up the stairs. The carpenter scrambled and slipped, landing hard on his hip as the noxious cloud crashed over him. He coughed and choked, squinting through the smoke, and glimpsed a shape like the head of a bull, plunging its horns through a figure in the doorway. The monster lifted the impaled figure and gave the writhing body a shake, then stampeded down the stairs with its bloody prize held aloft, like a locomotive carrying the corpse of a man struck at speed down the tracks.

As it passed, Joe saw that the body had been grievously damaged before the flaming horns pierced it. Half of the man's head was gone, leaving a gaping cavity of jagged bone and gory pulp. The one remaining eye stared wide and wild at the ceiling as the ghostly body was carried away into the smoke.

Turning away from the ghastly spectacle, the carpenter's gaze fell on the shadowy interior of the tower room. A white crescent gleamed at the edge of the blood-shadowed moon in the window. In front of it, Annie stood in her plain white dress, staring at him in horror. The most substantial figure in the room, she was surrounded by translucent phantoms: an adolescent girl, an Indian with braided hair, a woman in a blood spattered dress. Each had been blown open by gunshot wounds. The crescent moon emerged from the earth's shadow, and the company faded, but their wounds lingered, imprinted on the carpenter's fractured mind.

CHAPTER ONE

April 18, 1906

Father Diego Montero awoke with a heaving breath to the ringing of bells. He fumbled for his pocket watch atop the Bible at his bedside. Squinting at the black hands through the scratched glass, he angled the watch face toward the scant gray light spilling through the window. It was barely a quarter past five. Too early for the tower bells, though the disruption was a mercy as it had shattered a nightmare in which a snuffling beast pursued him through a labyrinth. As he set his watch down and lay back on the worn pillow, a tremor passed through the walls and floor, as if the monster from his dream growled in frustration at his escape through the veil of sleep. The bells rang on, and now he noticed their discordant rhythm—long tones interrupted by stammering shorter notes, the striker swinging wildly, hammering a mad telegram across the iron sky.

Was the bell even manned? Or had it been set swinging by the same tremor that now shook the wood and plaster of his cell?

Shouting voices across the campus. He rose and hurriedly dressed, watching out the window as lamps were lit in the college building across the grounds.

When he reached the courtyard, he found an assembly of fellow priests milling around, searching the sky as if some sign from above would explain the event, though clearly it came from below. Here in the open air, they need not fear a collapse of the old wood and adobe structure. The giant cross beside the bell tower remained upright, defiant.

When no further tremors followed, the hushed conversation among his brothers rose to a chatter, as if to a man they had stopped listening with one ear cocked for further calamity. Father Diego was inspecting the whitewashed plaster of the main building's facade for cracks when a horseman approached at a trot. The animal was wild-eyed with fear, and the sweaty rider was hardly better composed. By now students were joining the crowd, asking questions for which the priests had no answers.

When the rider had caught his breath, it came out that he'd raced from the Agnews Asylum for the Insane, where aid was needed as fast as could be managed. The quake that had only rung the mission bell and shattered some glassware here had wrought havoc on the four-story brick buildings at the neighboring hospital, sending towers tumbling through the rooftops and floors collapsing into basements. Scores had been killed, wounded, or trapped in the wreckage.

Father Xavier, the senior priest, quickly took the lead, ordering the students to ready as many carriages as they could and load them with first aid supplies and flasks of water and brandy. "Father Diego," he called, "Gather everything needed to administer last rites. Take all that we have, and take Peter with you. *Quickly* now!"

Diego had been staring at the pale sky, where black smoke rose in plumes to the north. The command broke his paralysis and he started for the chapel, but his senior stopped him in his tracks with another order. "Dress first, or you're liable to forget to."

The priest looked down at the nightshirt and trousers he'd pulled on in the dark, then hurried back to his room and traded them for his black cassock, forgoing the cap at the last minute for fear that it would tumble from his head on the frantic ride to the asylum.

In the chapel they filled baskets with communion wafers and vials of wine. The sounds of horses and young men arguing over how best to make haste drifted in through the windows. Diego couldn't help the nagging fear that he was forgetting something they would need at the scene, but he couldn't think of what it could be. His mind kept returning to the black smoke over San Francisco. Was the city burning?

"Father Montero? Did you hear me?" Had Peter asked him something while his mind was elsewhere? Focusing his attention on the young scholastic for the first time, he noted the stark fear on the man's face and admonished himself for not being better attuned to it. Today would bring many encounters with suffering and death. He would do well to remember that for Peter these would be a first, though they would leave a permanent impression on his psyche. How Father Diego treated him in the midst of it likely would as well.

"What is it, Peter?"

"How will we know who can receive the rites? How will we know who's been baptized?"

"We will ask them."

"But what if there aren't enough consecrated hosts?"

Was his assistant worried that some unbaptized lunatic would sneak into heaven on a lie?

"Don't worry, lad. There are provisions for circumstances such as these. All who seek the Lord's grace shall have it. Let us go. The wagons are waiting."

When Father Diego first laid eyes on it, he thought the Agnews Asylum for the Insane looked like a sinking ship whose timbers had been battered by cannon fire. As the carriage rumbled up the gravel drive toward a central tower flanked by crumbling wings to either side, he could see where the roofline had buckled and caved in. The corner of one wing had been shaved clean off and dumped in a pile of rubble. The abundant windows meant to provide light and air for the patients lay shattered in glittering shards on the ground. Wild-eyed men and women ran to and fro, some chasing the carriages and pawing at the horses as they slowed. Most were dressed in whatever bedclothes they'd been wearing when the trembler struck, making it nigh impossible to tell the staff from the patients. Many appeared to be in shock, their eyes glazed over and detached from their surroundings. But who could say for whom this was a daily state and for whom it was owed to this fresh trauma?

Bodies lay on the ground, tended by men and women who may have been doctors and nurses, though their attire gave no clue. Some were covered in blood-stained sheets and breathed no more. Screams, cries, and even mad laughter ricocheted off the brick walls and slouching roof tiles.

Off to the side of the triage area, an orderly struggled to tie an agitated patient to a tree trunk where three others were already restrained. His fellows, still dressed in their night shift uniforms, chased other wandering madmen across the grounds, though it looked as if the prospect of rounding them all up again was doomed from the start.

Diego searched the chaos for an authority figure, but before he could get his bearings on the scene, someone had clutched his sleeve and tugged him over to the body of a dying man sprawled on the dewy grass, his face caked with mortar dust turned muddy with blood. The man's breath came in erratic, labored gasps.

The priest knelt beside him and made the sign of the cross. "Are you Catholic, my son?"

"Baptist," he whispered.

"All right. I can recite the Apostle's Creed with you."

"My last rites?"

"Yes. It doesn't mean you'll die, son. You can receive the rites even if you'll recover, you underst—"

"No time for bunkum, Father. I won't live to see the noon. Feed me the body of Christ."

The morning was a blur, a whirlwind of pained faces and last words. Some of the gravely injured clung to life after he'd finished the rites, others died before the rites were complete. There were those who gripped his cassock with a strength that belied their condition and would not let go. In these cases, young Peter applied compassionate force to extract him. There were those who coughed up the wafer in a bloody spray, and a woman who rejected his offer of blessings with curses when he refused to let her drink the sacramental wine from his flask. And there was a litany of sins that only the mad could produce, some confessions so outlandish he felt sure they must be fantasies.

The work exhausted him when the adrenaline rush of walking onto what felt like a battlefield was depleted. The odors of stale sweat, blood, and human waste clung to his clothes, undefeated by the tendrils of frankincense rising from the thurible Peter swung in his wake.

With a nurse to guide them, the pair worked their way through the bodies strewn across the lawn and then into a gash in the corner of the men's ward, where more lay trapped and dying. Stepping over the rubble and ducking under collapsed ceiling timbers, Diego noted the absence of any steel reinforcements in the brick structure. Despite the grand architecture and extravagant budget, the hospital had been built without sufficient support, and too high to withstand a seismic event of such magnitude.

He ministered to staff and patients alike, and offered prayers for the unbaptized. He watched their store of communion hosts dwindle, and thought of the tale of Jesus with the loaves and fishes, but there was no miracle of multiplication to be had today.

The last wafer went to a man whose terrified face was the only visible part of him, gazing out from a gap between a splintered beam and a heap of broken bricks. A pair of brawny teen boys from a local farm struggled with the debris, but when their efforts resulted in the bricks shifting to crush the man further, they backed off and waved the Jesuits in.

"Do you know his name?" Diego asked one of the boys who'd been wrangling the wreckage. The boy shrugged and gestured at an older man in a sweat-soaked dress shirt. Diego guessed he might have been a psychiatrist.

"Joe Colton," the man said.

"Is he a patient of yours?"

The man shook his head. He looked numb and exhausted. "I'm an administrator. He's Catholic, if that matters."

Joe Colton's eyes had closed. Diego wondered if he'd already passed. A tangle of black hair was plastered to his forehead with congealing blood.

"Joe? I'm Father Diego Montero. Are you with us? Can you speak?"

No reply.

"How do you know he's Catholic?"

The administrator's fist was clenched at his side. He opened it now and showed the priest a rosary of black beads with a silver cross. "He passed it through. Asked me to see that his daughter gets it. I tried to make him keep it until... But he was worried it would be lost in the rubble."

Diego knelt beside the gap. He made the sign of the cross, and recited the Lord's prayer with his own eyes closed, opening them again when the trapped man's voice joined him for the final lines: "Lead us not into temptation but deliver us from evil. Amen."

"I'm here to guide you to the Lord, Joe. Through this holy anointing may the Lord in his love and mercy help you with the grace of the Holy Spirit. May the Lord who frees you from sin save you and raise you up. Have you any sins to confess before you receive the sacrament?"

He nodded and coughed. "Forgive me, Father, for I have sinned. It's been too long since my last confession."

"What have you to confess?"

The man grimaced, working his jaw. Diego thought he was summoning the courage to speak, but then he spat a thick wad of bloody phlegm into the dust. Something inside him was ruptured. "Closer, Father," he said in a frayed voice.

Diego braced his hands on the gritty floor and inclined his ear toward the hole.

"I'm listening, Joe. Confess your sins to the Lord."

"I've collaborated in the Devil's business, Father. God have mercy on me, I've communed with spirits and served a witch," Joe sobbed in Diego's ear. The other men had stepped back to grant the pair a moment of privacy, but a peculiar silence had settled on the scene, and Diego knew they were listening with rapt fascination. Was Joe Colton insane? The priest wished the man's doctor were present.

"Calm yourself, son. Tell me what you mean by that and don't exert yourself. Maybe you imagine you've done something that isn't true."

"No, Father... She's as real as you are. I did her bidding...as a carpenter, and now it's too late to make proper penance."

"Who is *she*? Whom do you speak of?"

"Mrs. Winchester, Father. I built a labyrinth for the crazy old witch. To trap souls and hide them from God. I...thought I could help the girl, thought I could save her, but I couldn't save anybody. This whole calamity is probably from Sarah's demon banging on the gates of Hell."

"It was a trembler, my son. That's all. A terrible one, but an act of God, I'm afraid."

Joe's bloody fingers crawled out of the hole like a spider, reaching for the priest's sleeve, a weak effort to seize hold of him and make him listen. "They say I'm crazy talking about ghosts and demons, about time and space folded up like a newspaper. But it's the house that's insane. She built a wicked thing. And I helped her do it."

"Easy now. You're talking about the rifle heiress with the big estate?"

Joe nodded. It was getting harder for him to muster the breath and strength to continue. He might have mere minutes remaining, and Diego wanted to administer the man's last communion while he could still receive it.

"I...worked for her. She fired me for trespassing."

"It doesn't matter now what you've done, my son. You've confessed it. And the trauma has you confused. How could you be trespassing in the house if she hired you as a carpenter? I'm sure you did no wrong. Ease your mind now and pray with me."

"She caught me talking to her daughter through the speaking tubes. Little Annie. You have to believe me! No one ever believed me."

"I believe you, Joe. Did you say something bad to the girl? Is that what you need to confess? Did you...*touch* her?"

Now the man looked horrified. "Annie's no little girl...She's forty-years-dead. And it ain't right for a man of the cloth to lie to a dying man. You *don't* believe me. I can see it in your eyes, and—" he coughed a mist of blood into the dust, "let's be honest...they're the last pair I'm ever gonna see."

Father Diego took a handkerchief from his pocket and wiped the man's lips. "I'm sorry. I'm trying to give comfort. Confession is a powerful act, Joe. It will purify you for the journey that awaits. And if your confession is sincere in your heart, it doesn't matter what I believe."

"It does, though. I can't make amends once I'm gone. Someone has to understand, or there's no hope for redemption. I could have prevented this if I managed to convince a single soul I wasn't crazy."

"You can't dwell on that. Even if you weren't hospitalized when the tremors struck, you might have been somewhere else that crumbled. All of San Francisco looks to be burning in the aftermath."

"I might have stopped the earthquake from happening is what I'm telling you. This is from the...*cough*... abominations in that damned house. Mark my words, Father. I have proof. And there's men here who have heard it and done nothing about it."

Joe stared at the space beyond the priest, at the spot where the administrator had stood a moment ago. Turning to follow his gaze, Diego saw that the man had moved on.

"The administrator?" Diego asked.

"The man he works for. Abercrombie...the director. Doctor Burchard is in league with him. Keeping my proof locked away same as me. Proof of life after death, Father. A phonograph recording."

Conspiracies and fairy tales. There were other casualties of the accident in need of his aid and comfort and he'd been waylaid by this? He caught himself wishing that Joe Colton would fade.

"Annie's ghost predicted the trembler. She told her mother it would happen like it happened before, only worse this time. And Sarah recorded the warning with a phonograph. She keeps a library of those sessions on wax, but that one cylinder I stole. It's another of my sins, Father. But I took it to warn others."

"Easy now, Joe. Save your breath."

"She's a witch, Father. A sorceress. Obsessed with mystic numbers. The length of every beam we cut, the number of nails in every room. The whole house is built on the Devil's accounting... *Thirteen*...everywhere. The 'key of death,' she calls it. Something to do with a nun and a fish. I've seen her notes laying about." He broke into a coughing fit, having rushed to get it all out.

Father Diego felt a chill spread through his chest at the reference to mysteries that only an initiate would know. He pushed these thoughts aside and focused on the troubled man. Colton's breath came in ragged gulps. His eyelids fluttered as he fought oblivion.

"It's not your burden anymore, Joe. You've confessed your part in it. You can rest now." Turning to his assistant, Diego took the phial of consecrated oil. He dabbed a drop onto his finger and traced a cross on the dying man's forehead.

"Through this holy anointing may the Lord in his love and mercy help you with the grace of the Holy Spirit. May the Lord who frees you from sin save you and raise you up."

He exchanged the oil for a host and held it up to the sun. "This is the Lamb of God who takes away the sins of the world. Happy are those who are called to his supper."

"Lord, I am not worthy to receive you," Colton whispered, "but only say the word and I shall be healed."

"The body of Christ."

"Amen."

Father Diego placed the eucharist on the carpenter's tongue, but the man's mouth remained open. He was already gone.

DEATH AND DESTRUCTION HAVE BEEN THE FATE OF SAN FRANCISCO. SHAKEN BY A TEMBLOR AT 5:13 O'CLOCK YESTERDAY MORNING, THE SHOCK LASTING 48 SECONDS, AND SCOURGED BY FLAMES THAT RAGED DIAMETRICALLY IN ALL DIRECTIONS, THE CITY IS A MASS OF SMOULDERING RUINS. AT SIX O'CLOCK LAST EVENING THE FLAMES SEEMINGLY PLAYING WITH INCREASED VIGOR, THREATENED TO DESTROY SUCH SECTIONS AS THEIR FURY HAD SPARED DURING THE EARLIER PORTION OF THE DAY. BUILDING THEIR PATH IN A TRIANGUAR CIRCUIT FROM THE START IN THE EARLY MORNING, THEY JOCKEYED AS THE DAY WANED, LEFT THE BUSINESS SECTION, WHICHTHEY HAD ENTIRELY DEVASTATED, AND SKIPPED IN A DOZEN DIRECTIONS TO THE RESIDENCE PORTIONS. AS NIGHT FELL THEY HAD MADE THEIR WAY OVER INTO THE NORTH BEACH SECTION AND SPRINGING ANEW TO THE SOUTH THEY REACHED OUT ALONG THE SHIPPING SECTION DOWN THE BAY SHORE, OVER THE HILLS AND ACROSS TOWARD THIRD AND TOWNSEND STREETS. WAREHOUSES, WHOLESALE HOUSES AND MANUFACTURING CONCERNS FELL IN THEIR PATH. THIS COMPLETED THE DESTRUCTION OF THE ENTIRE DISTRICT KNOWN AS THE "SOUTH OF MARKET STREET." HOW FAR THEY ARE REACHING TO THE SOUTH ACROSS THE CHANNEL CANNOT BE TOLD AS THIS PART OF THE CITY IS SHUT OFF FROM SAN FRANCISCO PAPERS.

AFTER DARKNESS,THOUSANDS OF THE HOMELESS WERE MAKING THEIR WAY WITH THEIR BLANKETS AND SCANT PROVISIONS TO GOLDEN GATE PARK AND THE BEACH TO FIND SHELTER. THOSE IN THE HOMES ON THE HILLS JUST NORTH OF THE HAYES VALLEY WRECKED SECTION PILED THEIR BELONGINGS IN THE STREETS AND EXPRESS WAGONS AND AUTOMOBILES WERE HAULING THE THINGS AWAY TO THE SPARSELY SETTLED REGIONS. EVERYBODY IN SAN FRANCISCO IS PREPARED TO LEAVE THE CITY, FOR THE BELIEF IS FIRM THAT SAN FRANCISCO WILL BE TOTALLY DESTROYED.

DOWNTOWN EVERYTHING IS RUIN. NCT A BUSINESS HOUSE STANDS. THEATRES ARE CRUMBLED INTO HEAPS. FACTORIES AND COMMISSION HOUSES LIE SMOULDERING ON THEIR FORMER SITES. ALL OF THE NEWSPAPER PLANTS HAVE BEEN RENDERED USELESS, THE "CALL" AND THE "EXAMINER" BUILDINGS, EXCLUDING THE "CALL'S" EDITORIAL ROOMS ON STEVENSON STREET BEING ENTIRELY DESTROYED.

IT IS ESTIMATED THAT THE LOSS IN SAN FRANCISCO WILL REACH FROM $150,000,000 TO $200,000,000. THESE FIGURES ARE IN THE ROUGH AND NOTHING CAN BE TOLD UNTIL PARTIAL ACCOUNTING IS TAKEN.

ON EVERY SIDE THERE WAS DEATH AND SUFFERING YESTERDAY. HUNDREDS WERE INJURED, EITHR BURNED, CRUSHED OR STRUCK BY FALLING PIECES FROM THE BUILDINGS AND ONE OF TEN DIED WHILE ON THE OPOPERATING TABLE AT MECHANICS' PAVILION IMPROVISED AS A HOSPITAL FOR THE COMFORT AND CARE OF 200 OF THE INJURED. THE NUMBER OF DEAD IS NOT KNOWN BUT IT IS ESTIMATED THAT AT LEAST 500 MET THEIR DEATH IN THE HORROR.

AT NINE O'CLOCK, UNDER A SPECIAL MESSAGE FROM PRESIDENT ROOSEVELT, THE CITY WAS PLACED UNDER MARTIAI LAW. HUNDREDS OF TROOPS PATROLLED THE STREETS AND DROVE THE CROWDS BACK, WHILE HUNDREDS MORE WERE SET AT WORK ASSISTING THE FIRE AND POLICE DEPARTMENTS. THE STRICTEST ORDERS WERE ISSUED, AND IN TRUE MILITARY SPIRIT THE SOLDIERS OBEYED. DURING THE AFTERNOON THREE THIEVES MET THEIR DEATH BYRIFLE BULLETS WHILE AT WORK IN THE RUINS. THE CURIOUS WERE DRIVEN BACK AT THE BREASTS OF THE HORSES THAT THE CAVALRYMEN RODE AND ALL THE CROWDS WERE FORCED FROM THE LEVEL DISTRICT TO THE HILLY SECTION BEYOND TO THE NORTH

THE WATER SUPPLY WAS ENTIRELY CUT OFF, AND MAY BE IT WAS JUST AS WELL, FOR THE LINES OF FIRE DEPARTMENT WOULD HAVE BEEN ABSOLUTELY USELESS AT ANY STAGE. ASSISTANT CHIEF DOUGHERTY SUPERVISED THE WORK OF HIS MEN AND EARLY IN THE MORNING IT WAS SEEN THAT THE ONLY POSSIBLE CHANCE TO SAVE THE CITY LAY IN EFFORT TO CHECK THE FLAMES BY THE USE OF DYNAMITE. DURING THE DAY A BLAST COULD BE HEARD IN ANY SECTION AT INTERVALS OF ONLY A FEW MINUTES, AND BUILDINGS NOT DESTROYED BY FIRE WERE BLOWN TO ATOMS. BUT THROUGH THE GAPS MADE THE FLAMES JUMPED AND ALTHOUGH THE FAILURES OF THE HEROIC EFFORTS OF THE POLICE FIREMEN AND SOLDIERS WERE AT TIMES SICKENING, THE WORK WAS CONTINUED WITH A DESPERATION THAT WILL LIVE AS ONE OF THE FEATURES OF THE TERRIBLE DISASTER. MEN WORKED LIKE FIENDS TO COMBAT THE LAUGHING, ROARING, ONRUSHING FIRE DEMON.

The Call=Chronicle=Examiner

SAN FRANCISCO, THURSDAY, APRIL 19, 1906.

EARTHQUAKE AND FIRE: SAN FRANCISCO IN RUINS

CHAPTER TWO

"Fiends battling a demon, eh? It's awfully breathless writing." Father Xavier folded the newspaper and tossed it on the table between the coffee cups.

Diego snapped out of his own musings at the sound of paper smacking wood.

"*You're* in your own world today."

"I almost wish I were," Diego muttered. "Were you not moved by the horrors we witnessed yesterday? It's a wonder there's any newspaper to read at all."

"True. The delivery boy said it was printed on a press borrowed from a paper in Oakland. Of course I was moved by the suffering. But do *you* not take comfort from how many souls we ushered into paradise?"

Diego nodded. "A painful passage for most. I hope they were well received."

Father Xavier took a sip of his coffee and leaned forward. He clapped Diego on the shoulder. "I can promise you that more of them were than at the last massacre I witnessed. Glorieta Pass, 1862."

"I didn't know you were a priest in the war."

Xavier grunted. "I carried a rifle, not a rosary. And last rites were for a lucky few. You did your best, Diego. Take some solace in that. And remember: those who died at the asylum were suffering long before disaster struck. The Lord has released them from that."

Diego stared at the skin of milk that had congealed on the surface of his coffee before it had cooled, untouched. "I heard the survivors are living in tents."

"The ones they could round up are. There will be lunatics roaming the valley for years. Try not to forget that in the course of your daily errands."

Peter appeared in the doorframe. Now *there* was a face haunted by the horrors of the previous day. Had the lad slept at all? "Excuse me. There's someone here to see you, Father Diego. A doctor from the Agnews Asylum."

"He asked for me by name?"

"Yes, Father. He's waiting in the chapel."

Diego excused himself from the breakfast table. Father Xavier watched him leave without comment, though it was obvious the old man was musing on what harm Diego might have done the previous day that would cause a doctor to make the trip to the mission. Surely there was much urgent business to attend to at the asylum in the aftermath of the disaster.

In the chapel, Diego found the doctor stooped over a statue of Saint Clara, whom the valley had been named after. The man's hands were in his trouser pockets, a posture that to Diego signaled an attitude of arrogant curiosity. The sound of the door creaking open did nothing to alter the man's posture, though he turned and offered a smile and a handshake when the priest drew near.

"Father Montero. Thank you for making time for me. I'm Dr. Evan Burchard."

"From Agnews, yes. Peter told me. How may I be of assistance?"

"You already have been. I wanted to personally thank you for comforting so many of our patients in their hour of need."

Diego nodded. "We were fortunate, in a way, to be so close when the call for aid came. As you can see, the mission was largely spared. But it was the young men from our college who were the real heroes of the day. They extracted many of the injured from the wreckage."

"And I plan to pay my thanks to them as well before I return."

Diego smiled. An awkward silence filled the space. At last he said, "You needn't have come all this way to convey your thanks, Doctor. I'm sure you have much to attend to."

The doctor shrugged. "My surviving patients are in good hands. The care that I provide will be needed more when the dust has settled. In fact, that's partly why I'm here. Your students and clergy were exposed to some terrible sights yesterday. I know the church can provide some solace for the traumatized, but if there is any aid our psychiatrists can offer to return the favor…"

"I see. That's kind of you. I will be sure to pass the offer on to Father Xavier. He's the senior priest here at the mission. I was told you'd asked after me by name, but I'd be happy to introduce you."

"Perhaps before I leave. But there is another matter I wish to speak with you about. You tended to one of my dearest patients at the moment of his passing. A man by the name of Joseph Colton, though I'm told you ministered to so many, I don't expect you to remember them all by name."

"I remember Joe."

"He was a very troubled man. I regret that I didn't have more time to help him find peace of mind in life. Perhaps you helped him to find it in death."

"I imagine it's hard for any man to face sudden death with peace of mind."

Dr. Burchard expelled a sharp breath through his nose, not quite a laugh. "I suppose that's true. I like to imagine I'll have time to prepare myself, but we never know, do we?"

"Are you a religious man, Doctor?"

"Not especially. I try to remain open-minded, but my mortality is something I'll have to come to terms with using the tools of my own vocation."

"Well, thank the Lord you were spared yesterday. Were you at the asylum when the trembler struck?"

"At five in the morning? No. I was at home in bed. The roads were impassible. By the time I arrived, many of my patients were lost. It's hard to swallow…that lack of resolution. So much unfinished business."

"You seem especially troubled by the death of Joe Colton. I sense there's more that you wish to ask me about his death, but you're reluctant to speak plainly."

Dr. Burchard spun his wedding ring with the fingers of his right hand. Diego observed that one need not be a psychiatrist to recognize a nervous habit.

"Did Joe say anything about Mrs. Winchester?"

"Yes. He was quite agitated about her."

"Right to the end, then. He was obsessed with her and her strange, rambling house. It was the reason for his commitment. And I know there has been all manner of gossip and speculation about her own obsession–her endless building project. But as I understand it, she's considered a generous employer to her staff and the small army of carpenters Mr. Colton was a part of. The widow may be eccentric, but I believe she is entitled to her privacy."

Again, Diego nodded. "I've heard that she's dedicated a good deal of the Winchester fortune to philanthropy. Has she donated to the Agnews Asylum?"

"Indeed she has. And it would be distressing to the board of directors if the delusional ravings of a patient once employed by her were to find their way to the tabloids. I'm sure you understand."

Diego straightened his spine. "Confession is as confidential as therapy, Doctor Burchard. I take offense at what you're implying."

"You asked me to speak plainly, Father. Now, I don't mean to question your integrity at all—"

"Good."

"But I understand that your assistant, the young priest who summoned you for me today, was also privy to Joe's confession."

"Peter is trustworthy."

"That's reassuring, because some of these papers pay a handsome fee for gossip about lurid subjects."

"And what subjects would those be?"

"Tales of seances and such. Allegations of witchcraft and dealings with the Devil. We've all heard the stories. Mrs. Winchester has been plagued with wild claims ever since she moved to the valley. Rumors that the strange, labyrinthine architecture of her home is meant to evade the vengeful spirits of the dead killed by Winchester rifles. To the enlightened man of science, such allegations are patently absurd. But...for men of the cloth, claims of the supernatural might even seem credible. So my advice is that you should take anything Joe Colton told you in his fevered final moments with a large grain of salt."

"I understand your concerns. And they must be quite urgent to you if you feel that the person most in need of your protection this morning is Sarah Winchester. I will only say this: I have a duty to take a man's confession seriously if he believes he has committed a mortal sin. But honestly, the most intriguing thing about Joe's confession was that he claimed to have physical proof of a ghost. All gossip and politics aside, I must admit that is of great professional interest to me."

"Proof?"

"A wax cylinder recording made at the Winchester House. He said it was in your possession for safekeeping."

"Did he also tell you that this recording was the source of his rift with her? That she fired him after accusing him of stealing it?"

"No."

"Apparently she made a number of such recordings of seances. One went missing."

"Do you have it?"

Dr. Burchard gazed up at the ceiling mural—angels flanking the risen Christ among the clouds—and sighed. "You must understand that because Mrs. Winchester is a patron of the hospital, the director—my boss—feels protective of her. She is more than a neighbor. She holds shares of one of the most successful manufacturers in the country. If the rumors of her odd beliefs and practices were supported by a recording... it could severely damage her reputation. And given her immense wealth, there are surely some who might even seek to blackmail her. *If* such a recording existed."

"Joe said the spirit heard on the recording warned Mrs. Winchester of the earthquake."

"I've told you, Father: I don't believe in spirits."

"Not even if you heard one prophesy something that later came to pass?"

"Belief is a powerful hallucinogen. People hear what they want to hear. Especially people like Joe Colton."

"So there *is* a recording," Diego pressed.

"There's a recording of...*something*. Likely a hoax. Someone projecting their voice."

"I'm only asking to judge it with my own ears."

Burchard shook his head. "I don't know you well, Father, but in my experience, priests tend to indulge in the one vice the good Lord allows them. The next thing you know, they're sermonizing into the bottom of a bottle at the local saloon."

The Jesuit laughed. "You're not wrong. But I'm afraid there aren't any saloons left standing after yesterday."

Father Diego had always been attracted to the intersection of science and religion. He didn't need evidence to have faith, but if evidence came to light that proved his articles of faith, or more importantly helped others to shake off the shackles of skepticism...that would be a powerful thing. Still, the doctor had heard this recording and he at least *claimed* to be unmoved by it.

"Might I judge this recording for myself? I'm an educated man, Dr. Burchard. If your patient was delusional about its contents, I will recognize that, and you won't have to worry about my imagining there's something there that simply isn't. But keeping it from me only throws fuel on the fire of my imagination. Treat me as a colleague. Please. Indulge my professional curiosity and perhaps I will even have something to contribute to your own understanding."

"Of what? Spirits?"

"Of Joe Colton's mind at the least."

"You make a persuasive case, Father Montero. But the truth is, the earthquake may have decided the fate of the recording already. I haven't been allowed back to my office yet, but I'm told the damage could be considerable. If you have no pressing business today, you're welcome to join me on the ride back. We can find out together if there's anything for you to listen to."

When Dr. Burchard's carriage reached the asylum, they found the place in a more orderly state than the day before. There were still workmen clearing debris, but the search for survivors was over, the bulk of the rubble and wreckage gathered into heaps. A line of white canvas tents had been erected on the lawn to house the remaining inmates, and even their vocalizations were more subdued than when Father Diego had left the previous evening. Perhaps the midday heat had a sedative effect, or the exhaustion of the disaster had provided the same, but the wailing and shouting had given way to moaning, weeping, and even soft singing that mingled with the birdcalls in the trees.

The doctor led the priest through a side entrance of the main building. They encountered no orderlies, but soon came upon a foreman directing laborers filling wheelbarrows with broken bricks and carting them out the main entrance. Burchard conferred with the man, who asked the location of his office.

"South corner, you say? Getting the doors open to check those rooms was the hard part, but believe it or not, they were mostly spared. There's no basement under that section, so you don't have to worry about the floor giving out. Tread carefully on the way there, though." The man coughed and spat brick dust on the tile floor. "Least you've got a priest if you need one." He laughed at his own wisecrack as the pair proceeded down the hall.

The door of Burchard's office hung ajar at a cockeyed angle. The oak slab was wedged against the buckled floor in its cracked frame, but the gap was wide enough to squeeze through.

The ceiling had fractured in a web of jagged lines, raining plaster dust on the furniture and rug. Diego followed the fault lines with a wary eye, while Burchard picked through sheaves of paper on his desk, shaking them out, and blowing puffs of dust from them. Framed photos and certificates were hung askew where they hadn't tumbled to the floor and shattered.

The doctor fished a key from his pocket and unlocked a filing cabinet in the corner. He removed what looked like a suitcase from the bottom drawer and set it atop his desk. The lid was emblazoned with the words *Edison Home Phonograph* in gold leaf. A stubby hand crank protruded from the right side. Burchard popped the latches and removed the lid to reveal a shiny black control surface with a steel spindle.

"I hope the trembler didn't put the device out of alignment. I rely on it to record sessions with my patients."

"Like Dr. Seward's voice journal in the novel *Dracula*," Diego said.

Burchard scrunched his dark eyebrows at the reference. "I've heard of the book, but not read it. Is this Dr. Seward a psychiatrist?"

"Yes. In London. Although, now that I think of it, he records his observations after the fact, not the patient's voice directly."

"I see. I find the direct recording allows me to devote my attention to my subject's emotions, rather than scribbling shorthand while they talk."

"The machine itself isn't a distraction to them?"

"Quite the contrary. The monotonous rhythm tends to be less troublesome to them than the scratching of my pen. It also gives me a verbatim record and mitigates their worry that I may be judging or commenting on their words."

"But isn't it your job to judge their condition?" Diego asked.

"To diagnose; not to judge."

"Then we have something in common. We both hear confessions without judgment."

"I suppose that's true enough," Burchard said. "Though the higher authority in my profession is a body of knowledge. In yours, it's…"

"The same."

"I was going to say *God*."

"I imagine we both rely on the authority of a book and consultations with our superiors to decide how best to help heal a man's wounds."

Burchard absorbed this. "I hadn't thought of it that way before." He took a funnel horn from the filing cabinet and screwed it into place on the phonograph. "Sometimes wounds of the mind can be as invisible as wounds of the soul, I suppose. Though the same deed may cause both. Assuming you believe, or rather the patient believes he *has* a soul. I am unsure of that, though I must admit that my science often feels as intuitive as an art, and on occasion a mystical one at that. Even if I don't have any use for the trappings of the Theosophists with their spirit tables and animal magnetism."

Burchard twisted the lid off a cardboard jar and removed a brown wax cylinder from within, handling it with his fingertips so as not to damage the grooves etched in its surface. He slid it onto the steel mandrel and adjusted the reproducer.

"Do you think this recording was made among the trappings of spiritualism?" Diego asked.

"According to Mr. Colton it was. He claims to have watched the session from a hidden cubby with slits for viewing. The house, as he described it, was full of such odd features. Secret rooms and passages, listening tubes for conversing from one room or floor to another. Supposedly, the lady of the house herself had lost track of which rooms she'd built and where, and lacking a definitive blueprint, she sometimes had the carpenters build new rooms and features that covered over and blocked off older rooms, like layers of geologic sediment hiding the treasures of an earlier period."

"That sounds fantastical."

"And it may well be. Consider the source. But if true, a master carpenter like Mr. Colton could be one of the only people in a position to keep track of that history. Which would present him with countless options for spying. The speaking tubes were especially useful for the eavesdropping he became obsessed with after overhearing the session I'm about to play for you. But yes, to answer your question, he claimed the recording was made in Mrs. Winchester's temple room, amid snow white silk-draped walls. To the Japanese, white is the color of death, did you know?"

"Not black?"

Burchard shrugged. "Apparently Mrs. Winchester only introduced color when it suited the astrological forces she was calling on."

Father Diego could picture the scene in vivid detail. The widow and her favored medium dressed in white gowns, seated in the inner sanctum of the sprawling house. The smell of wax would be thick in the air, from both burning candles and the recording stylus shaving off twists of the stuff from the blank cylinder. Incense drifting on the air in undulating currents, shifting only if one of the women moved.

And what stood—or hovered?—in front of the phonograph horn? Was it merely a gathering of that same incense, a condensed cloud in the dusky air from which one might extrapolate the smudged features of a face amid the shifting shadows? Or was it something more substantial? If Sarah Winchester could afford to build a mansion and outfit it with such technological wonders as electric lamps, phonographs, and a network of speaking tubes...might there not also be photographs of ghosts in her keeping?

Burchard had picked up a hand broom from somewhere. He brushed plaster crumbs from a sofa and invited Father Diego to take a seat. It must have been the very place where patients sat when making their confessions into the horn. Diego couldn't help feeling that he was being placed under the doctor's microscope as he settled on the thick cushions. Was his sanity also being assessed, if not quite judged? The feeling was only exacerbated when the doctor turned to look at him while winding the hand crank and asked, "Did you come by those scars on your hands in the course of your priestly duties? If you don't mind my asking. I wondered if yesterday wasn't your first time ministering to the dying in a disaster zone."

"No. I've never tended to a disaster... I burned them in a campfire when I was a boy."

"Witnessing the kind of suffering you encountered yesterday can leave a different sort of scar. On the mind. Of course, the bodies are still being counted throughout the valley and it will be some time before we know the true toll of the event, but it seems likely that we were hit hardest here at the asylum. I do hope you'll keep my offer of help in mind."

Father Diego shifted in his seat. The sofa was too low to the ground. He couldn't quite get comfortable in it, and felt awkwardly aware of his height disadvantage. He was relieved when the doctor turned his penetrating gaze away and focused on the machine again. Without another word of introduction or context, he flipped a metal switch and the wound spring set the wax cylinder turning. A crackling, like rain pattering on gravel, poured from the horn.

Then a woman's voice, thin and metallic: "Did you hear that?"

There was a rustling, as of papers rubbing together, and a second woman's voice, lower in pitch, replied, "There is something here…a presence. I can feel it."

The first woman, in a high, wavering tone commanded, "By the power of the angel Metatron, and in the name of the Lord God, Adonai, I call upon any spirits who are present. Reveal yourselves. Speak through me so that we may converse and bring you solace."

An interminable silence unspooled in the crackling air as the wax cylinder turned.

Then a third female voice emerged. Younger. Barely more than a girl. "I'll talk in my own voice, thank you. Why wouldn't I?"

On the heels of this statement, Father Diego thought he heard a moan, though he couldn't say which of the women had uttered it. It seemed that the woman who'd made the ceremonial commands was the medium. Perhaps the other, with the deeper voice, was Sarah Winchester.

"Who are you?" the medium asked. "Name yourself."

"My name is Annie Pardee Winchester, and I'm forty-years-dead."

"Annie," the medium said, "have you come to us from a realm of light? Have you come to visit us from heaven?"

"No." The girl's voice was thin and frayed, a ragged whisper. "I was a long time under the ground with my Daddy. But then I come up into a root where I could travel and still be in my element."

"A root? Like the root of a tree?"

"It was a mandrake root I lived in. Dark and cold. It was better when the milk and honey refreshed me, but I couldn't stay in there forever."

"She's talking nonsense," Sarah said. "Children do that if you don't focus them. Take some control, Nancy."

"I almost got free of it, when there was a clips, but then I was caught in a spider web and now I'm here in this house where there's lots of webs. Webs of light, and webs in the glass. There's even pretty rainbows caught in the webs."

"Annie, that's very interesting," the medium said, "but I need to make sure that it's really you I'm speaking to and not a mischievous imp. Can you tell me when you were born?"

"June 15, 1866."

"And when did you die?"

"July 25, 1866."

"Is that correct, Sarah?"

"Yes."

"That's very good, Annie, dear," the medium said. "Spirits remember everything. It's fragile human brains that forget. Even though you only lived for a month, you might remember many things from your little spell on Earth. Do you remember your doctor's name?"

"Doctor Ivy?"

"It was Dr. Ives," Sarah said. "The same who tended your Aunt Annie, whose name we gave to you. She died giving birth to her third child."

"I was named after my auntie?"

"Yes, dear."

"Were you named after someone?"

"Yes, dear. My mother."

"Annie," the medium interjected, "How did you learn to speak so well? Did the angels teach you languages?"

"I don't know what angels is. I learned words from listening to mother. Listening from her locket whenever she brought me along. I've been lots of places in mother's locket."

There was a pause, and then Sarah said, "I kept a lock of her hair with me."

"Oh, how fortuitous," the medium said. "It served her well."

"It was cold in the locket, and nothing to see, but lots to hear. But ever since I got caught in the spiderweb, I have a whole house to explore. Mother built it for me. A whole wide world just for me."

"You're a very lucky girl."

"It's called *Llanada Villa*. That's Spanish for *The House on the Plain.*

Mother speaks lots of different languages. How many languages do *you* speak?"

"Just English and a little French, dear," the medium answered. "And you?"

"I know English because that's what my ancestors knew. And all of the tongues of the legions under the earth."

"Do you know the language of the angels?"

"What's angels?"

"Creatures of light, child. Servants of the Lord."

"Well, I've never met one, so they never taught me their ways."

"Never mind them," Sarah said. "If you see one scratching at the windows, you tell me, dear. They like to take little girls from their mothers."

"*Sarah,"* the medium said, "How could you say such a thing? The servants of the Lord could be among us right now in this room!"

"Not in *this* room, Nancy. Maybe in your White Temple up the road, where they're welcome, but not here. Now do allow me to speak with my daughter.

"Do you like the house I've built for you, Annie?"

"Yes, mother."

"You mustn't stray from your special rooms for too long. Do you understand? You might fade if you wander too long. But I promise you there will be much to explore when exploring is allowed. There are gardens and a music room, and so many beautiful things to see and hear and smell. I've had such wonderful things brought here from all over the world so that you might *see* the world without ever leaving your home. Now it's time for you to return to your room. I'm afraid all this talk has exhausted you, dear."

"I don't feel tired."

"Yes, well, you're looking a bit thin."

"Am I?"

"Yes, dear. You need your rest."

"The other one that roams the house gets thin sometimes, too. But he *never* rests."

"What other one?" the medium asked.

"The beast."

"Turn off the phonograph, Nancy," Sarah said.

"Him that gets fat with the moon, and from supping on them that died bloody."

"Turn it off, damn it!"

"Wait, Sarah. We should hear this."

"When the beast gets strong, the walls shake. One day when the full moon is bloody enough, he's going to crack the earth and tear the whole house down, he told me so..."

There was a rustling and the crackle of the background noise ceased. Dr. Burchard flicked the switch to stop the cylinder turning.

"Incredible," Diego said. "Is there more?"

"On this cylinder? No. But according to Joe Colton, Mrs. Winchester had an entire cabinet filled with similar cylinders and the labels on the canisters suggest they were all recordings of spirit communications, though whether she believed they were all conversations with her daughter, I can't say."

"Whether she *believed*, you say. I know you aren't a religious man, but that truly was remarkable. How do you explain the voice of the girl, coming from a mere cloud of incense, into the funnel horn?"

"The medium, a Mrs. Nancy Roberts, is well known in the San Jose spiritualist community. I have to be aware of such people to keep track of what sorts of delusions are being propagated in the local population, and as I'm sure you know, they're abundant in Southern California. Rosicrucians, Theosophists, every stripe of ghost hunter and fortune teller preying on the unlucky and the bereaved. There was a boom of interest in these subjects following the loss of life in the War of Rebellion. So many lost husbands and sons. Out here, at the farthest edge of America, we also had desperate pioneers chasing fortune in the gold rush colliding with the most extreme religious factions driven westward when they were exiled from more conservative communities. It's as if the entire past century has been a perfect breeding ground for gullible marks and unscrupulous charlatans. Anyway, this Mrs. Roberts and her husband operate a church called The White Temple, just up the road from the Winchester estate. They claim to perform spirit channeling for the bereaved, as well as *angelic healing*, whatever that's supposed to mean."

"And you believe she's a fraud."

Burchard turned his hands up and shrugged. "It's a difficult discussion to have with a priest. I'm sure some mediums honestly believe in what they espouse. Some may even enter self-induced hypnotic states in which the messages they perceive from the depths of their own mind are experienced as coming from outside. But to produce a voice that can be recorded on a dictaphone, one needs to employ the trickery of a stage magician. It requires an accomplice. A small woman or child who can be concealed and conversed with according to a prearranged script."

Father Diego tried to sit up straight on the sofa, struggling against the thick cushion to perch at its edge. "But the things the girl said were so specific. And Mrs. Winchester didn't refute any of them. The dates of her birth and death, the name of her doctor...how could a fraud know these things?"

"You must remember, Father, that Sarah Winchester is as close to an aristocrat as we have in America. Births and deaths are recorded in the newspapers. With a little ingenuity and persistence, a charlatan could obtain the relevant papers from the time when the Winchesters lived in New Haven."

The priest scoffed at this.

"I'm not claiming it would be easy, but with a considerable fortune dangling, it would be worth the effort. These are the methods of the spiritualist's trade."

"I get your point, Doctor, but this Nancy Roberts doesn't seem to be telling Mrs. Winchester what she wants to hear, exactly. In fact, they have a disagreement about the benevolence of angels. And there are even times when Sarah seems to be steering the conversation away from certain details, as if she doesn't want the medium to hear what Annie might have to say. She even shuts the whole session down to keep Annie from talking about this beast at the end. Would you play that part again?"

The doctor sighed. "No, Father Diego, I'm afraid not. I had hoped that hearing it once would be enough for you to see the fallacy Joe

Colton's obsession was rooted in. I'd heard that the Jesuits are relatively rational men, as Catholics go. But if you can't agree that it takes physical lungs and lips to move the air that moves the knife that cuts the wax on a phonograph spool, then we have a fundamental difference. I won't encourage your misapprehension any further."

Diego rose to his feet, regaining dignity with every inch. "You claim to be a man of science, but to dismiss evidence... It only reveals that your own biases regarding what's possible are as dogmatic as those of the most fervent fanatic."

Burchard stood and straightened his jacket with a tug. He waved a hand at the jammed door. "I can see this was a mistake. My driver will return you to the mission."

"I see. Well then, good day to you, Doctor."

Father Diego was halfway down the rubble-strewn corridor when Burchard called after him. "If any word of this appears in the press, I will know the source. Please do keep that in mind. My superiors prefer harmonious relations with our neighbors. I imagine yours do, as well."

Father Diego kept walking through shafts of dusty light, out into the day.

CHAPTER THREE

That night, the lingering odor of smoke from the burning city tainted Diego's sleep, and the old dream returned.

It is the last carefree day of his life. The sun blazes in the blue sky, flashes like a million silver coins spinning on the wave peaks of the pacific. The white sand is hot beneath his callused feet, the salt crust a thin film on his sun-browned calves as he takes Julia's hand in his and leads her down the beach to the dock. She is laughing, teasing him, her brown eyes so big and deep he could fall into one like a bottomless well and never hit the bottom. Gulls cry overhead, and in the dream their angry shrieks sound like a warning, a prophesy, but he helps her into the little red boat unheeding, the part of him that knows what happens next unable to stop it. And yet, the part of him that is an observer of this memory also wants to relive this one taste of Eden, wants to savor the original sin that comes before the fall.

The breeze on the water is gentle when he unties the ropes and pushes off from the dock. He sits facing Julia, his back to the ocean, and takes up the oars. She smiles at him through dark hair teased by the salt air.

The bay is almost deserted at midday. Too late for fishing boats.

Most of the fishermen, like his father, have taken their catch to the marketplace in town. Only a solitary sail cuts the skyline, so far away off starboard that it looks like a dorsal fin.

"Will your father be angry if he comes home early?"

"Don't worry," Diego says. His father had a good catch this morning. "He won't come home until he's had a few drinks on his earnings."

"He drinks a lot?" There's concern in the furrows of Julia's brow. He hates to see it there and regrets mentioning his father's habits. The old man does drink a lot since the cancer took Mama, but Diego doesn't judge him for that. He just doesn't want to think about his father, his mother, or his sister right now. Not for the next hour. Not while he's with Julia on the open water, where there are no reminders. So he decides to make a joke out of it. He reaches under his plank seat and rummages in a bag. He pulls out a corked bottle and shakes it at the sky, sunlight shining through the amber liquid—a third of rum. "Not enough to finish this! Have a sip." He passes it to her and she smiles, eyes the bottle in her hand as if she's tempted but unsure, then pulls the cork and tips it to her lips. Just a taste before handing it back.

Diego shakes his head. "You hold onto it," he says. "The old man won't miss a few sips."

Julia takes another, then puts the cork back in the bottle and returns it to the canvas satchel under Diego's seat. Her arm brushes the inside of his thigh and he feels a tingle at her touch.

They're far enough from the shore now that his house looks like a toy poking out of the sawgrass. He pulls the oars up and leaves them pointed at the sky in their locks, the boat bobbing on broad swells. Looking at the house, he feels a pang of conscience. Have they gone too far out? He's supposed to be watching his little sister while Papa is at the market. He told Estella he would be right back. She'd told him not to go, almost cried over it, but he'd promised to make her favorite lunch when he returned and she'd relented. He has tried to place the boat far enough out that Estella won't be able to see him kissing Julia if she comes out to look for him, but near enough to the shore that he would still hear her if she came down the beach and called out for him. She's a good swimmer, but he made her swear she wouldn't go near the water while he's out. He doesn't fully trust that she will obey this rule, but if he sees her anywhere near the water, he will cut this pleasure cruise short and row back. Already the tide is pushing the boat back in that direction with no help from him.

"You're distracted," Julia says. "I thought you wanted to spend time with me."

"I do," he says. "More than anything."

She follows his gaze back to the house. "You're worried about your sister. Should we go back?"

Diego shakes his head. "It's okay. We just can't stay out long. Sorry."

"We shouldn't waste any time, then," she says, and then her hand is on the bulge in his shorts and her lips are tangled with his. He fumbles with the buttons of her clothes, but she stops him with a firm hand on his wrist. "No," she says. "No time for that. Just relax and let me take care of you."

The boat rocks as she settles on her knees between his legs. He looks around at the open water. The solitary sailboat is nearer, but not near enough to see the people on it, meaning they can't see him either with the naked eye. He leans backward and braces the heels of his hands against the gunwales as she unbuttons his shorts.

Julia takes him in her hand, then her mouth. She teases out the pleasure, prolonging it until he can't hold back any longer. The gulls cry and the boat rocks, but his eyes are closed and he can't tell if the wake of another craft is responsible for the rocking, or if it's the motion of what they're doing.

He lets go, leaning forward with the spasm, then opens his eyes on a plume of black smoke rising from the beach. From the house. Where his little sister, Estella, has been left alone.

The knowledge that it wasn't a gull cry that cut the sky a moment ago sluices through him like ice water.

He pushes Julia away and pulls up his shorts. She makes noises of offense, and he rises from his seat as if he could run to the shore, throwing the boat off balance for a stomach lurching instant and almost tipping it over before falling back on the bench. Julia reads the horror on his face and turns to see what he's looking at. She stares back at him wide-eyed. Everything he feels is reflected in that wild stare: the fear, the cost, the regret. He takes up the oars and spins the boat around, heaving it toward the beach with all his strength.

He doesn't hear Estella's scream again. Doesn't know if that's good or bad. Doesn't see her on the shore waving her arms at him as they get closer and the fire blooms ever larger—growing with proximity, but also spreading and consuming more of the house, the black smoke churning against the blue like a genie tumbling out of a bottle.

He drives the boat up onto the beach, the hull scraping the sand, and leaps over the side into the water. The tide has receded in the time they were away, leaving a longer stretch of beach between the shoreline and the burning house. He runs, feet pounding the wet sand until they're sliced on broken shells and then thwacking through the tall grass. The blackened wreckage of his home towers above him, crackling and collapsing, scraps of burning fabric tumbling skyward on the plume.

The heat dries the sweat on his face and threatens to singe his hair. How could it have caught so fast? Did someone douse it in fuel?

No. The truth is simpler than that. The truth is a hard stone at the bottom of his stomach. There will be no denying or escaping what happened. Estella tried to cook her own lunch because he wasn't there to do it for her. His sister was hungry, and she died for it. Because he neglected her in his selfish lust. She spilled the cooking oil on the stove and the flame spread, ravenous, throughout the house. Because the Devil's appetite is bottomless, and his claws find purchase in every human failing, every bad idea.

Diego screams her name. He circles the house, searching for her. But she is nowhere to be found. And only the gulls scream back.

Diego tossed and turned in his bed at the mission, dream and memory interwoven in fitful sleep, the girl's voice from the phonograph recording echoing in his mind, mingled with the cries of seagulls. Such a raw voice. Childlike, yes, but also guttural. Like a half-formed thing cracked out of an egg.

He lay awake now, damp with sweat, pondering that voice. The idea that it had been projected by the medium in an act of ventriloquism seemed absurd. Would the medium have been sitting directly in front of the funnel horn? And if she had brought a girl with her, a young actress who had been trained to answer questions with just the right answers to satisfy the bereaved mother… How likely was that? The voice itself had been strange, but not in the way he would expect from a ventriloquist pitching their own voice in mimicry. He was no expert in such matters, but Annie Winchester's voice sounded more like the voice of a young woman who'd had little experience with speech and whose mind had only developed as far as that of a child. It also sounded fundamentally *wrong.*

Was he projecting his own imagination onto what he had heard? His own interpretation? The girl, or woman, or whatever she was, explained that she had learned to talk from listening to fragments gleaned through a locket, as if her consciousness had been contained within the lock of hair her mother had carried for years. Then there were the references to a root, which made no sense to Diego. If the medium was staging an elaborate ruse, wouldn't she have provided a more coherent dialog through the false ghost? Perhaps the incoherent parts were things that would have made sense to Sarah Winchester, things that could be learned by someone who'd researched her family history in Connecticut as Burchard believed the medium had done.

He doubted that his own efforts would turn up the same details. All he knew about Mrs. Winchester was that she'd inherited a large stake in her husband's family industry, the Winchester Repeating Arms company, which had produced the most successful firearm in America. That, and the obvious fact that when she'd moved to California some years after the deaths of her husband and child, she'd employed a small army of carpenters to pursue her obsessive building project. They'd worked around the clock, adding rooms, towers, turrets, and all manner of patchwork architecture to what had been a modest two-story farmhouse at the end of Los Gatos road.

Some said she'd been told by a medium that she would die when her house was completed, and that this was the explanation for the endless construction. Was Nancy Roberts that same medium?

Diego fussed with his pillow and stared at the ceiling. He fidgeted, reached for his rosary on the nightstand and thumbed the beads, whispering prayers to settle his mind, but to no avail. At last, he threw off the bedsheet and blanket and went to the window. It was here that he'd stood at dawn a mere two days ago shaking off the fog of sleep, puzzled by the ringing of the tower bell. How long ago that seemed now. His beliefs hadn't been changed by his experiences of the past two days, but his faith—and more, his curiosity—had been rekindled with an intensity greater than any he'd felt since his secret initiation into the Rosicrucian society.

Though his life was openly devoted to God, his membership in the mystic order remained a secret shadow side of his spirituality. From within the sanctuary of the rose cross, it seemed absurd to him that it should be necessary to hide his initiate status from his brethren in the Jesuit order. Both fraternities were filled with sincerely devout men seeking a clear path to the divine. Yet, as was too often the case throughout history, he knew that his superiors in the priesthood would condemn any rites and symbols that diverged from their officially sanctioned ones. Anything that smelled of the occult.

Every time he snuck out of his room after midnight and walked the dark road to meet the carriage of a fellow mystic, every time he returned from such a meeting before dawn and slipped back into his room past Father Xavier's door, he risked expulsion. At times he thought he must be crazy to take that risk. He'd even asked himself on sleepless nights if he was intentionally sabotaging his career by tempting fate until his luck ran out. Did he want to provoke a conversation with Xavier about the legitimacy of the occult path? Had he decided on some deeper level that getting caught out pursuing it was the only way he could muster the courage to have that conversation?

On nights when a secret carriage ride couldn't be arranged, he had even risked taking a horse from the college stables, and had befriended a favorite—a black mare with a quiet demeanor and a coat that blended into the night. Her name was Bronte, and he was thinking of her now. Thinking of the apple he'd tucked under his pillow before bed because a part of him knew he would be feeding it to her as he coaxed her out of her stall and saddled her in silence.

Treading lightly on the floorboards, he dressed and slipped the apple into his jacket pocket. He found her alert in her stall, as if she could read his mind on such sleepless nights and anticipate his coming. Considering some of the other things he had come to believe and suspect about the wonders of creation, why should that seem so strange?

CHAPTER FOUR

He was a shadow among shadows when he reached the wrecked asylum beneath a sliver of waning moon. The tents housing the inmates were dark swathes of rough fabric rippling in the night wind. Only one of these was lit from within by a lantern that projected the silhouettes of an agitated patient and his handlers in a warped pantomime of lament and restraint on the canvas. Though this was the most dramatic disturbance, the moaning, singing, and raving that he'd heard during his previous visits also continued, as if it never ceased.

Perhaps it doesn't, he thought as he pulled on the reins and slowed the horse to a trot, guiding her in a wide arc around the building, under the cover of the palm trees that lined the road to the main entrance.

Diego dismounted and tied Bronte to a tree near a pile of rubble where the outer wall of the asylum had collapsed. He petted her nose and fed her a handful of grain he'd brought along for her reward.

"There there, my good girl. We're both going to follow an old hermetic axiom this hour: *to dare, to will, and to keep silent.* We'll be back home before you know it."

She nickered. He patted her neck and crept away, navigating the now familiar ruins with a light, careful step, and relying on his black clothing to blend in with the darkness.

The broken building appeared empty this deep in the night. He found a few extinguished lanterns on the floor of the first corridor he stepped into, indicating that the workmen might have continued their efforts to repair the damage for some hours after sunset, but he saw no active lights and heard no voices echoing through the halls. He picked up one of the lanterns and considered using it to help get his bearings to search for the doctor's office, then dismissed the idea and set it down where he'd found it. There were too many places where a caved in ceiling might allow light up through the windows on the upper floors, like a beacon announcing his presence. The candle he carried in his pocket would have to be enough when necessity called for light, and he would save it for as long as he could.

The corridors looked too alike for him to tell if he passed through any he had traversed in the daytime. He wandered for the better part of an hour before a familiar tangle of splintered wood and wiring caught his eye and enabled him to chart a course for the door marked with Dr. Burchard's name plaque. It was still wedged ajar. Diego slipped through the gap and found himself staring at the lumpy sofa he'd perched upon to listen to the phonograph.

The desk appeared to be cluttered with the same papers that had littered it during his afternoon visit. The file cabinet stood in the same corner, black and monolithic, the drawers closed and locked. Through the window, he had a view of the tents. A buttery light still cast a shadow play onto the canvas at one end, but the figure animating it moved in a more docile manner than when he'd first arrived, swaying back and forth like a mother rocking a babe to sleep.

The relative peace was a disappointment. An agitated patient would have drawn more attention away from the building and masked any noises he might make in his attempt to penetrate the locked cabinet and gain access to the wax cylinder. The office window, which he'd paid little attention to in the daylight, was now likely to broadcast the light of his candle, if he used it. He looked around for a curtain to drape over the frame, but found none. His jacket wasn't big enough for the job, nor was the moonlight spilling through the window sufficient to work by.

And what was that work? He'd put the bare fact of it out of mind while tending to the obstacles of the journey. Now that he'd arrived, he had to face it: He meant to break into the file cabinet and steal the phonograph recording.

But how? Pick the lock of the bottom drawer? He had no such skills. He'd come here on an impulse, thinking that he would somehow solve the problem when the time came.

Burchard had unlocked the cabinet with a key from a ring kept in his pocket. Did the doctor keep a spare hidden somewhere in the office? It seemed like his best hope, slim though it was, but he would have to conduct the search largely by touch, which would take more time than he had.

Maybe there was another way. He braced the file cabinet between his hands and rocked it from side to side, testing its weight to see if he might lower it to the floor on its side and try to access the lock mechanism from below. The cabinet was heavy enough that the likelihood of dropping it with a crash and arousing attention from the tents seemed high, even if the orderlies there had become accustomed to sounds from the wreckage as it continued to settle. There was also the possibility of damaging the wax cylinder to consider. If the heavy suitcase phonograph were to crush it from an odd displacement of weight, the whole effort would be wasted.

He considered returning to the mission empty-handed. If he cut his losses here, at least he wouldn't be caught trespassing or thieving. And even if he succeeded in stealing the cylinder, did he think the doctor wouldn't suspect him when it was found missing? He was, after all, the only person who'd heard it since the quake. Possibly one of only a few people who knew of its existence and where it was kept.

Jesus, what am I doing here?

It was time for a dose of his own medicine – the self-reflection he was always encouraging in others.

What was his justification here? A mere thirst for more of the ghost's voice was not enough. And it *was* more than that. It was proof he wanted. Proof that spirits persisted beyond the border of life. That it was possible for the dead to commune with the living.

Proof. A guilty indulgence for a priest. If faith was his bride, proof was his mistress.

Was the craving for proof a justification to covet his neighbor's property? To steal it? Of course not. But the rationale that had whispered in the back of his mind on the ride to the asylum returned to him now, full-throated: The cylinder *wasn't* the doctor's property. It belonged to Sarah Winchester, and the fact that it hadn't been promptly returned to her when Joe Colton revealed it to his doctor was evidence that someone at the hospital – maybe Burchard or even the director – was keeping it as leverage against the heiress in hope of pressing her for more money if the well of her charity were to run dry in the future.

Father Diego knew in his heart that these men wouldn't dare openly accuse him of stealing something that they had in turn stolen from its rightful owner. Even if their theft was by omission.

Thus far he had soothed his own conscience with the vague notion that he might return the recording to Mrs. Winchester, but also with a clearer motive – to use the cylinder as a key. A key to unlock the doors of the sprawling Winchester mansion and gain access to the famously reclusive widow. In so doing, he might keep his promise to the dying carpenter. It was impossible from this vantage to imagine exactly how, but he might even find a way to liberate Annie Pardee Winchester's ghost.

Turning to the doctor's desk, he opened the center drawer and felt around inside, touching writing utensils, a letter opener, a pipe and a pouch of tobacco. There was an assortment of those ingenious new paperclips in a carved well, along with some spare coins, but no key to the filing cabinet. In the side drawers he found a flask, bottles of ink, and a stack of notebooks. The bottom left drawer had no keyhole on its face but it was locked by some hidden mechanism. There were no other cabinets or drawers in the room. Only a bookcase heaped with stacks of academic journals and rows of leather-bound books.

Diego went down on his knees and huddled in the footwell under the desk. He fumbled in his pockets, then struck a match and lit the candle he'd brought with him. It was a short pillar, fat enough to stand upright on the floor. Sitting in its sheltered light, he examined the stack of notebooks he'd removed from the desk drawer. They were labeled with the names of patients, and filled with Burchard's observations and diagnoses, with references to what appeared to be wax cylinder numbers corresponding to the recorded sessions. The doctor's scrawl was largely unintelligible. Diego searched the covers for the name Colton but failed to find it.

Did Burchard keep his records on the carpenter locked in the file cabinet with the recordings? Diego took a paperclip from the center drawer and unfolded the thin loop of wire. He tried picking the lock of the file cabinet, but with no success. After a few minutes of unskilled effort, breath held and ear cocked for the sound of a latch turning over, he gave up with a sigh. The candlelight flickered over the floorboards at his feet, shielded by the heavy desk.

The desk with one stubborn drawer.

Was it jammed by swollen wood, or by some hidden latch?

He moved the candle aside and laid on his back in the footwell, searching the underside of the drawer. His upper body blocked most of the light in the small space, making the candle more of a liability than a help. He pinched the wick, snuffing out the flame, and ran his wax coated fingers along the edges of the drawer until they came upon a metal bolt threaded through a hole in the frame. It could only have one purpose – a quick and primitive privacy measure that kept the drawer from sliding on its track when inserted. Diego removed it with one hand and tugged the drawer handle again with the other. It slid freely open.

By now his eyes had adjusted to the darkness enough that he could discern another stack of journals. He placed them on the floor and relit the candle.

This stack of notebooks lacked the uniform style of the patient logs from the other drawer. The first one he opened contained a series of dated entries in the doctor's familiar script, but the contents – to the extent he could decipher them – were nonsensical, even phantasmagorical. Diego decided this must be a record of the doctor's own dreams. The dates were from the previous year. There was likely a matching journal sitting at the doctor's bedside wherever he slept at this very moment.

The second book was labeled COLTON and appeared to match the kind of diagnostic observations he'd found in the other patient records.

Closer examination revealed a timeline of the carpenter's employment at the Winchester House, as well as a series of dated references to "encounters."

Diego caught his gaze lingering uncomprehendingly on the list of dates and closed the journal. The lateness of the hour was catching up with him, his eyelids growing heavy, his joints aching from crouching on the hard floor. Flipping open the final book from the bolted drawer to a random page, he saw that it was written in pencil in an entirely different hand.

Today we cut and laid the beams for a new room on the south wing. Been waiting all week for new wood to be delivered after Mrs. Winchester rejected the last delivery for knots in the boards. As usual, she insists on very peculiar measurements we must abide by.

Another random page contained the following lines:

Even with the gas and electric lamps, I don't like to be in that house after dark if I can help it, but the work is endless. I know I should thank the Lord for the income, and there's little urgency to ever finish it, but the madness of the project gets under my skin. Rooms built on top of rooms. Windows built into floors. Doors set into second story walls with a sheer drop to the ground over the threshold. The men say there's no rhyme or reason to it, but there is for her. I think some of the plans come to her in dreams, and others I don't like to think what's behind them. All I know is it doesn't always seem like Llanada Villa was conceived as an abode for the living.

I never feel truly alone here, no matter what part of the house I'm in. There's strange noises that come and go, like machinery deep in the walls. And a smell like copper and charred flesh that hits you like walking into a wall of fog when you turn a corner. I never know when I'll encounter it, and I'm always on my guard. The job pays well, but no amount of money would be enough for me to sleep there.

Diego's heart fluttered, his aches and fatigue forgotten. The candle had burned down enough that the liquid wax pooled around the wick was spilling over onto the floor. He returned to Burchard's session notes for Joe Colton and again found the list of encounters. Picking a date from the doctor's list, Diego searched Colton's journal for the same. It corresponded to a short but chilling entry.

Annie revealed herself to me again today. In the garden. At first, I thought she was a neighborhood girl trespassing. She saw me, too, this time, and smiled like she had a secret. I swear it almost stopped my heart. She walked around a pear tree, and when I got up the nerve to follow, she'd vanished on the other side. I guess that answers the question of whether or not she can leave the house, but the gardens were laid out with the same odd designs as the house, so maybe she's constrained to the grounds.

But the strange thing was that I found a pear on the ground with what looked like faint teeth marks surrounding a rotten spot where the skin was bruised black. I know it figures that a fallen fruit would start to rot in a place where someone broke the skin, but I couldn't shake the feeling that it had happened right there and then, that the ghost girl tried to take a bite of that pear and turned it black as soon as she kissed it.

Running my thumb over the bruise, I poked right through to a rotten core crawling with maggots and dropped it like a hot potato. I know rot can't bloom like that in a heartbeat, but I swear it did.

Diego flicked the pages with his thumb, scanning for the last of Colton's entries, but before he reached a blank page, he heard a clattering noise from the hall outside. He started and dropped the book, almost setting it alight when it knocked the candle over and the flame guttered out. Scrambling in the dark, he gathered the other books and stuffed them into the open drawer. There was no time to replace the bolt or scrape the wax from the floor beneath the desk. In a harried moment, he stuffed the candle back into his pocket and the carpenter's journal under his arm, sprang to his feet, and cast about for a hiding place.

Was the crash he'd heard from a falling piece of debris that had finally let go? Or an interloper? Crouching beside the file cabinet, he held his breath and listened.

There was a shuffling sound, as of footsteps sliding through the cement dust in an effort to be quiet.

Had an orderly seen the flickering light of his candle and come to investigate? The staff was probably still rounding up prodigal patients who'd gradually wandered back to the only home they knew. Was it possible that the person in the hall was one of these? A lunatic come home to roost? He wasn't sure if that prospect was more comforting or alarming than getting caught and having to explain himself. What would he even say? That he'd lost something valuable and come back to look for it? Not likely given his vow of poverty. And in the deepest hours of the night?

An orderly might entertain a strange claim, but when the doctor whose office he was found lurking in was informed, there would be no denying what he'd done. The wax on the floor...the open drawer...the journal in his hands.

He couldn't be caught with it. But neither could he give it up. Not after all the risk he'd taken to find it. The answers to the mystery of what the carpenter had witnessed at the Winchester House were literally in his grasp, and whatever they were, Dr. Burchard had gone to some trouble to conceal and protect them, sequestering them away in a locked drawer.

Diego's pulse pounded in his ears. He remembered to breathe, and a prayer of protection came to his lips, but he stopped himself before he could whisper it. It was a petition to Saint Dismas, the patron saint of thieves, who had been crucified beside Jesus. Surely asking to escape detection was a bridge too far.

The cylinder that remained under lock and key was Mrs. Winchester's rightful property; that much was true. But the journal?

It belongs to a dead man to whom you made a promise. If keeping that promise requires you to take it, would that be so wrong?

He waited for the shuffling sound in the hall to pass by, but whoever was out there had paused, as if listening.

His gaze settled on the window. The lantern in the tent had gone out, leaving only a thin scrim of moonlight to trace highlights on the broken pane. At ground level the only injury he'd likely suffer if he jumped through it would be lacerations from the glass. That and self-incrimination. He took a deep breath and stepped out of hiding, an excuse rising to his lips.

A coyote stared up at him, startled. It dropped the sack of potatoes it had been dragging down the dusty corridor and fled, its mangy tail swishing around a corner at the next open door. A stray potato rolled across the floor and bumped the priest's shoe. Diego slumped against the wall and put a hand to his racing heart. Chest heaving, he gazed at the ceiling and laughed like a lunatic.

CHAPTER FIVE

From Joe Colton's Journal
April 29th, 1904

I saw the ghost again today.

I think she's getting more solid, though I don't know why that would be. You might think a ghost would fade with time, the longer she was dead. Living things get weaker the longer they live. But who knows how death works? I've always sort of believed what the Bible says about that, but Annie is the first dead person I've actually met. What a strange thing to write, but it's true.

I'm writing things down in this journal so I won't forget them or start to believe they didn't happen. Like how dreams fade the longer you're awake. Maybe ghosts don't fade, but memories do. If I can't look back at the details, I'm afraid I'll try to convince myself it didn't happen for real. Right now, I know what I saw and what I heard, and there's no other explanation for it.

I don't plan to show this to anyone. I must remember that so I won't be embarrassed to tell it plainly. No one ever has to see this book but me.

The first time I heard Annie's voice and saw her phantom, I was spying on Mrs. Winchester in her séance room with Mrs. Roberts, the psychic from up the road. I never put any faith in the Roberts woman's claims before that day, but I heard a girl's voice coming from a wisp of smoke during their session. A whole conversation, and I heard every word. The ladies even recorded it. And that whole time, the white smudge in the air just hung there like how a person would stand in one spot to give a speech right into the phonograph horn. The smoke wasn't damaged by the air currents, not even with the Chinaman working the bellows to blow the wax trimmings from the cylinder.

I'm sure Mrs. Winchester picked the Chinaman because he couldn't understand what the ghost said. She speaks enough languages to give orders to all the Chinese and Japanese housekeepers and gardeners. But I'm sure the Chinaman understood the sound was coming from a spirit even if he couldn't make heads nor tails of the words. He quit the next day and I've never seen him since.

At the seance, Annie said she was 40 years dead. I've been wondering ever since if ghosts get stronger with age, or if something about this house made her more substantial. When I saw her again today, I knew it was her even before she spoke to me, even though she looked more like a girl than a smudge of smoke. Not a forty-year-old woman mind you, but maybe twenty. So I don't know what to make of her age. She talks more like a child than a woman. Maybe she's confused and can't make sense of time since she died. Or maybe time works differently for the dead. Who can say? I'm just a carpenter.

I saw her because Mrs. Winchester sent me to the Grand Ballroom to try and figure out what was buzzing when she played the pipe organ and if anything could be done about it.

Now that I think about it, I wonder if Annie was lingering in the ballroom because she hears music differently from how normal people do. Living people, I mean. My grandmother used to say that spirits in the old country could take sustenance from the incense and organ music in a church, and even from food offerings left out for them on holidays in graveyards. I always thought those were old wives tales, folklore and such. But now I find myself wondering about it all the time. In any case, I guess Annie had been listening to her mother play the organ.

Mrs. Winchester doesn't play music very often. There are instruments all around this house—organs, pianos, even a harp. But

I guess those are mostly for the entertainers she sometimes hires for private concerts when they're visiting San Francisco and she can coax them down to Llanada Villa for a late night encore. I've usually gone home for the night by then, but I've heard rave reviews from her niece, Daisy, a couple of times.

Most of them that make the trip and play for the ladies in that ballroom don't ever come back a second time. I don't know if that's because they're touring musicians who don't happen to find themselves in the valley again or if it's because they got the same weird feeling I get working in there.

The ballroom is the heart of the house. It's not central—if *anything* can be called central in a house that keeps sprouting limbs in all directions—but the ballroom *feels* like a heart. Covered in gold patterned wallpaper and red velvet curtains, it's located on the first floor right above the main boiler in the basement. It has a large fireplace flanked by Mrs. Winchester's crown jewels—the tiffany glass windows she had designed special, each with a strange quote on it. Most of the other stained glass panes throughout the house have spiderweb designs and what look like stars and planets *caught* in spiderwebs. The pair in the ballroom are the only ones with a message written in English, but I'll be damned if I can say what they mean to her. The words give me an uneasy feeling, nonetheless.

There's a crystal chandelier hung from the fancy tiled ceiling that also feels like a centerpiece of the house. It was imported from Germany with twelve gas lamps, but Mrs. W had a thirteenth added to go along with all of the other thirteens throughout the house. That number echoes over and over in the architecture.

Rumors about Mrs. W's obsession with certain numbers and symbols is a plague among the servants and work crews. Most are just guesses, but they say she went to the Ladies' school at Yale where the leadership is mostly men with affiliations to secret societies such as the Masons and Rosicrucians. People in love with mystic numbers and secret codes. I heard from an actual stone mason that the Founding Fathers were Freemasons and that the Masons have handed down secrets from the Knights Templar about the builders of King Solomon's temple, which was also based on the number thirteen. Maybe that's all just tall tales, but other tall tales say that Solomon employed demons to build his temple, for whatever that's worth.

Other rumors I've heard from the housekeepers hold that Mrs. W had a hidden safe installed behind one of the wood panels in the Grand Ballroom, and that there's a second safe inside the first one, so whatever she keeps in there must be either diamonds or something horrible and damning. But one of the maids claims she walked in on Mrs. W handling a box she took out of there one time and it looked to her like the lady had a tangle of roots or human hair in her fingers.

I don't know why, but that's an image that gives me a chill. I've lain awake many a night thinking about it and I must admit that it may have colored my feelings about the room.

The great organ in the grand ballroom also feels like part of the house's heart with its pipes and valves reaching toward the carved ceiling. The wall behind it is reinforced with an arched panel of hardwood designed to project the sound, and like everything in that room, all of the joints are fitted together tight and precise. Going in there to diagnose a rattle, I doubted it would be anything architectural. More likely a crystal from the chandelier buzzing against its neighbor. Or one of the vases or statuettes that fill the nooks in the mantle shelves vibrating in its housing.

I was taking my lunch in the basement when one of the housekeepers came down and told me what the lady wanted me to do, and when I stuffed the last couple bites of my sandwich into my mouth, I dripped mustard onto the leg of my trousers. The housekeeper loaned me a handkerchief to clean it up with, but I didn't want to stain something so fine, so I took a minute to find a rag and dip it in a bucket of water to clean the stain before we went upstairs together.

I usually feel self-conscious tromping around indoors in the house in my work boots and dungarees, and now to top it off, I had a wet spot on my leg along with the sawdust and dried paint.

Thankfully, we didn't cross paths with Mrs. W or her niece on our way to the Ballroom. I brought a small toolbox with everything I expected I might need in order to tighten up whatever was buzzing.

I told the housekeeper I didn't need her to show me to the room, but she said she was supposed to play the organ for me to demonstrate the problem.

That she did, and she wasn't half bad. Said she used to play the hymns at Sunday services when she was a teen. But she wasn't there to entertain me, and we soon got down to the business of trying different notes until the effect was triggered by a black key in the bass. I don't know much about music, but I know opera singers can shatter glass, and something in the room was vibrating with just that note.

I moved around the room, listening to the buzzing, trying to pinpoint where it came from while she held the key down. I felt odd about touching Mrs. W's trinkets. Eventually I got over it, but no matter which ebony figurine or china sculpture I touched, the buzzing didn't stop until at last I put my hand against part of the fireplace grate.

I told the housekeeper she could leave. I knew the key now and could play it myself to test it again when the repair was complete, and so she left me to it.

I opened my tool kit and found a set of fasteners to secure the rattling grate. But while I was setting the screw holes with my hand drill, I noticed a figure out of the corner of my eye near the paneled wall. Thinking that the housekeeper had lingered, I got aggravated and determined to ignore her. Did she not trust me to be left alone with the precious books and sculptures in the room? Or had Mrs. W told her to watch over my shoulder and supervise my work?

When I'd driven the screws for the fasteners, I looked up, prepared to give her a piece of my mind, only to find that the figure was gone. It was unsettling because there was nothing else there I could have mistaken for the housekeeper—no curtain, coat, or shawl draped over a music stand.

I turned back to the task at hand and my heart jumped into my throat. There was a young woman on her hands and knees beside me, licking the mustard stain on my pant leg like a dog.

I jumped back from her and nearly crashed into the rack of fire tending tools.

I'd felt no pressure from her touch. As if she was too thin and wispy to make an impression on my nerves, even though she looked as solid as anyone I've ever seen. Her dark hair looked greasy and unwashed, and her pale skin showed blue veins in her throat and temples. Her cheeks were hollowed out and her lips as gray as worms, but the hunger in her eyes shone like embers from the hearth beside her. Simmering coals in deep, black wells.

She crawled toward me on all fours as I scampered away, the red light of her eyes stretched wide, like rays of the setting sun smeared through thick glass.

I fumbled for a fire poker and pulled the first iron rod my trembling hand could find. It jammed in the rack, and by the time I dislodged it and looked back at where the girl was, she'd disappeared.

I stumbled out of the ballroom, the fire poker clenched like a sword in my fist. There was no sign of her. I caught my breath and touched the spot on my leg where her mouth had been latched on. The fabric was still damp from the wet rag I'd used to clean it. If the phantom girl had added saliva to it, there was no way to tell. My skin crawled at the thought, and for a moment I thought I might be sick on the fancy Persian rug.

I felt shame that I'd been startled like a nervous cat. Guilt, too. Like I'd been left alone with Mrs. Winchester's daughter and allowed her to do something indecent. Crazy, but I knew that was who it was. It was Annie's ghost. The same one whose voice I'd heard in the seance room that night when I let curiosity get the better of me. When I lurked in a forgotten passage and listened through the slats.

"Can you play for me?" That same voice. From across the room. Now the girl was seated at the pipe organ. She patted the bench seat beside her, inviting me to sit and join her for a duet.

"I'm hungry," she said.

I didn't know how to reply to that. Even if I'd had an inkling of what to say, I don't think I could have found my voice. My hands felt cold, and the thought came to me that once a man started having conversations with ghosts, there was no going back.

"I couldn't digest the milk," she said. "That's why I died. Mother told me so. And I've been hungry ever since. My belly's like a pit that aches all the time."

She said she could take some nourishment from smells—things like fresh baked bread or the mustard on my clothes. She said she could even taste music sometimes and asked me if I could play.

I shook my head and backed away from the organ, my fingers clenched tight around the iron poker, my jaw clenched almost as tight around my tongue.

There was a sound then that rumbled through the ballroom floor. At first, I thought Annie must have put her foot down on one of the bass pedals, as if her spirit limbs could move such a thing. But her feet were on the floor. I could see them, bare, below the lace hem of her plain white dress. Somehow, a part of my mind was still capable of reason in the face of the impossible, because I puzzled out that if the organ wasn't making that rumbling, maybe the boiler in the basement below was in distress. But before I could run down the hall and the stairs to check on it, the ghost sat up straight as a statue and looked me dead in the eye.

She was scared. I could see it writ in every muscle. She was as afraid to move as I was. It occurred to me then that her posture was like someone in the wild who'd caught sight of an approaching predator and froze on the spot, trying to go unnoticed.

"Did you hear that?" she whispered, barely moving her lips.

I nodded, and the flesh on my arms pricked up.

"It found me," she said.

The vibration under the floor moved toward the hearth, rattling the china and trinkets with more force that the organ could muster.

"Don't let him see me," she said, and I felt strangely compelled to protect her, though from what, I didn't know. I moved to the fireplace, to where it seemed that whatever was rumbling under the floor would emerge, putting myself between the girl and whatever was on her trail. I was on the verge of nervous laughter. Me, a carpenter, standing there with a fire poker in his hand like a knight with his trusty sword, waiting for a dragon to emerge from a cave mouth. Defending a fair maiden. It was absurd.

"Hold him off," she said, "while I lose him in the labyrinth. He has no dominion over you."

By now the vases and statuettes were shaking so hard I feared they'd topple off the shelves and shatter and I'd be blamed for making a wreck in the course of my repairs. And I remember thinking that if that happened, I'd tell Mrs. W it wasn't me, it was the trembler, because surely she would have felt it too. It had to be a trembler shaking the house. It was crazy to think it was a monster like the dragon from the Book of Revelations or a demon or a Minotaur, like from that story about Theseus I read about in that Bullfinch book at school. And why was I thinking about those things, anyway? She hadn't told me what was after her, had she? Maybe it was her calling the house a labyrinth that put those pictures in my head. It's funny the things you can accept for real and how fast it can happen when you know in your bones that something dangerous is near.

She said the rod would hold it back, but I didn't know why it should. The girl wasn't made of flesh, and by some magical reasoning, I knew that whatever threatened her wouldn't be either. I started to recite the Lord's Prayer.

The other iron tools in the rack rattled. The crystals in the chandelier chimed.

Did I hear laughter mixed in with those chimes? The prayer dried up in my throat as I listened for the sound of something human or beastly under the rumbling. I sensed that the ghost girl had fled, but I couldn't take my eyes off the hearth and the stained glass windows to either side of it.

WIDE UNCLASP THE TABLES OF THEIR THOUGHTS
THESE SAME THOUGHTS PEOPLE THIS LITTLE WORLD

All at once the rumbling ceased, the trinkets settled on their shelves, and in the silence I pondered what those words could have meant to Mrs. W.

I had no earthly idea, but they seemed in that moment to be taunting me with meaning. As if puzzling out their message would break the spell and banish the threat, or release me from where I felt my feet were nailed to the floor.

I'd seen the lines before, written in a winding ribbon from top to bottom of the tall panes of glass, but I'd never cared what they meant.

Now, though, they seemed to flank the gates of Hell. Taunting me.

A man's mind makes strange connections under stress, and that notion—of gates—shone a light on the word UNCLASP. I didn't know where the words came from. Didn't recognize them from the Bible, but they had that style of language, with the ring of an incantation. And the image they called to mind was of thoughts made flesh rushing through gates thrown open. I pictured demons loosed from Hell.

I squatted and peered into the dark opening, half expecting to catch the glint of light from the Devil's own eyes. Instead, I was blinded by a cloud of black ash billowing out on a gust of wind down the flue, hot as a beast's breath. In the swirling particles, I fancied I saw a shape: the horns and snout of a bull rushing over me as I rocked back on my haunches and held up the poker.

Then it was gone. The charged atmosphere in the room fell flat, and I was just a dirty workman jumping at shadows, out of place in a grand ballroom in mustard stained pants.

I put the poker back in the rack, packed up my tools, and hurried out of the house to let the sunlight clear my head. I can't remember ever being so scared. Not since I was a boy. And here I am at home, hours later, still shaken by the encounter. I'd hoped putting it down on paper would make the absurdity of it plain, but I don't believe it has.

CHAPTER SIX

"What do you make of it?"

Diego sat in the vestibule of a private hall that had somehow been spared by the earthquake. Beside him on the bench was his mentor, a man he knew only as Frater H. Following the initiation ritual of a new candidate, the brethren of the Rose Cross had hung up their ceremonial robes and milled out into the moonlit night around them while Frater H read the carpenter's journal entry. Now, only the two men remained, and they could speak openly.

Frater H scratched his beard. "Well, there is a tradition which holds that iron is baneful to demons. Perhaps the fire poker performed the function of an amulet in that regard."

"I hadn't thought of that. I wonder if Mrs. Winchester kept it there for that purpose, though there's certainly nothing special about keeping a fire poker beside the hearth. But the carpenter's interpretation of the verses on the Tiffany glass suggests that the lady may have intended the house to be a welcome abode for spirits of all kinds."

The older man considered this with a frown. "I wouldn't assume too much," he said. "Just because she welcomes her daughter into her own home doesn't mean she would throw the windows and doors wide to all the beasts of the earth. I would expect the same rules of hospitality to prevail on the spiritual plane. Especially where it seems this other entity was predatory to the girl."

"What do *you* take the verses on the windows to mean?"

"They're from Shakespeare. But each is from a different play. One is from *Trolius and Cressida;* the other from *Richard II.* They're totally unrelated, and yet Mrs. Winchester has combined them as if they were from the same monologue. Why she would choose to do so and what they might mean to her when taken together... That much is a mystery. And you say there are other elaborate Tiffany windows throughout the house? Perhaps the sense of these lines can only be deciphered in relation to a larger puzzle."

"The carpenter's journal describes many stained glass windows adorned with symbols and geometric shapes, but he is very clear that only these two contain words. Most are of spider web designs and daisies. Two themes that recur throughout the house in the carved wood finials and wrought iron gates as well. You're a master of symbolism, brother. I'd hoped you might be able to tell me what they represent."

Frater H rose from the bench and set the book down. He paced the vestibule with the slow step of a man moving his legs merely to help exercise his mind.

Diego remained seated, allowing his mentor the time to formulate his thoughts.

"I would have to walk the rooms of this house myself to glean even an inkling of how the symbols relate to one another. And even then, I could only speculate about precisely what they mean to *her*."

"But surely she must be a mystic? The design of the house may seem chaotic to the uninitiated, the project of a madwoman, but I sense an underlying grand design." Diego opened the journal to a page he'd marked with a slip of paper. He rotated the book and presented a drawing to Frater H.

"This is another of the windows." The carpenter's sketch was precise: a spider web pattern in which thirteen orbs were caught like jewels of morning dew. "The number thirteen recurs throughout the house. It's everywhere. The carpenter said Mrs. Winchester referred to the number as 'the key of death.' He said she also used the word *nun* in connection to thirteen, which he thought referred to a sister of the church. But it's a reference to the tarot, isn't it?"

Diego had made a study of the symbols encoded in the ancient oracle. Each card of the major arcana was connected to a letter of the holy Hebrew alphabet. The letter *nun* related to the thirteenth card, Death, depicted by a skeleton wielding a scythe. The letter was also symbolic of a fish, which connected it to Jesus and the twelve apostles.

The old master nodded, pondering the design. "The number appears often in myths of the spiritual quest. King Arthur was the thirteenth to sit at the round table among his twelve knights. Gautama Buddha was said to have had twelve disciples as well. But never mind that. This design looks more like a calendar to me."

"But there are only *twelve* months."

"Twelve months in a year, yes, as there are twelve signs of the zodiac. But there are thirteen moons."

"You think it's a lunar calendar? That at least has some connection to another event described in the journal—a lunar eclipse that seems to have precipitated the carpenter's firing and banishment from the house."

"Tell me more."

"Do you remember the eclipse that happened in February? The newspapers called it a blood moon. It was visible all across the country."

"Yes, I watched it from the balcony off my study. That red moon. You could see why such an event would have inspired dread in the ancients."

"The carpenter refers to eclipses throughout the journal, but it seems that the full eclipse of this past February is when things took a turn at the Winchester House."

"What kind of a turn?"

"He doesn't say exactly what happened the night of the eclipse, but he alludes to how Sarah's demeanor changed in the days following the event. She became paranoid of the house being breached, and short-tempered with the work crews. There are only a few direct quotes, but the way she speaks of securing the house, it's impossible to say if she's trying to protect it from human interlopers or some kind of demonic infestation. Violent noises are heard from empty rooms, objects crash to the floor as if shaken by the sort of trembler we only recently suffered…

Colton says it's like living with an invisible bull in a china shop, which harkens back to his first encounter with a demonic force, two years prior, when he imagined he saw the head of a bull in a cloud of ash emerging from the grand ballroom fireplace. Comparing the carpenter's journal to the Farmer's Almanac shows that that event happened on the first full moon following a penumbral eclipse on March 31st, 1904."

"A bull in a cloud, you say?"

"Yes. Does it mean anything to you?"

The old man shrugged. "You've described the house as a labyrinth, so of course I'm reminded of Theseus and the Minotaur. Do you know if the carpenter was educated in mythology?"

"He at least had a passing familiarity with that tale. He mentions it."

"So we can't rule out the contents of his own imagination skewing his perception."

"I suppose that's true." Diego sighed. Every solution only raised more questions. "It's a strange case," he said. "I'm afraid to talk about it with my superiors in the Church, but it has awakened a powerful spiritual paradox in me. I'm driven to pursue evidence of an afterlife beyond the bounds of heaven and hell, but I'm worried that the mystery of the house is luring me out of my depth and the bottom will drop out beneath me at any moment."

"Come. Walk with me in the temple, where we can discuss what troubles you among the symbols of the craft. May I see the book again?"

Diego handed over the journal. Frater H flipped through the pages as they entered the shrine room.

"It looks like a novel in places. What are these passages of dialog?"

"For a few years, Joe had brief random encounters with Annie's ghost. Then, in the weeks before his termination, they had a series of conversations conducted through a speaking tube from the tower room that apparently serves as the girl's bedroom."

"A speaking tube?"

"It's one of the more advanced features of the house. Not only did Mrs. Winchester have some electric lights and even a shower installed, she also hired a plumber to run a series of pipes fitted with acoustic horns, like on Edison's phonograph. She used them to communicate with servants between the different floors of the house. Joe Colton heard whispering from one of these pipes while working in the basement. He thought it was his employer at first, but came to believe it was Annie, locked in the tower room her mother had confined her to after the eclipse. Though I can't imagine how one confines a ghost to a single room. Apparently she was lonely. She trusted him from their first meeting when he'd helped her escape whatever was pursuing her. They conducted a series of dialogues that he transcribed in this journal."

"Did Mrs. Winchester find out about the book?"

"I don't believe so. I can't imagine she would have allowed it to leave the house if she knew of its existence. She fired Joe when she caught him listening to the horn connected to Annie's room. He stole the wax cylinder on his way out of the house. I'm sure he would have kept the journal a secret."

Frater H closed the journal and waved a hand at their surroundings, the Hall of Initiation.

"Do you remember how you felt when you first entered this room?"

Diego thought about it. "I was afraid."

"As you are again. At the threshold of a mystery. May I suggest that a man unafraid at such a threshold is one who has closed off his heart and mind to the wonder and terror of the unknown?"

"You may. But I'm supposed to have the answers, to reassure others that the universe is knowable, that man's place in God's plan is knowable. I've faced down demons as an exorcist, and I won't lie and say I wasn't afraid, but the weapons of my faith steadied my hand in those dark hours. This, though…It feels different. Like I've stumbled blindly into what I thought was a familiar room only to find that not only has the furniture been rearranged, but it's all on the ceiling, and so am I."

"Your world has turned upside down. And why is that?"

"Because I don't understand what's happening in that house. If the carpenter's story is to be believed…it suggests cycles of power in the Winchester house, tied to the phases of the moon. Strange and even calamitous events occur at intervals following each eclipse. And the effect seems to be growing stronger over time."

They had arrived at a marble cube topped with a bronze brazier now gone cold. The ashes from its fire had been swept up and disposed of at the conclusion of the evening's ritual.

"It sounds like you understand more than you're willing to admit to yourself. What if you were chosen by the Almighty for this encounter with the house? I dare say it is no small coincidence that a carpenter named Joseph should have handed you the task."

Diego opened his mouth to argue the point but then scoffed, finding he had no retort. "If…*if* the spirit is who she claims to be, and not some imp of hell playing games with a widow and her carpenter, then she is the ghost of a child who died one month after her birth in New Haven Connecticut. She was unbaptized, and so should now be in purgatory, and yet we find her chased through a labyrinth by a demon? That the Lord would allow such a thing… I cannot fathom it."

"It sounds as if Mrs. Winchester tried to keep her daughter's soul for herself, to conceal it from God. Isn't that what the carpenter believed? What he asked you to put right?"

"It is. And yet I feel unmoored. Am I to cast a demon from a body of wood and nails?"

"The cross, made of wood and nails, is a symbol of the holiest sacrifice, is it not? Imbued with power beyond its components."

Diego continued as if his mentor hadn't interrupted him. "And what of Annie? She is not the ghost of an infant but has grown somehow. Has she also sinned in the years that her mother has kept her caged like a pet? Sinned without a body? I do feel that I've been put here by God to act, and I do feel a duty to fulfill Joe Colton's dying wish, and yet I find myself wracked with doubts."

"What do you fear, brother?"

"Most of all? That I may make things worse. That I may play into the Devil's hand and give him what he wants."

"Do you believe Sarah Winchester has made a pact with the Devil?"

Diego considered this. He shook his head. "I won't know what I think until I've met her."

"So you intend to approach her. You *have* decided to act, then, and are only delaying accepting your decision."

"I must confront her. But by all accounts, she shuns visitors. I've no idea how to go about it."

Frater H waved a hand at the temple room around them. "What does this room represent?"

"The tabernacle in the wilderness. The first temple of the wandering tribes."

"Yes, the thirteen tribes of Israel encircling the holy fire in the temple. It is all the same quest, Frater D. Your public path through the Jesuit Order, your private path through the Brotherhood of the Rose Cross, and now your path through this labyrinth. But in that temple on the plain, the ancients approached first the fire of sacrifice, a foul fire, shrouded in smoke." He gestured at the brazier that stood between them. "One must pass through that first trial before proceeding to the inner temple, where the clear light of a pure flame burns..."

"And eventually pass beyond to the invisible light of spirit," Diego finished.

"Yes. But we must begin in darkness. Just as the candidate approaches this shrine on the night of the dark moon. We must meet the profane where we find it. On its own terms, as you once approached this first flame thick with smoke. And what did the ancients do by the law of Moses when they approached that first fire?"

"They made offerings," Diego said.

"Yes. Animal sacrifices. And in this we see the symbolic sacrifice of the pleasures of the flesh. Who knows what Sarah Winchester has sacrificed on the altar of that house for the preservation of her daughter's spirit? But to enter her sanctum, you must make an offering *she* will accept."

"She's rich. I've taken a vow of poverty. I failed to retrieve her phonograph recording. I have nothing of worth to offer her."

"I wouldn't be so sure of that," Frater H said, and placed the journal in Diego's hands.

CHAPTER SEVEN

That night at the temple would come to feel like a last remnant of a strange dream to Diego in the weeks that followed. A little island of time granted to him for pondering the tantalizing and terrifying mysteries of the Winchester House before the aftermath of the great quake tugged him along like an undertow into the heart of the broken city, where his priestly duties exhausted and consumed him. Everywhere he was sent he found the vacant eyes of people shocked by loss, the pained expressions of those broken and grief-stricken. The death toll had been greatest at the asylum, but countless survivors had lost homes and businesses in the conflagration that followed the cataclysm.

Diego had left the Rosicrucian temple empowered by Frater H's conviction that he would find the answers to his questions if he had the courage to pursue them. It had all sounded so simple. He possessed something the heiress wanted—a record of her daughter's secret confessions to the carpenter, her private hopes and fears. It seemed strange that a ghost could even have hopes and fears, but this one did. He'd felt like a voyeur reading those pages, but once he'd accepted that they were the words of Annie Pardee Winchester and not the fictions of a madman, it was impossible to ignore the sadness, terror, and longing for freedom that infused them. Surely the book would be a key to the house. A key to Sarah Winchester's confidence. And would Annie's words unlock her mother's heart to the necessity of finally letting the girl's spirit go? He had lain awake that night, staring at the cross on his bedroom wall, imagining what that encounter might look like. Him passing through the wrought iron gates of the sprawling mansion and knocking at the door with Joe Colton's journal in his hand.

What he would tell Father Xavier about his errand, he didn't yet know. His preference was to offer some version of the truth, but he would have to improvise, depending on whether or not the lady accepted his offer to banish the demonic force that threatened Annie's ghost and guide the girl to salvation. It was a night for wild dreams of spiritual heroism, but the next day dawned on the same old labors as the day before. Tending to the horses, sweeping the chapel, and then riding out with Peter to minister at funerals and console the sick and wounded.

The worst visits were to those who didn't die of their injuries or perish in the fire, but who withered away in makeshift hospitals until their lungs failed under the weight of the black smoke they'd inhaled.

Everywhere he and Peter went, they saw signs of utter destruction beside buildings that had been spared, as if a wanton God had rolled dice at every street corner. The chaos, the apparent randomness of it, troubled Diego deeply. But he soon found himself too busy for contemplation.

Before he knew it, weeks became months. The valley slowly nursed its wounds and rebuilt its towns and cities. One beam at a time—as if the endless construction at the Winchester House had spread like a virus through the region. Then, one night Diego happened to stumble upon the carpenter's journal again—it fell out of a cassock he'd wrapped it in when he removed the garment from his bottom dresser drawer—and it struck him with a flash as he recalled his fervor over the house in the earliest days following the earthquake.

Looking back, he wondered if he had obsessed over Joe Colton's story to distract himself from the tragedy that had surrounded him on all sides. Were these fantasies of good and evil a mere diversion he'd latched onto to dwell in abstractions and delay his confrontation with the pain and suffering of his neighbors? And if so, why had his mentor in the order encouraged him?

As life gradually turned toward some semblance of normalcy, he found himself returning to the journal, reading through it in private moments, tracing the spider web lines of pencil sketched stained glass windows with his finger. Puzzling over the lines from Shakespeare, the numerology of the architecture, until it dawned on him that these mysteries had been fermenting in the back of his mind the entire time he'd thought himself too busy to entertain them. His thoughts had matured, but not fully ripened yet. And this, he realized, was the real reason why he hadn't made time to visit Llanada Villa—the unshakeable feeling that he would be turned away at the door, journal or no journal, unless he could say something to Sarah Winchester in the minute or less he might be granted the opportunity that would convince her he knew enough about her grand design to help her.

In the pages of that notebook were trees he could identify root, branch, and leaf, but he couldn't grasp the scope of the forest, or tell where one path connected to another.

Then came a day in July, on an errand to San Jose for groceries, when he caught his first glimpse of Mrs. Winchester, and with it, an epiphany.

He was loading bags of vegetables into his wagon when the sound of strong horses trotting down the street reached his ears. Looking up, he saw a glossy Victoria approaching, drawn by a pair of sleek, black carriage horses. A driver in black livery with silver buttons sat atop the coachman's box, his passengers concealed by the canopy.

Diego wasn't the only one on the street to turn his head at the sight. Most of the adults maintained some discretion in their furtive glances, but the children chattered excitedly about the gold harness, and he was sure he heard the name Winchester more than once in their piping voices. For his part, the coachman kept his posture straight and his eyes fixed on some invisible horizon beyond the burned and wrecked buildings. A young woman in a gray hat and dress disembarked and approached the curb. The carriage had pulled up to a bookseller hawking newspapers, periodicals, and novels out of a street cart with an awning to shelter his wares from the weather.

An aged but elegant sign that might once have hung above the door of a now ruined shop proclaimed E. GRANT & Co. BOOKSELLERS.

Diego wasn't near enough to hear the exchange between the young lady and the bookseller, but the man seemed to know her and to have set something aside for her in advance. Was she Sarah Winchester's niece or secretary? He studied the lace-draped canopy of the Victoria and thought he could discern the shape of a black clad passenger wearing a veil over her face. Or was this his imagination filling in the details of obscure shadows? Mrs. Winchester's enigmatic appearance was, after all, legendary in the town. He'd been acquainted with the rumors passed among his congregation long before his encounter with Joe Colton.

Speculation about the lady's use of a veil and long gloves when she ventured out in public was especially prevalent. Some said her flesh had been badly burned in an accident before she moved to California, a detail that made Diego's own scarred hands tingle when he first heard it. Others, who claimed to know from the accounts of acquaintances employed at the estate, said she suffered from severe arthritis and was self-conscious about her bad teeth. In any event, she seldom stepped down from her carriage, preferring to send her assistant to gather and pay for goods, while she waited, sacrificing little privacy while remaining close enough for consultation.

In this case, none was required. Mr. Grant appeared to have just what the lady had ordered, despite the devastation to his shop. The vendor produced a hardbound book from his wagon and displayed it for the lady in gray. Diego took the opportunity to walk between the stall and the carriage, close enough to read the title over the woman's shoulder before the bookseller set it down and wrapped it in brown paper and twine before handing it over like a butcher delivering a prime cut.

The book was *The Way of the Spirit* by H. Rider Haggard. Diego had only read the author's most popular novel, *The Mines of King Solomon*, a fantastic adventure story set in North Africa with a plot worthy of Kipling. This new book was apparently the latest offering in a long line of adventure romances. Staring at the cover, Diego nearly tripped on the curb, but he righted his step at the last second and avoided spilling his grocery bag into the gutter.

He cut a straight line across the street, and resisting the urge to look back at the scene he'd just passed, he caught himself judging Mrs. Winchester's taste in literature. This popular fiction felt at odds with the idea he'd constructed in his mind of a woman absorbed with deeper intellectual pursuits. Was the book for her niece? Or did the title indicate a theme that aligned with Sarah's spiritualist inclinations? If he hadn't been acquainted with the author, he would have assumed exactly that.

When reading the carpenter's journal, Diego had pictured the bookshelves of the Winchester House lined with classical works and treatises of theology and philosophy, perhaps even demonology. The Grand Ballroom especially, he imagined, would be stuffed with such treasures among the panels of colored glass quoting Shakespeare.

And then the epiphany struck him all at once, and he nearly dropped his groceries again, like a drunkard who couldn't walk a block without stumbling. The meaning of those lines, which had eluded him for months, flashed upon his mind.

Books! The composite quote was a metaphor for books. The ballroom was also a library, and the lines from the Bard referred to the inhabitants of that room.

Wide unclasp the tables of their thoughts.

These same thoughts people this little world.

The reclusive lady was making reference to opening books, which when clasped shut imprisoned the thoughts of their authors. But to unclasp them, to open them wide, was to populate her mind and her home—*this little world*—with the characters and ideas they held. Books were her company, her estate a little world.

Diego realized he was smiling like a drunken fool and fixed his face, but the euphoria stayed with him. She couldn't possibly know it, but he suddenly felt closer than ever to the mind of the woman hiding behind layers of black lace behind him.

A moment later, he heard the music of harness and hoof overtaking him. As the shadow of the stately carriage cast a chill over the priest, Mrs. Winchester's silhouette appeared to turn in his direction, her inscrutable gaze fixed upon his face from behind the black veil as she passed.

CHAPTER EIGHT

On Friday, July 27, Father Diego Montero approached the Winchester House for the first time. He was dressed in the black cassock and cap of the Jesuit order, and carried the journal of Joe Colton, as well as his personal Bible, crucifix, and other tools of the exorcist's art in a slim briefcase at his side. The day was overcast, the air stagnant with a thick fog, when he arrived at the iron gate and found it ajar, as if in a mocking gesture of welcome. All accounts of unsolicited visitors he'd found in the tabloids told of locked gates and sentinels on the lookout. Expecting as much, he'd come prepared for a lengthy exchange relayed back and forth to the house by some sort of guard. When no such obstacles appeared, he found his hackles raised in wary suspicion.

A wagon of the sort used to transport building materials trundled up the gravel drive away from the house. Diego stepped aside, allowing it to pass through the open gate, and now he could see the signs on the wrought iron bars: NO ADMITTANCE and BEWARE OF THE DOG. When the wagon had exited, a boy in overalls jumped down from the empty bed, and Diego cast any fears he might have harbored about a guard dog aside. Seizing the moment, he stepped swiftly through to the grounds before the lad could latch the gate behind the wagon.

Maybe it was his age or the uniform of his office that kept the boy from questioning him, or maybe this team from the lumber yard had no interest in who came and went. In any case, realizing that his timing had been serendipitous, Diego strode across the lawn with renewed purpose and a silent prayer of thanks to Saint Francis.

A line of cypress hedges had obscured the details of the house from the road, but now they overwhelmed him. His eye was drawn first to the red shingle rooftop. Its jagged line described a zig-zagging path from the highest spindle-topped turrets and gables down through a proliferation of columns and gingerbread layers, endless panes of glass reflecting the gray sky in their blank eyes, and an impossibly convoluted pattern of brown cornices outlining multi-layered recesses and extruded features—towers, doors, and balconies in asymmetric profusion giving way to swathes of pale yellow shingles, rounded at the bottom, like sections of dragon scales.

Workmen, like the silhouettes of knights attacking that dragon in the mist, stood on scaffolding swinging hammers, or on the ground in nests of lumber. The shriek of an electric saw cut the air. And the ringing of hammer on nail punctuated the muted shouts of workmen lost to sight around the endless corners and wings of the rambling mansion.

The sharp odors of fresh paint and turpentine slithered into the priest's sinuses as he trod a path across the dew-jeweled lawn between towering palm trees and approached a pair of garden statues flanking a fountain – two women, the one on the left in a feathered turban holding a basket of flowers, the one on the right in a Greek gown holding a shallow bowl aloft. These were apparently the only sentinels standing guard at the front entrance. The fountain was dry. Algae stained the concrete basin. Corrosion marred a copper pipe protruding from the mouth of a creature that could have been part dolphin, part sea serpent from the corner of some antiquarian map of uncharted lands.

The front door of the house was an imposing slab of dark wood within a covered porch. Set with panes of beveled glass in a fleur-de-lis motif, it was framed by an arch of matching wood carved in a pyramidal pattern that repeated along the bottom of the door. The effect was jarring, and one that echoed throughout the architecture—a feminine floral theme offset by jagged aggressive shapes, hints of predatory energy barely concealed by whimsical and decorous distractions.

Father Diego mounted the porch steps, took a breath, and rang the doorbell.

The percussive rhythms of the work crew continued around him, masking any sound from within the house, but a moment later he glimpsed shadows shifting through the great crystal windows. The door swung wide, and he was faced with the same flaxen-haired woman he'd seen conducting Mrs. Winchester's business with the bookseller on the street in San Jose. She was young, and likely pretty when in a favorable mood, but her quick, blue eyes took inventory of the priest in less than two seconds. With a curt nod of her head, she said, "Mrs. Winchester already has a church, thank you."

And with that, the heavy door began to glide shut on well-oiled hinges.

"*Wait!*" Diego said. "I'm not here proselytizing." He shifted his briefcase to his left-hand and extended the right, fingers unfolded, for her to shake. "Father Diego Montero," he said, "from the Mission of Santa Clara, to see Mrs. Sarah Winchester."

The woman returned a handshake as curt as her previous assessment of his attire and said, "Pleased, I'm sure, but I'm afraid you haven't made an appointment."

"And how would one go about that, Mrs. ..."

"Weatherlake. Mrs. Winchester's secretary. And in answer to your question, one would not. Mrs. Winchester isn't seeing visitors at this time."

"I see. And when might she be seeing visitors again?"

"I can't answer on her behalf, but experience suggests, well... perhaps when Christ returns. Good day, Father. I'll certainly tell her you called."

The door swung toward him again. This time he caught it with the heel of his hand. His strength was greater than hers, but he felt immediately embarrassed by the use of physical force, and fearful that the secretary would cry for the workmen to drag him from the porch and toss him through the gates. "Please, Mrs. Weatherlake. Hear me out. I'm afraid my attire has worked against me today. You see, my philosophy is not as black and white as my dress. And you'd be forgiven for doubting it, but I come here as a kindred spirit to your employer. A fellow traveler."

The secretary squinted at him.

"If you live in this house," he continued, "then surely you're aware of Mrs. Winchester's spiritualist practices. They're hardly a secret."

"Rumors," she said, her jawline tense.

"Would you please tell her that I bear a message from her daughter."

"How *dare* you?"

This time she shut the door in his face.

He raised his fist to knock but stopped in mid-air. Was Mrs. Winchester watching him from one of the multitude of windows? Peering at his distorted image through a shard of crystal? He took a few steps back and scanned for a sign of movement in the glass. There was none he could discern, but that didn't mean he wasn't being watched. Had she heard what he'd said to her secretary? Or was Sarah in some far off wing of the house? If she wasn't eavesdropping on his interaction with Mrs. Weatherlake, would his words even reach her? The younger woman had obviously been offended by them and taken him for a charlatan. Why would she trouble her employer with something she'd dismissed?

This was all going so wrong. He'd imagined it differently when he'd resolved to introduce himself, though now he found himself unable to recall what that other, better version of events looked like. He knew only that his long season of meditation on Sarah Winchester's perilous spiritual ambitions had convinced him it was within his power to help her and her daughter. His time spent pouring over the carpenter's journal had led him to feel as if he'd met Annie already. Maybe that familiarity had made him overconfident. It was frustrating to be turned away by a secretary when he knew in his bones that he had found what he believed were the keys to reaching Mrs. Winchester, if only he could speak with her directly.

But the heavy door stared back at him implacably, the cold glare of its gray glass unmoved.

And why should she welcome him in? Why should she trust a man with a briefcase—like a traveling salesman in priest's garb—when he'd made no effort at correspondence and had slipped furtively through her front gate at an opportune moment? She wasn't even Catholic! He'd asked around and found out that she attended Saint Paul's in Burlingame on the rare occasions when she attended church at all.

He'd gone about this all wrong. Repairing the damage might call for desperate measures, but a girl's mortal soul was at stake.

Without pausing for further thought, he laid his briefcase on the deck boards, unlatched it, and removed the carpenter's journal. By now he knew the book by heart and it took scarcely a minute to locate the well-thumbed page he'd often pictured himself showing Mrs. Winchester in one of her sitting rooms over tea and biscuits. He tore the page from the book, folded it in half, slid it under the door, and rang the bell again.

No turning back now. The die is cast.

The hammering of the carpenters counted out an interminable interval while he waited for a response.

When the door swung open, it was not the secretary or the lady of the house standing before him, but a stocky man in overalls and a cap. The man seized him by the collar and dragged him over the threshold and down the hall, the toes of his shoes catching on a Persian carpet runner and bunching it up until the man lifted him over the little woven waves with a quick, "Sorry, Ma'am," before setting him down again and shoving him forward with two hard palms to the shoulder blades.

Diego stumbled down the hall, his briefcase lost somewhere behind him. Glimpses of opulence flashed past him on both sides—dark wainscoting and flower-patterned plaster, a piano, at least two fireplaces, a grand staircase. A dining room with a chandelier flashed by, the long table draped with a canvas tarp, the walls cracked by the earthquake. A second dining room followed, similarly damaged and draped, like a reflection in a giant mirror.

The man clamped a hand on Diego's shoulder and dug his fingers and thumb into the bundle of nerves under his clavicle, steering him around a tight corner and into a vast kitchen, where the work of servants echoed from the tiled ceiling and walls.

"Take a break," a woman's voice said, and the kitchen staff scattered, leaving half washed pots lying in the sink basins, and half-chopped vegetables scattered beside a knife on a cutting board.

The brute, whose face he'd barely caught a glimpse of, spun Diego around to face him—bushy eyebrows and black razor shadow framed the ruddy face of a drinking man. The smell of coal and coffee wafted from him as he slammed the priest backward onto a bloodstained butcher block.

"Well done, Clyde. We can't have him pissing himself in the foyer." And then, in a volume that suggested she'd turned her head to address someone else: "Why do you suppose interlopers never approach the back of the house?"

"I don't know, Ma'am." This sounded like Mrs. Weatherlake.

"I'd much prefer to have them marched into the stables. Fetch Duke, would you?"

"Yes, Ma'am."

"Please, Mrs. Winchester," Diego said, struggling against the man pinning him down. "There's been a misunderstanding. I want nothing from you but a moment of your time."

"Is that so?"

A side door opened and closed and the room erupted with the fierce barking of a dog. The man Mrs. Winchester had called Clyde took his beefy hand off Diego's chest, allowing him to lift his shoulders off the butcher block. But as soon as he'd come up far enough for a level look at the room, the dog lunged forward—a snapping German shepherd straining at the end of a chain held by Mrs. Weatherlake. Diego scrambled backward. It seemed absurd that the small woman could restrain such a beast—maybe it was trained to put on a show and only attack on command—but its fangs chomped at the empty air mere inches from Diego's crotch.

"Heel, Duke," Mrs. Winchester commanded. The dog settled on its haunches with a low growl. "You were saying that you want nothing from me, Father..."

"Montero," the secretary offered. "Father Diego Montero from the Santa Clara Mission."

"Then what exactly is this?" Mrs. Winchester shook the fold out of the page from Joe Colton's journal and thrust it in Diego's face. "Because it looks very much like a blackmail threat to me."

She was shorter than he'd expected, a petite woman with a straight spine and regal bearing in a plain black dress, her gray hair pinned up in a bun, her eyes more fierce than the dog's. The paper in her clawed hand showed not the slightest tremor. The carpenter's transcription of his conversation with the ghost.

Where are you, Annie?

A: I'm in the tower. Mother says I must stay in the tower until she traps the monster in one of her webs. I'm safe in the tower because of the wards. Maybe you could visit me, Joe? I'm lonely here.

I don't think I can do that. If I was caught up there, I'd get fired and then we couldn't talk at all. But I'll use this tube when no one's watching. I'm glad you're okay.

A: You saved me, Joe. You held it at bay when it sniffed me out in the ballroom.

What is it? A Minotaur?

A: Mother says it's a demon, but the other ghosts say it's a god. One of the oldest gods. The child eater.

There are other ghosts in the house?

A: Yes, but they're so thin I can't hardly see them. Like moth-eaten curtains. They say the monster can eat me because I'm neither here nor there, but they say Mother sacrificed them to it to fuel the house. The house runs on them that died bloody. I'm trapped here, Joe. Can you help me escape?

I don't know, but I have to go. Someone's coming.

Diego knew the words by heart. He'd spent many a late night pondering them.

"Where did you get this?" the lady demanded.

"From a carpenter who worked for you. Joe Colton. He died in the earthquake. I performed his last rites. He transcribed his conversations with your daughter."

Someone had picked up his briefcase from where he'd dropped it in the hall while being dragged. Now Mrs. Winchester placed it on the kitchen counter, popped the latches, and opened the lid. After a cursory examination of his priestcraft tools, she removed the journal from which he'd torn the page and flipped through its contents.

"What were you planning to do with this? Threaten me with selling it to the tabloids?"

"No, ma'am. That was not my intention, I swear."

"They'd pay a pretty penny, I'm sure, for a firsthand account of my sorcery. I'm well aware of the rumors. But why the holy water and other paraphernalia? Do you bring them everywhere you go, even on the Devil's errands?"

"I want to be of service, Mrs. Winchester. As a priest and exorcist. I want to help you…to help your daughter. But I've gone about it all wrong. You're a difficult woman to approach." He blurted this out quickly, hoping that some piece of what he said would buy him the time needed to explain his motives in greater depth.

She placed the folded page inside the cover of the journal and closed it, taking time to consider her next words.

"Mr. Colton died in the earthquake? You were there when he died?"

"Yes."

"I'm sorry to learn this. He was a troubled man."

Mrs. Weatherlake chimed in. "Ma'am, if I may… It will be a matter of record that Joe was institutionalized shortly after you let him go. Even if the papers were interested in publishing the diary excerpts of a madman, no one would believe them."

Mrs. Winchester sighed. "You might be surprised by what people will believe if it suits what they *want* to believe. What they already imagine. The papers would suggest that working on my house was what drove Joe mad. That he'd seen things here that shattered his mind. After a fortnight of scandalous revelations, half the population of California would believe *I* caused the trembler."

Mrs. Weatherlake scoffed. "That's absurd."

"Absurdity is no impediment to a good rumor. The mystery is half the fun for them. *How did she do it?* Interview the local psychics and mediums. Perhaps she cast a spell. Or raised a demon that cracked the foundations of the earth."

At this, Mrs. Weatherlake turned away and stared at the floor, as if Mrs. Winchester had confessed to some private fetish. Diego noticed that despite the slackening of its chain, the dog remained rigidly poised on its haunches, waiting for a command, though its growling had subsided.

"*Why* did she do it?" Mrs. Winchester continued. "To punish one carpenter who betrayed her confidence? Her wrath has no sense of proportion. The widow's grief has been inflicted on the entire valley... Do you see? An act of God offers no such profitable speculation. But the act of a crazy woman? Of a witch? It provides endless entertainment. I'd wager this isn't the first confession you've spun into gold, Father. But it must be the most ambitious. So, what's your price?"

"I have none. I swear by all that is holy, you've misjudged me."

"I don't believe you."

The dog might have waited for a more direct command, but this was apparently enough for Clyde, who seized Diego's wrist and pinned it to the butcher block. The brute fished a long, thick carpentry nail from the breast pocket of his overalls and held it clenched in his fist like a railroad spike above Diego's writhing palm. "Shall I give him a taste of his Lord's suffering, Ma'am?"

The dog barked, as if goading him to do it.

"*Please,* hear me out!" Diego pleaded. "You pretend to jest about what caused the quake, but I know what forces you've snared in this house. Now your wards are failing and you're running out of time. You need my help! Let me help you before the blood moon on the fourth. Before your defenses are breached again."

Mrs. Winchester's nostrils flared.

"Put the nail away, Clyde. Your poetic mind is wasted on physical labor, but I've no further need of your assistance here. Take Duke back to the barn."

The henchman was visibly disappointed, but he dropped the heavy nail back into his breast pocket and let go of Diego's wrist. The priest's hand tingled as the blood returned to his fingers.

"What about him?" Clyde asked.

"I've changed my mind. I'm going to hear his story. Mary? Call the kitchen staff back and have them prepare tea for two."

CHAPTER NINE

They dined in a room Mrs. Winchester referred to as "the Venetian," a dark wood paneled space with a low ceiling that made Father Diego feel as though they were on a boat except for the greenery and statuary he could see through a large picture window to the right of the lace draped table. The long room was divided by a partial wall and a set of carved wooden arches. Beside a fireplace of ruddy Italian marble, a cabinet set with glass windows allowed the chef to pass plates through from a sliding door on the kitchen side, where they waited for a servant to remove them from the cabinet and carry them to the table. Apparently, this was a smaller kitchen than the one in which Diego had been interrogated, set deeper in the house, away from the east facing side that had suffered the most damage during the quake. The larger dining rooms in that wing had been shuttered for renovation, and the lady had since taken to receiving her meals in this central dining room.

The walk to the Venetian room had been disorienting, with too many twists and turns for Diego to maintain any sense of where he was in relation to the rooms he'd seen upon entering. They passed what had to be the ballroom described in the journal, and at least that room appeared to have sustained no damage in the quake. A good part of the first floor was devoted to the operations of the staff, with narrow corridors twisting off in all directions, odd little changes in level with a step up or down here and there, diamond shaped windows in walls that looked into adjacent rooms, as well as apertures in the ceiling that allowed light to stream in from the upper floors. There were doors too small to make sense even as closets or cupboards, and long stretches of the building where the wood was painted in creamy yellow hues lit by abundant natural light through a seemingly endless procession of windows. The resulting effect was a sensation of plunging through alternating passages of glaring light and oppressive darkness, unsettling emptiness and tight confinement.

When Mrs. Weatherlake finally offered Diego a chair at the dining room table, he felt awash with relief at the chance to settle in one place and focus his attention on the details of a single room. Once seated, Mrs. Winchester dismissed the secretary, but that didn't leave Diego alone with the lady of the house. A Japanese manservant poured tea and delivered trays laden with baked apples and cakes before retreating to busy himself with polishing the silverware at the far end of the dining room. He looked cleaner and less intimidating than Clyde, but still managed to telegraph a wary attention that led Diego to contemplate the sharpness of the steak knives that were the objects of his attention.

"Don't mind him," Mrs. Winchester said. "My staff is very protective of me."

"I noticed." Despite the change of tone, Diego felt sweaty and anxious. A chemical taste lingered in his mouth from the nervous excitement of the violence he'd been threatened with only moments ago.

"Clyde does get a bit overzealous at times. He's not unlike the dog in that regard."

"What is his job, exactly? Bodyguard?"

Mrs. Winchester laughed. Diego noticed that her teeth were crooked, but the sound was infused with a relaxed warmth. This was a woman with confidence in her own home. "Clyde is a general handyman. He maintains the fireplaces and furnaces, empties the ashes from the chutes, tends to interior repairs and plumbing. I have no proper security guards on the payroll, but most of the workmen pitch in when the need arises. They're a very loyal crew. With few exceptions over the years."

"Such as Joe Colton."

"Yes. Which pains me because loyalty is a two-way street. I take a genuine interest in improving the lives of my employees."

"I've heard that you pay most of them twice what they would make for the same work elsewhere."

"That's true. I provide housing as well where there's a need."

"In this house?"

"Not often. I've built smaller houses on the grounds for carpenters and gardeners. How is the tea?"

"Delightful, thank you."

"I've always felt that the British were onto something with afternoon tea. It's a civilized custom."

"Have you visited England?"

She nodded. "Most of Europe and Persia. Most recently Paris before moving to California."

"I understand you speak several languages."

"My parents raised me to be a socialite. Language and music lessons were par for the course."

A moment passed while they sipped the tea. A clock ticked on the mantle.

Diego shot a furtive glance at the man polishing the silverware. "I'm grateful for your hospitality, Mrs. Winchester. But I must say, it's a little disorienting…adjusting to it after the way I was greeted."

She patted her lips with a napkin and set it down on the table. "Please accept my apologies for the rough handling, Father. I get all kinds trying to pry into my business and I daresay your strategy was provocative. You must have known it was fraught with risk."

"I didn't know how else to capture your attention."

"Well, you certainly succeeded in that. And please don't misunderstand your current status, despite the hospitality. You've said some things that earned you an audience, suggested that you may be of assistance, but I've yet to buy anything you're selling, or to reach a verdict on your sincerity."

"I can assure you I am quite sincere in my desire to help. I only spent a few minutes with Mr. Colton, but they were the last minutes of his life. I don't claim to understand your history with him after reading only his side of the story, but you should know that when he faced death, his greatest concern was for your daughter's soul. That must count for—"

"Enough. We will not speak his name in this house, Father,"

Diego's briefcase had been placed on a sideboard by Mrs. Weatherlake, but he doubted the carpenter's journal was in it. The contents would be an impossible subject to avoid if they were to converse in any depth about what was happening in the house.

"You spoke of the blood moon," Mrs. Winchester said. "Please elaborate. And remember that you stand on very thin ice."

The priest sat up straight and cleared his throat. "I believe that you, like me, are a student of the ancient mystery schools..."

"Go on."

"You have a fascination with the number thirteen. This represents the annual lunar cycles. You have a love of knowledge and philosophy. Perhaps your travels and fluency in classical languages has served to deepen this knowledge. Your love of books is proclaimed even in the Tiffany glass windows of your ballroom, which also serves as a library."

She raised an eyebrow at this. "You saw them in passing and believe you've decoded them?"

"No, I'm not that quick-witted. I read about them, and other features of the house."

"In the diary."

"Yes. So I've had time to contemplate their meaning. *Wide unclasp the tables of their thoughts*. In *Troilus and Cressida,* this is a reference to the lewd thoughts of the soldiers being unleashed by Cressida kissing each of them, but I think for you, it refers to opening books and setting their contents loose. That rings true for me, based on what little I know of you."

"Please. Before you go on, do tell me what you know of me."

"That you are well-educated, a reader and thinker, a worldly woman with an interest in the esoteric."

"And you, Father, are a politician. But continue. Tell me what the second verse means."

"Once I deciphered the first, the second was easy. The two are harmonious taken together. *These same thoughts people this little world.* Every character in a book or a play… They are all thoughts, first in the author's mind and then in the reader's. And it could be said that they populate our imaginations when we read. For a solitary person such as yourself, it seems that these would be companions populating your house through the books on your shelves. But I believe that's only the first level of meaning."

"Not bad, so far as it goes. But now you walk a perilous path. What is the second level of meaning?"

"There are books in this world that aim not to conjure fictional characters but other creatures of the mind and spirit—angels, demons, and gods. I don't know if you keep such books in your collection, but we've all heard fairy tales about such creatures escaping their paper prisons."

"Don't all of the fairy stories about *me* say that I'm haunted by ghosts, not angels or demons?"

Diego nodded. "That would be the third level of meaning. That each human soul is an idea in the mind of God, and that some of these populate your house as ghosts. Certainly your daughter falls into this category, and if the rumors are true, possibly also the ghosts of Winchester rifle victims, though I find that idea less likely."

"Hmph. Again, not a bad theory. I am a student of the mysteries. I do like a good theory, a good story, even if it isn't true. But this one feels a little thin."

Diego took a sip of tea. There was something oddly floral in the flavor, but he found it complimented the cakes perfectly. "I could flesh it out, if I'm not altogether on the wrong track."

"You may be so far-off the track that you need a machete, but I'd still like to see where you're going."

He leaned forward and held her gaze. "Just as these two windows are meant to be taken together for their meaning, I would be surprised if the other windows you've commissioned aren't part of a larger code to which they're connected. In a temple of the mystery schools, every object is symbolic, all of them sign posts on the path of the initiate toward greater wisdom. The Freemasons speak allegorically of building the temple that is the perfected man. They liken it to the building of the temple of Solomon. And your magnum opus, this eternally unfinished house…it is also a temple, is it not?"

Now it was Mrs. Winchester's turn to sip and remain silent.

Diego took it as a sign to continue. "Many of the windows depict spider webs, because, as in a spider's web, all points are connected. A fly touches the web in one place, and every thread of silk is set thrumming. In this way, the spider knows everything that happens in her domain, every disturbance, every fly trapped. One of your windows depicts thirteen orbs caught in a web. I believe these are the thirteen moons of the lunar year."

"And what is the significance of that?"

"Primitive peoples have always observed a connection between the lunar cycles and the ability of spirits to pass in and out of our world. Whether they be demons, the faery folk, or the ghosts of the departed, traditions from all across the globe acknowledge those moments when the membrane between worlds is thin. This lore is found in the folk magic of the medieval witch and the tribal shaman, but the occultists of the Renaissance elaborated on these celestial correspondences. Heinrich Cornelius Agrippa provided the tables by which a magician might calculate the hours when such forces were present according to the planets and their houses. Pyramids, ziggurats, and stone circles across the globe were aligned precisely to the positions of celestial bodies at the solstices and equinoxes that their high priests might harness these powers from beyond."

"Fascinating, Father Montero. Truly. And surprising to hear from a man of the cloth. But what has any of it to do with my house?" The lady seemed amused, though whether because she found his ideas ludicrous or accurate, he couldn't tell.

"The Winchester House is one such temple. Its main entrance faces east, the direction of the rising sun. I would imagine that the elaborate door of beveled crystal panes refracts that light in a scintillating display of rainbows at dawn on a clear day—the white light broken into shards of every hue, a symbol of the mind of God fractured into myriad imperfect spirits. *These thoughts people this little world.* But what if the house is more than the temple of an initiate recently returned from Paris where the Masonic orders are known to admit women? What if the house, like an Egyptian pyramid, is a resurrection engine? This is what I've been pondering for months. What if the architecture of the house is designed to trap souls in its web? In a precisely calculated occult labyrinth? What if every angle, every corner and tower, was placed in alignment with the celestial cycles, so that souls otherwise bound to other planes could be bound to *this* place, and drawn into it on moonbeams through these fine-tuned crystal windows?"

Father Diego paused for a reaction, but Mrs. Winchester only stared at him, her breath slow and deep, her gaze opaque. Did those eyes brim with barely restrained fury? Or was it awe at being truly seen and understood, maybe for the first time?

"My *theory*..." Diego continued, "is that Annie is not fully manifest in this house at all times. I believe that, like the tides, her presence swells and withdraws with the waxing and waning of the moon. The dates in the carpenter's journal bear this out. But there are other presences that have contaminated your web, and they have their own cycles of power. I don't know if you accounted for these in your calculations and some flaw has undermined your control, or if your web caught something you didn't expect alongside your daughter's ghost. But what I'm almost certain you *didn't* account for is the disruptions in the cycles of darkness and light that come with eclipses.

"There was an eclipse on February 8th. You fired the carpenter soon after, and judging by his journal entries, he witnessed something that night that traumatized him and precipitated his mental breakdown. Approximately two months before the earthquake. As if something unleashed by the eclipse continued growing in strength until it shook the earth and almost brought the house down. You believe Joe was interfering with your daughter, trespassing on your privacy, maybe even turning her against you, but I believe he was trying to protect her. I also believe that just as the moon waxes and wanes gradually, the ability of ghosts and other spirits to manifest in this house is a process that can take weeks or even months to reach fullness and remission. Is it the same for whatever demon used the eclipse to slip past your defenses?

Did it linger? Is it still here, roaming your labyrinth in shadow form, waiting to gain strength from the next event?"

Mrs. Winchester looked past Diego's shoulder, presumably at her man in the corner. He didn't turn to follow her gaze. If she was summoning help to eject him from the house, if he had overstepped his bounds and failed to prove his worth, he was at least determined to finish presenting his thesis before they dragged him out. "The next total eclipse will happen one week from now, on Saturday August 4th. I believe I can help you prepare for it, help you fortify your already weakened spiritual defenses. I have that authority."

"Authority granted by *whom,* Father? Does your Jesuit order know you're here? Do they know you dabble in the occult? That is what you're describing, is it not? You wish to establish magical wards against demonic forces. You've clearly read your Agrippa. And while you may be a church appointed exorcist, I doubt the Pope would approve of *that.*" She arched her brow and the corner of her mouth curled up with it, taunting him.

"My authority is from God. Yes, I admit I've augmented my education with sources outside the canon, but that is to your advantage. I present myself only to offer my services. I ask nothing in return. Please accept my help. Allow me to finish the work that Joe Colton wished he could do. He lacked the skills to truly protect your daughter's soul, though his heart moved him to try."

Mrs. Winchester laughed. A cold sound. "You men of the cloth are so arrogant. Do you think you can splash some holy water around my house, recite some psalms, and banish the evil that thrives like black mold in dark corners? You have guessed much, Father, I'll grant you that. And your intellect is a pleasant surprise. But the truest thing you've said is that you know only one side of the carpenter's story. Nor do you have more than an inkling of the powers I'm up against. You fancy that ghosts and demons pop their heads up like groundhogs when the luminaries allow it…" She scoffed. "This house is a precision instrument and there are monsters in the machinery. The spirit that surged during the February blood moon *does* have its own cycle of strength, but you have no idea how great that strength is. The echoes of its last emergence caused the quake that trapped me in one of my own rooms! You've seen the physical damage with your own eyes." She shook her head. "If you truly believe you're up to the task of confronting such a power, I have a little test for you first. We'll see if you scurry out the gates of Llanada Villa with your tail between your legs."

"A test? What would you have me do?"

She looked at the clock on the mantle. The ticking echoed in Father Diego's ears with an aching throb that sounded as if it issued from the bottom of a deep well.

When her head turned to face him again, it left a gray trail in its wake. She smiled, and said, "If you pass, you may call me Sarah."

CHAPTER TEN

When Diego regained consciousness on the dusty floor of a bare room, the first thing he saw was a man sitting Indian style in front of him. A silver object lay on the floor between them. Another glowed between the man's hands in the dim light. The Jesuit's vision was cloudy at first, but as the drug wore off and adrenaline surged with his dawning awareness, the room and its occupant resolved into greater clarity.

The man was the Japanese servant from the dining room. He even continued his chore of polishing the knives he'd been working on while Diego sat for tea with his mistress, as if he'd merely been transported to another room of the house with no interruption to his work. Diego watched him warily. The man's eyes and hands remained fixed on the simple task with a meditative focus that lent the chore an air of religious reverence. The room, too, had something of the appearance of a temple or shrine. The lack of furniture and decor only added to this effect. Bare wooden boards and beams arched toward convergence at the peak of the circular room, the pattern interrupted only by the triangular entryway where Diego had been placed. Two windows, one on each side of the chamber, were covered in sheer curtains which allowed just enough light to describe the servant, his knives, and the object on the floor between them.

Diego took care not to move his head or body while sweeping his gaze from the peak of what was likely the house's tallest turret to the glowing silver box at eye level, two yards away from him in the center of the room.

Despite his discretion, the servant noticed the motion of his eyelids and paused in his work. He set the knife and polishing cloth in the velvet-lined case that held the rest of the silverware set and leaned forward, head cocked low in an effort to make eye contact.

"You're up," he said. "I thought maybe we got the dose wrong and you'd sleep through the night." The man did have an Asian accent, but his English was crisp and fluent. His voice was also subtly amplified by the strange acoustics of the circular room.

Diego abandoned pretense and sat up, bracing himself with a hand pressed against the floor. The boards were rough, like the rest of what appeared to be an unfinished attic space. He focused his attention on the silver object: a rectangular box with a hinged lid inlaid with a delicate Arabesque.

"What is that?" he asked.

"A music box. Mrs. Winchester acquired it on her travels in Constantinople. This was some years ago when her husband was selling guns to the Turks. She brought many treasures back from this journey. Books, jewels, carpets. But mostly knowledge. She is fluent in several Persian dialects. Enough to converse with an Iranian prince who briefly courted her sister. I served them tea."

Diego's throat burned. His parched mouth held a bitter tang. "I've heard that the serving of tea is a religious ceremony in Japan. Is that where you're from? What would your ancestors think of you serving it with poison to a priest?"

The man smiled. "Not poison, Father. Only a sleeping draught."

Diego's final moments of consciousness in the Venetian dining room returned to him. "Mrs. Winchester said she had a test for me. Is this it?"

"Yes. A test for both of us, I'm afraid."

"How so? Are we supposed to fight?"

"You and I? No. I will be as absent as you were until a moment ago. Your contest is with the creature in the box."

"What do you mean? There's something trapped in there? What is it? A scorpion? A snake?" He pressed the heel of his hand harder against the floor and prepared to launch himself away from whatever might spring from the box if the man flipped the lid.

"No, no. Something older, swifter, and much more dangerous."

"And you're to leave me here with it? How is that a test for you?" The priest rose slowly to his feet, wobbled for a precarious few seconds of overwhelming dizziness, and then moved to the door behind him. He braced a hand on one of the beams to steady his teetering body, then tried the knob: locked.

"My body will remain in this room," the servant said. "My mind will step aside for the thing in the box. *My* test is trusting Mrs. Winchester enough to share her faith in your ability to vanquish it."

Diego saw that the man's fingers trembled as he flicked the catch that held the lid secure. He lifted the lid and music emanated from the box—chimes produced by wound gears. They ascended an exotic scale defined by melancholy and yearning, echoing off the walls of the circular room. Despite himself, Diego was entranced by the sound.

So too was the servant. He stared into the box in his lap with an expression of rapt wonder, as if he could see some celestial figure weaving a spiral dance in accord with the uncanny tune. The man's features went slack for the space of a breath before transforming into something other, something his bone structure was ill equipped to represent, though it made every effort to do so. His eyes receded beneath the shelf of his brow. His temples rose in mimicry of horns. His cheeks hollowed, and his chin jutted to a sharp point. His physiology also morphed, muscles bulging as he rose from the floor, his spine arched in a way that called to mind hyenas and prehistoric predators. But if the transformation had regressed him to something akin to an animal, it did not prevent him from handling tools, for he snatched up the knife he'd set aside with new purpose, and brandished it at the priest, the blade glowing bright in the dusky light.

Father Diego was unarmed. There were other knives in the case at the servant's feet, but his chances of seizing one without getting cut were slim. He'd never been athletic as a young man, never learned to wrestle or fight. He also lacked the weapons of his vocation, the briefcase containing his bible, crucifix, holy water, and hosts hadn't been provided to him as the servant's knives had been. He raised his hands in a defensive posture, eyes darting around the room for an escape. If he was unwilling to crash through one of the windows to an unknown fate, he would be cornered prey in a room devoid of corners.

The possessed man lunged at him with a roar, slashing the air as Diego ducked and dodged. On the third swipe, the blade caught on his cassock sleeve. He tangled with his attacker, freed himself, and shoved the man, sending him careening toward the door.

Diego stumbled into the center of the room, wishing in vain for a table or chair—anything he could use as a shield. He ripped one of the curtains aside and saw rooftops sloping away beyond the glass.

The demon glared at him through the servant's dark eyes. Chest heaving with rasping breath, it approached with the slow confidence of a predator.

A burning thread of pain twined up Diego's right arm, and he saw that blood dripped from the gash in his sleeve, pattering on the floor between the case of silverware and the music box chiming its mournful melody.

He thought again of seizing a knife to defend himself, but this was not a test of martial prowess. He had so far reacted to the attack with physical responses to a physical threat, but his opponent's transformation was spiritual. Only a spiritual response could truly disarm him of the violent rage and superhuman strength he'd been empowered with.

And yet, even in that arena in which he *had* trained as a kind of warrior, he was disadvantaged. His consecrated tools had been taken from him, leaving only his hands, voice, and memory with which to devise a defense.

No sooner had he formed the thought than the demon lunged across the room, kicking the music box and sending it skittering across the floor into the peaked entryway, then driving the priest into the wall. Diego caught his attacker by the wrist and fought to hold the blade away from his own throat. The body that attacked him was that of a slim, lightweight man when it wasn't infused with the power of evil.

Nonetheless, he was driven to the floor with irresistible force. The jaws of the transformed face gnashed at the air inches from his eyes, spraying spittle across his cheek.

With his left hand he tugged at the breast of his own garment, ripped the buttons from their threads, and clawed frantically at the silver chain he wore around his neck. When the medallion emerged from the collar of his undershirt, his attacker recoiled at the sight: the Seal of Solomon, a silver pentacle adorned with divine names and sigils.

"By the power of Adonai, I command you, rebellious jinn! By al-Nur, do I banish you to the outer dark, child of Ibis!"

The servant shuddered and dropped the knife as if it burned in his hand. He hissed and gnashed his teeth at the priest.

But Father Diego brandished the medallion again, thrusting it at the possessed man, who flinched at the symbol. His voice rose to a bellow as the rest of the banishing surfaced from the recesses of his memory, and he felt that he too was possessed, with divine authority.

"By the force of the angel Gabriel and the rod of Melchizedek, I drive you out! Hear thou me and depart, for mine is the voice of fire, and every spirit of the firmament and of the ether, upon the earth and under the earth, of whirling air and of rushing fire, and every spell and scourge of God is obedient unto me!"

Whatever power had driven the servant's body to violence, it withdrew at the command, leaving the man to collapse like a marionette with severed strings.

Diego shoved the body aside, pushing the man by the shoulder and rolling him over onto his back. He looked dead but for his breathing, though Diego couldn't hear it over his own.

The music box played on, unspooling its icy chimes in an endless round.

The doorknob rattled and the door swung open. Mrs. Winchester swept into the room in her black mourner's gown. Ignoring the tableau laid out before her—the bodies sprawled on the floor amid a drizzle of blood in the dust—she extended one foot clad in a shiny black shoe and shut the lid of the silver box.

In the silence that followed, it seemed to Diego that more than sound had been snuffed out by the action. An oppressive trace of malevolence had vanished from the air with it.

The lady of the house regarded the priest.

"You may call me Sarah," she said at last.

Father Diego examined his wound. The cut was long and clean, but not deep.

"Let's get you cleaned up, Father."

"He could have killed me."

"I imagine that's an occupational hazard for an exorcist."

He staggered to his feet, dripping blood from his sleeve.

Mrs. Winchester called down the hall for a servant to take him to a washroom, and another to fetch clean bandages. As they ushered him past her, he held her gaze. "What would you have done if I'd failed to drive it out of him? Send him to the asylum?"

Again, she looked vaguely amused. It was infuriating. "Isn't your kind always going on about *faith?* I had faith in you, Father."

"And if I failed?"

She raised an eyebrow as if it should be obvious. "I'd have shut the lid sooner."

CHAPTER ELEVEN

The head housekeeper, a stout lady named Mrs. Brown, met Father Diego in the North Conservatory to bandage his slashed arm. The expansive greenhouse room was equipped with several large, low sinks and a tile floor, which enabled her to clean and dress the wound while keeping the mess away from the kitchens and bathrooms. Dusk settled on the grounds beyond the windows while she tended to him among an exotic collection of potted plants, the air in the room thick with their humidity. Mrs. Brown handled her patient gently but tied the bandage tight after irrigating the gash with a stinging antiseptic.

When the job was done, Mrs. Weatherlake escorted the priest to a bedroom on the third floor where he found his briefcase waiting on a small desk of blond wood. The secretary opened a closet door and waved a hand at an assortment of men's clothing: shirts, canvas trousers, and sleeping attire, including a luxurious plum velvet robe. "Mrs. Winchester has acquired some extra garments from her brothers-in-law. I've selected some that I think will fit you."

Diego turned his forearm to show her the faint pink bloodstain already showing through the bandage.

"Don't worry about that. They're only hand-me-downs. Yours to take with you when you leave. But I'll have Mrs. Brown check in on you again before you turn in tonight, to change your bandages. Will you be needing anything else?"

"No. Thank you."

"Very well, then. Mrs. Winchester would like you to join her for a nightcap in the Grand Ballroom at nine o'clock. She usually takes her meals alone, but I can have a light supper prepared for you in the Venetian where you took tea this afternoon."

His stomach groaned at the thought of food before he could reply.

"I'll take that as a yes and tell the kitchen staff to expect you within the hour. That will give you time to change and wash up. There are several bathrooms to choose from on this floor. The nearest is five doors down on the left. The staircase to the first floor should put you on familiar ground, but if you'd like a guide to the dining room, just press the button above the desk and someone will come."

Diego took in the bed, the open closet, and his briefcase on the desk. "Am I to..."

"Stay the night? Yes. Possibly longer, if your schedule allows. Mrs. Winchester will discuss the offer with you when you join her this evening, I'm sure."

It seemed to Diego that days must have passed since he'd met this young lady at the front door, though he knew it had only been hours. So much had happened already. His head ached and his arm throbbed. He wondered how the servant who'd attacked him was faring. He almost inquired after the man, but decided against it and merely thanked the secretary for her assistance. He had many questions she could probably answer if she felt inclined to, but now was not the time, and he sensed that a cold current still flowed beneath her polite manner. She withdrew, closing the door behind her.

The room he'd been assigned was small, with a low ceiling and an odd, asymmetric arrangement of decorative elements. Yellow wainscoting covered most of the lower half of the walls, but there were also sections of tile for no apparent reason. The doors were set with windows of leaded glass in a diamond pattern that also repeated in panels on the wall behind the wood-framed bed. Diego wondered if all of the windows let in light in the daytime. Through one of the more transparent panes, he could see the second story rooftop sloping away, and beyond it the lanterns of the carpenters, still working into the night.

The smaller panes must have offered distorted views into adjacent rooms where no lamps now burned. He wondered if the effect was intentional. It left him feeling exposed, though at least the windows in the doors could be covered by lace curtains. Surely Mrs. Winchester would have been consulted on which room to offer him, and he wondered at her intentions. The priest in him whispered that he should be grateful for any hospitality whatsoever, even if it was rendered with a motive to unsettle.

Maybe most of the bedrooms are like this. Who knows? She may have offered me the least strange among them.

In one corner the plaster had cracked and fallen away, revealing the wood slats, like ribs glimpsed through an open wound. Another thin crack described a meandering path along the ceiling. Mrs. Winchester had mentioned that the worst damage caused by the quake had been inflicted on the east end of the building, but clearly some had reached other parts of the house. Diego recalled the journal of Joe Colton stating that Sarah had fired her architects early in the project and had since done the job herself. Perhaps it was a testament to her instincts for a craft she'd never studied that so much of the house was still standing. Or maybe it was simply luck that in a house so prolific there would be many rooms that escaped the catastrophe largely unblemished.

The decor was minimal. Photos of people he couldn't identify were propped up in silver frames on the low dressers and tables. The walls were mostly bare, with the exception of a few short nails that might once have supported frames, and a Winchester rifle mounted above the desk, leaving the impression that whatever art or photography had once adorned the room had fallen and shattered in the quake. Diego went to the desk and opened his briefcase. As expected, his Bible and holy objects were untouched, but the journal was missing. He closed the lid, drew the curtains, and changed out of his cassock into a clean, white shirt and tan slacks before going in search of the washroom.

If he'd thought the bedroom was tight and oppressive, the angular corridors were even more so. Despite his best efforts to follow the secretary's directions, he soon found himself turned around and unsure of which direction he'd come from. The inconsistent lighting didn't help matters. Gas fixtures glowed at odd intervals, lending vivid detail to textured wallpaper and plaster, while other rooms and passages were cloaked in shadow so deep as to be unsettling.

He was on the verge of calling out for help when he chanced upon a bathroom with a sink and tub but no toilet. Soap and towels had been laid out, but whether they were meant for him or not, he had no idea. It didn't matter. He filled a porcelain bowl from the tap and set about scrubbing the sweat and dust of the attic wrestling match from his face and beard. In a few moments, he felt like a new man, his salt-and-pepper hair combed back and looking presentable in the candle-lit mirror.

He braced himself for further disorientation, but was surprised to find that when he emerged from the bathroom, the corridor had resolved into a sensible and familiar path back to his bedroom, where the lace curtain he'd drawn over the diamond grid window in the door glowed a buttery yellow from the lamplight within.

Half expecting it to be the wrong room after all, he was relieved to find his briefcase and cassock waiting for him. It felt like a lucky break, and rather than press his luck, he swallowed his pride and used the call button to summon the guide Mrs. Weatherlake had offered, to escort him to the dining room.

After a light meal, Diego found Mrs. Winchester waiting for him in the Grand Ballroom in a red leather chair beside the fire. Diego's eyes lingered on the iron tools arrayed in a rack by the hearth before noticing two glasses of red wine set on a low table between Sarah's chair and its vacant twin. She dismissed the guide and invited him to sit. When he'd settled in, his host raised her glass in a toast. "To the fates that brought us together," she proclaimed.

The crystal goblets clinked. Sarah took a sip. Diego contemplated the dark scarlet hue of the wine by the light of a baroque chandelier.

"Don't worry, there's no sleeping draught in it."

"I won't find myself locked in another attic room with a demon?"

"That was a djinn. And it's not an attic room, it's a witch's cap. The tallest point on the house after the catastrophe."

Diego swirled the wine and sniffed it.

"Oh, go on already. Unless you'd prefer cognac? I thought a nice bloody red was a safe bet for a priest."

Diego took a sip. The taste was exquisite—dark cocoa and oak.

"You did well today," Sarah said.

Diego took in the room. The pipe organ and inlaid wood floor were even more impressive than he'd imagined based on Colton's description. And there, at last, were the Shakespearian windows he'd thought so much about—oddly unsettling in the way the twin phrases snaked from top to bottom within winding ribbon designs that gave the appearance of being rendered backwards somehow. He wondered if the effect was meant to disorient the viewer, or if it was another clue to the puzzle of the house.

"How is the man who attacked me? Well, I hope?"

"*He* didn't attack you, Father. I wouldn't expect you to forget that."

"Sorry. It's just a simpler way of talking about it."

"He's fine. Right as rain. I gave him a bonus for going above and beyond the call of duty."

"Well, I don't think he likes me very much, possessed or not."

"As I've said before, my people are protective of me. They'll soon understand that you have a place here."

"Do I?"

"If you wish. Now that we've established your credentials."

Diego took another sip of the wine. A knot popped in the crackling fire, sending up a little shower of sparks. He turned toward it and stared at the dancing flames.

"Is it too hot for you?" Sarah asked. "I know it's a warm summer night, but it does get cold in the early morning hours. I like to heat the house a little before bed."

"It's fine. You say the spirit trapped in your music box is not a demon but a djinn?"

"That's what I was told by the Imam who sold it to me, though I suppose it's merely a matter of semantics."

"How do you mean?"

"The legends of King Solomon, and the grimoires that have sprung from them are the primary sources of demonology in the western world. But the demonic names found in those grimoires can in most cases be traced back to the names of Canaanite gods, goddesses, and djinn."

"Gods become demons. Like Ba'al?"

"You *are* more than a priest, aren't you? How naughty. If only they knew." Her eyes narrowed and focused on the collar of his borrowed shirt. "Show me your amulet. Don't be shy—I saw it before you tucked it back inside your robe."

Diego undid the topmost button and brought out the silver pentacle, dangling on its chain."

Sarah leaned across the gap between them and examined it. "The seal of Solomon. You carry a crucifix in your case, but it's this symbol that you wear under your garments. Closest to your heart."

"I carry both for protection, and what is closest to my heart is no talisman but the word of the Lord."

"And was it the word of the Lord that you resorted to in your hour of need? I don't recall reading *that* particular prayer in the Bible, though I may have encountered part of it in the *Greek Magical Papyri.*"

"You recognize the seal of Solomon and the Invocation of the Bornless One. I doubt you were exposed to such things at St. Peter's or the Baptist church of your childhood. Clearly your reading runs deeper than the King James and the *Thousand and One Nights.*"

Diego swept his gaze over the bookshelves that surrounded them.

His hostess nodded her chin toward a line of gilt leather spines. "Be my guest."

Diego set his glass down and approached the shelf she'd indicated. He ran his finger along the titles. Only a few were in English, and his own linguistic skills were limited to Spanish, English, and Latin. He tilted a black book with an Arabic title out of the line and cracked it open to a random page. Astrological and planetary symbols were interspersed with the flowing foreign script.

"*The Picatrix?*" he asked in awe.

Sarah nodded.

"And you can read it?"

"Well enough to absorb the general philosophy of stellar rays. Not enough to apply its lessons to architecture."

"In my boyhood I read the story of how King Solomon employed demons—or djinn, if you like—to build his temple. I imagined them physically moving the stones for him, that he would summon them like slaves to do the hard labor. But now I think that's a misrepresentation, that rather they instructed him in the sacred architecture, just as local legend claims you have had instruction from spirits in the building of this house. They say you fired your architects, but do you not consult with a different species of architect in your seance room?"

"Stop asking questions you know the answers to."

"They say you receive the plans from ghosts, but that's not true. Winchester House was conceived to house a ghost, a small world unto itself for Annie to inhabit, but its architects are what? Angels?"

Her mouth drew into a tight, thin line and she said, "Angels would not approve."

"Demons?"

"That's a loaded term. Let's have it your way and call them djinn. Creatures of smokeless fire. Astral intelligences with no allegiance but to those who feed them."

"Like horses and dogs."

"Nobler than that."

"And what, pray tell, do you feed them, Mrs. Winchester?"

Her grimace curved up into a smile and she sipped her wine in silence.

"You compare the spirits you've enlisted to djinn, but the one that pursued your daughter and caused the quake must have been something else, something more powerful." He returned the book to the shelf and paced the room. "My first thought would be a wrathful angel, but the description of horns doesn't fit."

"Why an angel? What makes you say that?"

"Because from Heaven's point of view, you've imprisoned your daughter's spirit. If the deception was discovered, an angel might be sent to claim her."

"Careful, Father..."

"You've invited me to speak candidly."

"Yes, but let's focus on why you're here. Is it to pass judgment on me and lead me to repentance? Or do you wish to *help me?* Because I don't need an exorcist or a magician or whatever you are to cast out an *angel.* Something infernal threatens her. Now tell me how you intend to constrain it, or I'll have Clyde see you out."

Diego gathered his thoughts before he spoke. This was the moment he'd hoped for, his chance to convince her he would be a worthy ally. "Give me access to the entire house, unrestricted use of your library. Let me investigate the mystic logic of it for any flaws. Answer my questions fully and honestly, and let me speak with your daughter when her presence is strong enough to allow it. Then I may be able to protect her. I'd be lying to promise that I can, but with your resources we might at least fortify a room for her to shelter in while I hold the thing back and try to banish it."

"I did fortify a room for Annie, with every ward I could conceive. In the highest tower of the house, on the seventh floor."

"Seventh? I saw only four stories when I approached."

"It was dashed to the ground in the quake and then I was the one trapped in a bedroom. The men had to pry the door open with a crowbar to free me when the tremors passed. Everything above the fourth floor that didn't fall that day has been torn down and hauled away."

Diego stared at the stained glass window above Mrs. Winchester's chair.

WIDE UNCLASP THE TABLES OF THEIR THOUGHTS.

He considered the depth of knowledge she would have needed to build such a labyrinth. Clearly she was no dilettante. Was he in over his head? If she, the creator of this spiritual trap, had failed to secure it against demonic forces, how could he hope to? His gaze dropped to the flames in the hearth, and he thought of Joe Colton, brave but ignorant. Joe, a mere carpenter, had stood against the power that threatened this house. And in return for his valor, he'd spent his last days in an asylum that ultimately couldn't shelter him from the demon's earth shattering hammer blows.

Mrs. Winchester's voice seemed to reach him through a fog of rumination. "Granted," she said. "Now get some sleep, Father. And I would advise you not to wander in the night. We don't want you getting lost in the maze. We will begin the work by daylight."

CHAPTER TWELVE

On his first night in Winchester House, Diego dreamed of his sister again.

He drives the boat up onto the beach, the hull scraping the sand, and leaps over the side into the water. The tide has receded in the time he and Julia were away, leaving a longer stretch of beach between the shoreline and the burning house. He runs, feet pounding the wet sand until they're sliced on broken shells and thwacking through the tall grass, the blackened wreckage of his home towering above him, crackling and collapsing, scraps of burning fabric tumbling skyward on the plume.

The heat dries the sweat on his face and threatens to singe his hair. Diego screams Estella's name. He circles the house, searching for her. But she is nowhere to be found. Only the gulls scream back. He falls to his knees in the sand, and stares up at the raging flames, the collapsing timbers. This is the moment when the neighbors came and tried to lead him away. When he broke free and burned his hands on the doorframe and they dragged him down the beach, kicking and screaming while the bucket brigade went to work dousing the flames. But no hands fall on his shoulders this time. In the nocturnal Hell where he relives that terrible day, there are no neighbors. He turns to look back at the beach and finds himself utterly alone. Even Julia has vanished from the little red boat like a wisp of smoke, a succubus swept away on the wind, bearing his seed to the infernal realm.

The sound of the blaze goes silent, like a door shut against a storm, and turning back to the house, he finds the smoldering skeleton of the only home he's ever known, the sky behind the charred beams heavy with fog. This is how it looked the day after, when his father combed the wreckage. But one thing is different. One unbroken window remains upright in its frame, centered before him at eye level, where no window had ever been before.

It is not the same as the other windows of the house as he remembers them—thick, imperfect glass that distorted the view and added waves to the ocean even on the calmest days. He was fascinated by the optical tricks those windows played on his young eyes, sitting beside them and adjusting the effect by how close he held his nose to the glass and the slightest tilt of the angle of his sight. No, this pane of glass belongs in no fisherman's shack. This is pure white Tiffany glass cut in the pattern of a spider's web.

A shadow moves behind the frosted glass—the shape of a body, though he can see no legs between the blackened studs propping up the frame. It grows larger, a head and shoulders leaning in to scrutinize his shape through the opaque screen. Diego sits back on his heels and claws at the sand, afraid of the presence, but also transfixed, unable to stand and flee.

The shadow of a child's hand smacks against the glass like a giant spider landing at the center of the web. Diego jumps and lets loose a cry. The petite hand rotates, leaving a smear of ash and blood, like some obscene flower. Then the hand withdraws and strikes the window again. He scrambles to his feet, unsteady in the shifting sand. On the third strike, the glass shatters and he lurches upright in bed, tangled in sweat-soaked sheets.

CHAPTER THIRTEEN

Dim morning light limned the unfamiliar room. Diego caught his breath, swept the bedsheet aside, and set his feet on the hardwood floor, taking comfort from the absence of sand between his toes. He rubbed his closed eyes with the heels of his hands and looked up at the window.

A smudge of ash marred the glass like a crudely painted black rose.

He stood up, went to the window, and rubbed his thumb across the stain. It was on the outside.

Through the window he could see the carpenters on the lawn below, unloading the day's timber. He thought of the scaffolding he'd seen them traversing around the house when he'd arrived the previous day, but that had been erected on the east facing facade, where the quake had caused the most damage. Here, on the south side, there was a narrow ledge beyond the glass before the roof sloped down to a drop, but nothing that a man could stand on.

What about a little girl? Or a ghost? What about Estella?

A shiver of gooseflesh crept over his damp skin. He shook it off like a dog and admonished himself. *You're not here for Estella, you're here for Annie Winchester. Your sister is in heaven or another life, not haunting a purgatory, even if her memory does still haunt your dreams. The smudge on the window was there before you took this room. You just failed to notice it last night in the dark.*

His wounded arm itched and ached beneath the stained bandage, but he resisted the urge to scratch it. Instead, he took his rosary from the nightstand where he'd left it atop his Bible, knelt beside the bed, and settled into the familiar rhythm of his morning prayers. The routine was soothing. It gradually brought peace to his agitated mind, and prepared him for the day to come, his first as a guest of Sarah Winchester.

After prayers, he found his way back to the Venetian dining room, where he was served a simple breakfast of oatmeal, coffee, and toast with jam. The cook offered to pile on meats, eggs and hash, but given the unease of his waking, Diego felt it best to go easy on his stomach. When the dishes had been cleared and his coffee cup refilled, Mrs. Weatherlake appeared as if on cue, bidding him a good morning and asking if he'd found the accommodations comfortable. He assured her that he had and that she need not fuss over the comfort of a simple priest, as he was accustomed to sleeping on little more than a cot in a drafty loft.

"Will Mrs. Winchester be joining me this morning?" he asked.

"She's meeting with the carpenters to set the day's agenda. I'm sure you'll see her this afternoon. She wants you to know that you have permission to explore the entire house, with two notable exceptions: her master bedroom and the room with the blue door on the second floor. You are also welcome to peruse her book collections, which are scattered about the house but are primarily shelved in the grand ballroom. Will you require anything else for your investigation?"

"Ariadne's thread?" He laughed, unsure if she got the reference. "No, thank you. I hope to start by simply getting the lay of the land, so to speak."

"The gardens are also available to you."

"I meant the topography of the house. I expect the gardens would be easier to navigate."

"You might be surprised, Father. But a compass might serve you just as well in the house."

"Are you jesting about the compass or do you have one I could borrow?"

Mrs. Weatherlake crossed the dining room and opened a small

wooden box on the mantle. She returned to the table with a brass pocket compass and set it down beside his coffee cup.

"And how will I know which is the master bedroom? I must have passed at least four bedrooms on my way to breakfast."

"Mrs. Winchester sleeps in whichever room strikes her fancy on any given night, but the one she favors most has a carved mahogany headboard set into the wall and ceiling and a photographic portrait of her late husband on the wall."

Diego picked up the compass and turned it over in his fingers. Even the smallest trinkets in Sarah's possession were engraved with elaborate detail. On the bezel and backing, the brass was ornamented with a fine oak leaf pattern. "You're familiar with the tale of Bluebeard?" he asked.

Did he detect the hint of a smile at the corner of the secretary's prim mouth?

"I am."

"Then you'll know that I must ask what's behind the blue door. Nothing stokes curiosity like prohibition."

"Well, you won't find bodies on hooks if you violate Mrs. Winchester's privacy, but you will most certainly void her hospitality, including an invitation to experience that room's wonders at nightfall."

"Tonight?"

"Yes. It's an extraordinary privilege. I don't know what you did to earn her trust, but I would advise you not to undermine it."

"I'll take that to heart."

Diego finished his coffee, then rose and dropped the compass into his pocket. The secretary watched him leave the room with an enigmatic expression on her face. He suspected she didn't share her employer's trust in him, and he couldn't help thinking that there was a suggestion of satisfied amusement in her eyes as she watched him setting out like a man with no map or provisions entering the Grand Canyon.

Her voice trailed after him down the hall. "If you don't turn up by lunchtime, I'll send someone to find you."

The next time Diego checked his watch, two hours had passed and he was hopelessly lost. Even with an abundance of windows looking out over the red tile rooftops, and the compass to aid in his assessment of which direction he moved in, the house seemed deliberately designed to disorient. For all its unique features, there was also a mind numbing repetition to elements of the design. Endless narrow corridors, an abundance of bathrooms, and tight flights of twisting stairs that turned him around until he'd entirely lost his bearings…it all conspired to leave him unsure if he was passing a series of rooms he'd already seen or entering a new section of the house. Like the trees of a forest, the doors all started to look the same.

It was also impossible to discern which architectural oddities had been deliberately embedded in the design and which might have been the result of improvisation or hastily implemented repairs to the extensive damage the earthquake had wrought. In places the walls showed faint signs of depressions where doors might have been removed, boarded up, and plastered or papered over. Stairs ended abruptly at the ceiling, where presumably a fourth floor turret room might have crumbled to the ground, leaving a gash open to the elements. Diamond shaped windows offered a view into an adjacent room or corridor, but even these only confused his sense of place. Skylights set into the floor seemed designed to allow light to reach lower levels of the house from above while keeping voices contained to the rooms they illuminated. In other places, open shafts might have existed for no other reason than to promote eavesdropping. He overheard fragments of chatter from the kitchen staff through one of these but hesitated to call down for help. Eventually, when he'd been turned around enough to be fairly certain he was retracing his steps through a familiar corridor, he came at last upon the forbidden blue door.

He almost walked past it to the next sharp turn before realizing it was the room Mrs. Weatherlake had warned him about. He stopped in his tracks and turned to face it, his hand hovering over the doorknob. The temptation to check if it was locked was almost overpowering, but for all he knew Mrs. Winchester might be waiting on the other side for exactly that—the taboo set solely as another test. Instead, he put his ear to the door and listened.

The only discernible sound was a faint clicking, like a tiny rodent scratching at a piece of glass. It took him a moment to trace the sound to its origin. It was coming from the compass in his pocket, the needle under the dome spinning frantically, the disc bobbing on the water like a tiny boat in a gale.

Was there some magnetic phenomenon reaching through the door to interfere with the instrument? He had vague images in his mind of Tesla's strange machines that he'd read about in the newspapers.

He might've stood there for five minutes watching the compass and listening at the door—time seemed to move slowly in this house, and sometimes not at all. Gradually, he realized there was another sound beneath the clicking, faint but growing louder: a murmuring voice, deep enough to be male, the words incoherent. And yet, something about the cadence and accent was familiar. Frost bloomed in his stomach with a sense of déjà vu, and he suddenly felt that he was an adolescent again. How many nights had he listened through his bedroom door to his father's drunken monologues? Too many. The man was always talking to himself, as far back as Diego could remember. He'd guessed it was a fisherman's habit. Out on the open water with no one to talk to, no one to hear his voice, a man might get into the habit of long-winded rumination on his life. But the habit got worse after the cancer took Diego's mother, and the alcohol fueled it. Midnight sessions of self-recrimination and regret when he thought his children were asleep.

Diego didn't know if his little sister, Estella, had heard the worst of it, but after she died in the house fire and it was just the two of them, Diego and his father living in an even smaller cottage, the rants ran louder and later, sometimes lasting until dawn. It was impossible to sleep through them. And not only because of the volume—the old man no longer cared who heard him—but because Diego was now the subject of the drunken vitriol.

The old man blamed his son for the loss of his daughter. Not enough to exile his last remaining family member from under his roof, but enough to torture him with indirect accusations muttered into a bottomless bottle.

Diego would have recognized that tone anywhere. No matter how heavy the timber that rendered the words indecipherable.

His hand trembled above the doorknob, as it had on so many nights when he'd been pushed to the brink of bursting out of his bedroom and confronting his father, having it out, coming to blows. But that had never happened. The old drunkard had been too cowardly to say these things to Diego's face, and Diego had been too cowardly to face them. Because some of them were true. And some were worse than the truth, but he deserved to hear them anyway, because the truth was terrible. There was no atonement for it, and listening to these litanies was his penance, and it would never end.

He pressed his trembling hand to the door, and did what he'd always done—knelt and listened through the keyhole.

"The best of us... She was the best of us. The last piece of her mother. The last piece of our family that wasn't...*poisoned* like me. The last pure thing, burned like a pig on a spit. And now there's nothing left but poison and bitter tears. And for what? I'll tell you what. For *lust.* For a filthy little sinner who couldn't lift a finger to help his family. A selfish little shit getting his dick wet while my sweet baby girl's skin cracked and her fat boiled. While her precious eyes ran like eggs. He probably thought it smelled good. The smell of char on the water like a pig roast. I bet it made his mouth water while that little whore–"

A hand touched Diego's shoulder and he spun around, reeling and vomiting on his hands and knees. A housekeeper looked down at him in sympathy and alarm. An Asian woman in a white apron, holding a feather duster. She shook her head sternly, waved a finger, and said, "No Blue Room." Then her face softened in sympathy.

"You speak English?" he asked.

The maid shook her head and held her fingers an inch apart to indicate, *only a little.*

Diego apologized for dumping his breakfast on the floor and tried to ask for rags to clean it up, but the woman shooed him away with gestures indicating that she would take care of it.

Embarrassed, he thanked her, decided that a request for directions to the grand ballroom would only lead to further confusion, and hurried down another corridor at random, wiping his mouth with the back of his hand. He was sweaty and anxious, his heart rate up and his guard down, the bitter taste of acid thick in his mouth. He needed a drink of water. He needed to get out of this maze and gather his thoughts. To sit and think.

The urge to retreat into the pages of a book was overwhelming. Unlike the house, the leather tomes he'd glimpsed the previous evening in the ballroom might contain mysteries he had some hope of navigating without becoming hopelessly lost.

Following turns that led to greater daylight, humidity, and floral scents, he soon found himself in the familiar environs of the North Conservatory, where Mrs. Brown had tended to his wound the previous night. He drank from one of the sinks, splashed water on his face, and caught his breath. With the familiar room as an anchor point, he was soon able to find his way back to the ballroom, which stood silent but not quite empty. It was filled with an air of anticipation, as if it had only been waiting for him.

CHAPTER FOURTEEN

The opulent details of the room were more apparent in daylight than they had been by the glow of the fireplace and chandelier the previous night, though the dark wood and red wallpaper did little to amplify the illumination. The checkered dance floor stood empty, the pipe organ bench vacant, and the fire grate cold. But when Diego's gaze had finished tracing the contours of the carved wood accoutrements and settled on the contents of the shelves, the barren room came to life, and he soon found himself slipping into a contemplative state—cataloging the spines and cross-referencing connections before he'd so much as tilted a single volume out of the neat rows for closer examination.

There were many familiar editions. Books he'd studied or skimmed in the basement archive below the Temple of the Rose Cross at San Jose. These included the *Zohar, The Golden Bough, The Papyrus of Ani,* and *Ars Almadel Salomonis*—this last tome an instruction manual for summoning angels into a crystal ball situated atop a wax tablet inscribed with names of God.

But the part of Mrs. Winchester's collection that might have been described as anthropological, cabalistic, or devoted to white magic and theurgy was vastly outnumbered by the *black books* Father Diego was familiar with from his training as an exorcist. Among these were such notorious grimoires as *The Lemegeton, Heptameron,* and *De Vermis Mysteriis.*

Had she read them all? He knew that socialites often had a habit of collecting books for show, to create the pretension of knowledge and culture, but such collections were seldom characterized by such a solitary focus on the dark arts. To be sure, there were also sections populated with novels, history books, and musical scores, but the occult collection had been granted pride of place—surrounding the hearth, beneath the Tiffany glass windows.

Diego selected an unfamiliar volume: *Grimorium Verum*. Opening to a random page, he found the text was in Italian, a language he was semi-literate with through inference from Latin. The section at hand was the sort of primitive catalog of spells cobbled together and furtively passed around in the sixteenth century, usually attributed to King Solomon. Recipes involving grave dirt, animal entrails, and items so difficult to obtain as to render verification of the formulas nigh on impossible. Most of the spells were dedicated to the satisfaction of the basest human desires.

To make yourself invisible.

To know whom you will marry.

To win at dice.

For discovery of a treasure.

To send three ladies or three gentlemen to your room after dining.

The mystery of the black hen for making a demon obedient.

Interspersed throughout were crude illustrations in the form of woodcut prints. The binding was tight, the pages unmarked, suggesting that Sarah had spent little time with this particular tome. He wondered how long it might take him to find signs of wear in other books here that might help him to identify her lines of inquiry without having to ask her directly about her research. What path through these texts had guided her in the construction of the house and the preservation of her daughter's spirit?

On a whim, he closed the book, balanced the spine in the palm of his hand, and allowed it to fall open to whatever page might have been consulted frequently, if any.

On the left hand page was a diagram identified as *The Appearance of the Green Butterfly*. On the right, in a section titled OTHER SECRETS, was the following spell:

For Protection Against Firearms

First say "God" three times, then taking the firearm in your hand, add, "I see the mouth of the musket! God watch the entrance, and the Devil the sortie!" Then apply to the chest twelve small leaves of grey-white paper on which you have written these words: *Armisi, Farisi, Mestingo.*

Diego closed the book and returned it to its place on the shelf. No wonder it showed little sign of wear. Manuals of this sort were rubbish. Had she obtained it in the interest of thoroughness toward assembling a collection of Renaissance magic books? Had she sought it out specifically for the firearms spell, read it once, and dismissed it? Or was there something truly useful elsewhere in the book? He'd picked it at random, but the questions raised by even one sampling drove home the point that he could spend all summer in the Winchester House and come no closer to solving the mysteries of what magical formulae undergirded its construction and occult functions. He put little faith in stock charms such as the one he'd just read, but that didn't negate what he knew from experience: supernatural beings—divine and infernal—were as real as men of flesh and blood. And with the right authority and theory, one could employ them as surely as Mrs. Winchester had employed a crew of carpenters to work her will on the material plane.

He scanned the shelves and sighed. Given free rein to satisfy his curiosity, such a rich collection of esoteric texts would ordinarily have thrilled him. But faced with the task of deciphering the secrets of the house, he found even the few well stocked shelves in the ballroom overwhelming. He had glimpsed similar shelves in other rooms of the house, and it was entirely likely that despite her invitation to explore her collection, she kept her most treasured volumes under lock and key.

Diego turned his attention to the corner of the room to the right of the fireplace, where according to the carpenter's journal, a carved wooden door concealed a safe. He approached the most likely door and opened it. Keeping one eye on the ballroom entrance in case anyone should catch him snooping, he opened a second door behind the first, this one a plain metal panel. He *had* been given free rein with only two notable exceptions—the master bedroom and the blue seance room. There had been no specific mention of the safe in the ballroom. But of course, that was because it would be locked tight, impervious to his curiosity.

There was, indeed, a safe mounted in the wall behind the second door, fitted with two combination dials. It crossed his mind to try various sequences of mystic numbers that might be meaningful to Mrs. Winchester, and he reached for the first dial with some trepidation.

The chandelier flickered.

A sign from Annie that he was on the right track?

Or a warning.

A rumble passed through the floor, like the growl of a dragon, and he hurriedly closed the door, turning back to the hearthside shelves, his heart beating fast in his chest.

But no horned cloud of ash issued from the grate as in the carpenter's tale, and he caught himself blushing despite his solitude. It was shameful that a servant of God, an exorcist—more than that, a brother of the Rose Cross—should be spooked by a ghost story in a workman's journal. But the body knew what it knew, and his was pricked with gooseflesh.

Was it because he felt out of his depth? Questioning every conviction of his faith? Whatever was happening in this house, it seemed to have little regard for the laws of God's kingdom as he understood them. His initiatory journey through the mystic grades had also forced him to question some core beliefs and church doctrines. If Father Xavier ever discovered that he'd entertained evidence of reincarnation, he would likely be defrocked as a heretic. So, was it too much of a stretch to entertain the idea that Sarah Winchester might have forged a pact with some force that was neither angel nor demon? Some elder god that powered the engine of the house and made it a sanctuary for souls outside of time, beyond the reach of both heaven and hell? A private purgatory built on occult architecture and sacred geometry? He'd read his Plato and Pythagoras. And wasn't it the Bard himself, whose words mocked him from the frosted glass panes flanking the fireplace, who wrote of "more things in heaven and earth than are dreamt of in your philosophy?"

What of things *beyond* heaven and earth?

He thought of the number that echoed throughout the house. Thirteen. Why had she chosen it? Was there a book on the shelves before him likely to at least shed a ray of sunlight through the clouds of this one little mystery?

A book, or a note in a book, that might lead him to a combination for the safe?

He reached into the collar of his shirt and removed the silver medallion he'd relied on during the trial in the witch's cap: the Seal of Solomon.

He slipped the chain over his head and let it dangle from his pinched fingers as he paced around the room, brushing the spines of the books with the fingers of his free hand. It was a kind of dowsing—using the medallion as a pendulum, holding it as steady as possible while watching to see if it swung in a spiral of its own accord. At times he had used the technique to answer YES or NO questions. A clockwise rotation indicated a YES, counterclockwise a NO. In this way, he had trained the amulet to respond in the affirmative when he was near the target of a search.

Some brothers of the mystic order argued that methods of divination such as the pendulum or tarot cards could only tell you things your own higher consciousness was already aware of. Others claimed that this was a meaningless point. If the highest part of your mind was the godhead, then it was connected to all the information in the cosmos, whether or not you had ever encountered it before.

As for Diego, he didn't know *how* the method worked, only that it did. Time and again, it had given him clarity at a crossroads. Now, strolling the empty ballroom beside the bookshelves, the silver medal swinging in small, random arcs at his side, he closed his eyes and formulated a question: *Which book contains the answers I seek? Which book will point the way?*

Eventually, as he walked, he felt the medallion graze his leg. He froze in place, the index finger of his left hand lingering on a cloth spine. He opened his eyes to see the pendulum tracing a vigorous clockwise circle at his side.

Diego tilted the book off the shelf, dropped the medallion in to his pocket, and examined the volume. It had the appearance of a custom binding. The title stamped on the spine was in English: *The Black Flame of Canaan Volume 1.* But flipping through the pages, he found that the text was printed entirely in Arabic, which he lacked fluency in. He had seen privately bound books before, and wondered if Mrs. Winchester had commissioned this one from a manuscript she'd obtained on her travels. Surely she had the means. And though she was clearly a collector of occult books, the care and expense required to preserve a manuscript in this fashion suggested that he'd stumbled upon a work of special significance to her. He checked the shelf and found no second volume.

Turning back to the text at hand, he discovered that his inability to translate the language was somewhat made up for by lavish illustrations and diagrams that at least hinted at the contents. Forced to guess, he would have said it was a historical treatise on the pagan practices of the pre-Christian Levant. Blasphemous cults that had persecuted the Hebrews and vied for power against the pharaohs.

There were maps of the fertile crescent, sketches of ziggurats and sacrificial pyres. Heathen temples adorned with alien alphabets and strange geometric forms. The sigils possessed an energy that transcended his inability to read the language, transmitting a malignancy in their lines and curves that made his stomach churn and the back of his head throb.

He swayed on his feet and almost dropped the book, recovering the tome before it could slip from his hands. The pages fluttered and a rain of loose newspaper clippings drifted to the floor. He knelt and retrieved one that had landed face up.

The article was from this year, just three months prior. Diego remembered reading it at the time it was published and feeling anguished for the family's loss. Why had Sarah saved it? And was there a reason she'd kept it in this particular book?

TODDLER KILLS HIS PLAYMATE

Boy of Six Picks Up Rifle and Sends Bullet Into the Side of Little Friend

SPECIAL DISPATCH TO THE CALL.

MODESTO, April 17.—The six-year-old daughter of Oliff Anderson, residing seven miles south of this city, was shot and almost instantly killed late this afternoon by the six-year-old son of a neighbor. The two children were playing together in the Anderson home, and had been left in the dining-room while Mrs. Anderson was preparing the evening meal in the kitchen. A small rifle was lying on a table in the corner of the dining-room, and the young boy got hold of it by climbing upon a chair. As he drew it across the table the charge in the weapon exploded, the ball striking the little girl in the side. With a cry the little one fell to the floor.

The frantic mother summoned help and a messenger went to Ceres, two miles away, and telephoned to this city for medical aid. Dr. Apple at once left for the Anderson home, but before he reached his destination the child was dead. The Anderson family came to this county from Stockton but three months ago.

Diego scanned the shelves again, wondering how many of the books might contain such clippings. Did she use them as bookmarks? But one didn't trim newspaper clippings for no reason. And this one fit the rumors about her guilt over Winchester rifle deaths a little too well. The article didn't state what brand of rifle had caused the fatal accident, but doubted she would have kept the article if it wasn't a Winchester. Was the bloody source of her fortune the reason why she donated so much of it to charity?

He gathered the other clippings from the floor and found that they also fit the pattern. Some were yellowed with age, others were recent like the first, but all were stories of people killed with guns, whether by accident or ill intent.

It was impossible to tell which pages they'd been tucked in between and what significance the locations within the book might have held, if any. Even if he'd found them before they spilled out, he wouldn't have been able to read the Arabic.

The diagrams in the book, on the other hand, recalled his conversation with Frater H. Many of these were of a man with the head of a bull, calling to mind the Minotaur and the horned cloud of black ash that Joe Colton had described in his journal. It had emerged from the fireplace in this very room.

But there was another association nagging at him as well, lurking in the shadows at the back of his mind. Another demon or horned god. Of course, horns were common attributes of pagan gods and devils, but there was something specific he'd read about a bull-headed deity. Something from the ancient mystery cults? Mithras, perhaps? The solar god who demanded sacrifices of cattle?

No, it was the opposite. A bull god who demanded the sacrifice of humans. Only, he wasn't just a hybrid of man and bull, he was…a *machine*. A clanging machine spouting fire from its brass furnaces. The memory came to him in the form of sound: deep drums and a cacophony of pipes and flutes. Legend held that the Ammonite priests in the hills near Jerusalem raised an unholy din to drown out the cries of infants sacrificed to the fires of the crimson king known as Ba'al or Moloch.

And on the tide of imagined drums and pipes, a verse from Milton recurred to him.

First MOLOCH, horrid King besmear'd with blood of human sacrifice, and parents' tears, Though, for the noise of Drums and Timbrels loud, Their children's cries unheard that passed through fire to his grim Idol.

Was the grimoire in his hands a tribute to Moloch? A manual for summoning him? Several of the woodcut prints depicted images of the bronze idol on the desert plain. A towering statue with flames raging in its belly, visible through the gaps between its great fangs and behind the faceted jewels in its eye sockets, but most of all through portals like the mouths of ovens cut in the torso for the transfer of offerings. For the roasting of children.

Diego had noticed a small alcove off of the main ballroom, where an assortment of musical instruments were displayed. A vision flashed in his mind, brief but vivid, of an infant burning in the fireplace while a string quartet and a flutist drowned out its cries.

Beads of sweat formed at his hairline. He tucked the news clippings into the back of the book and closed it. The leather cover felt sticky in his clammy hands as he returned it to its slot on the shelf.

Where was the second volume of *The Black Flame of Canaan?* And was there a third? He'd never heard of the book before. If Sarah had removed the second volume and hid it away somewhere, that would suggest that the tome was especially valuable or incriminating. Perhaps after researching the nature of Moloch in the first book, she had found a method for making a pact with him in the second.

He admonished himself for excessive speculation. This was only his second day in the house. He needed to get his bearings before formulating theories and jumping to conclusions. After all: why would she have summoned an entity that she considered a threat to her daughter's spirit? Unless it had somehow enabled the girl to linger for a time. For a price. Had Sarah thought she could make a pact with a devil with the intention of outmaneuvering it only to find that the eclipse tore a hole in the defenses she'd erected?

There was exactly one week remaining until the next eclipse. He'd promised to help her, but he knew he hadn't earned her full confidence yet. It was tempting to ask her these questions directly, but all too likely they would undermine the fragile trust he'd established. If she thought he was working against her to liberate Annie, he would end up tossed out the front door at best. If he had any hope of saving the girl's soul, it would require convincing Sarah that she was holding her beloved daughter back from a greater spiritual evolution. And that would call for a delicate touch. The clock might be ticking, but he couldn't rush the process.

The light flickered again, and, turning to look at the chandelier, Diego caught a glimpse of motion out of the corner of his eye—the figure of a girl in a white nightgown scurrying into the music alcove with the furtive demeanor of a child playing hide and seek.

The curtain dividing the alcove from the ballroom now appeared half drawn, as if the girl had given it a tug before disappearing behind it. But he hadn't heard the rings sliding across the rod. Had it been like that before? Almost certainly not. And the girl... She'd flitted through his peripheral vision in the blink of an eye, but something about her reminded him more of his dead sister than what he knew of Annie Pardee Winchester. Was it only the return of his recurring dream skewing his perception? He thought of the smeared handprint on the window and shuddered.

"Hello?" he said to the half drawn curtain, his voice barely more than a whisper.

No reply.

"Estella?"

Could she be here? Could her spirit have somehow taken up residence in this house? Or was it a trick played not by his mind but by something sinister? In his few encounters with demonic forces, none had ever plucked such a private and painful card from the deck of his own mind.

He moved to pull the curtain aside and jumped when a finger poked him in the spine from behind. For a moment he was tangled in the scarlet fabric. Then he was swatting it away and stepping through into the alcove, retreating from the brute who had terrorized him upon his arrival at the house. Clyde, Sarah's human guard dog, clutched his ample gut and laughed while Diego flailed to regain his balance, almost knocking a music stand over in the process.

"You sure are wound tight, Padre," the workman said. "Did you piss yourself?"

Diego hated the blush he could feel heating his face. He looked away. There was no girl behind the curtain.

"You startled me."

"No shit. What did you think was behind the curtain?"

"I don't know."

"Sure you do. If I hadn't embarrassed you, you'd be white as a sheet. It's okay, I get it. This place'll do that to you. Make you jump at shadows. Lotta the carpenters and housekeepers are superstitious. The gardeners? Not so much. Maybe the Chinese just don't mind ghosts. Or they don't get worked up about it because they can't understand half of what gets said around here. Man of the cloth, though? I'd expect you to take it all in stride. What with the Lord's protection and all."

Diego declined to take the bait. "And you?"

"What *about* me?"

"How do *you* feel about ghosts?"

He shrugged. "I figure what you don't believe in can't hurt you."

Diego smirked.

"Somethin' funny?"

"Your philosophy is. I'm sure the Indians didn't believe in the rifle before they encountered it on the battlefield. That hardly saved them."

"Well, I ain't never encountered a ghost. Just rich ladies who get attention from pretending they're possessed by them. Hell, maybe they even believe it."

"And how far does your skepticism go, Clyde? Do you believe in God?"

"That I do, Father. That I do."

"And the Devil?"

"Sure. I seen the Devil in a mean drunk's eyes as sure as the sun at noon. More real than any spirit in a medium. And you'll see him in *my* eyes if you take advantage of Mrs. Winchester. Just thought I'd drop by to remind you of that."

"I'm here to help Mrs. Winchester."

"Me too, Padre. Me too. She's a strange bird, no doubt, but she's good to her people."

"Did you know Joe Colton?"

Clyde spat into the fireplace grate. "Son-of-a-bitch betrayed her. I hope he suffered."

"I'm afraid he did."

The brute sniffed, satisfied.

A new idea occurred to Diego, and he spoke it aloud without pausing to think. "Did you terrorize him before he left the house? I mean, did you try to spook him with noises under the floor, blowing ash up through the vents?"

Clyde's face hardened, his mouth drawn into a tight line that suggested he was offended. "Do I strike you as a man who plays games, Father? If I knew what Joe was up to before she kicked him out, I'd have terrorized him plenty with my knuckles."

"You think he got what he deserved. But why? If you don't believe in Annie's ghost. Isn't that how he betrayed Sarah? By talking to Annie behind her back?"

"That's not what I'm talking about. He stole her wax recording and kept a record of her doings. What do you think the newspapers would do with all that if it got out?"

"I don't know if you get into town much, but the rumors are already rampant."

Clyde scoffed. "Rumors but not proof. There's always gossip and tall tales about the rich. But if people knew what she really believes? This whole thing could come tumbling down. And I don't mean the timbers and shingles. The lady employs a lot of people. I might not be schooled but I got enough history to know how witch hunts start. And I *live* in town, so I know there's already whispers about her causing the trembler. But people don't understand that the only danger here is within. The only things to be feared at Winchester House are what you bring with you."

"I didn't bring you or that dog with me."

Clyde grinned at this. His teeth were stained with coffee and tobacco. "True enough. True enough. But Joe Colton wasn't the first carpenter to end up dead. He's just the first to do it off the premises."

"There have been other untimely deaths among the crew?"

"Uh-huh. Accidents mostly. Like on any building site. Not *all* accidents, though. We've had more'n our share of suicides. Bodies hung from the scaffolding. Drowned in the fountains."

"I don't believe you. There would have been stories in the papers. Investigations."

"With enough cash in the right hands, anything can be wrote down as an accident. You'd do well to remember that before you think about crossing her."

"If what you say is true, then you're the one betraying her confidence now."

"Yeah, but proof is a fickle bitch, ain't she? Proof of suicide…proof of spirits. All I know for sure is that once a man starts down the path to madness, it's hard to turn back. And once you believe a place is cursed or haunted, it's like an infection of the mind. The fear festers. It'll make your foot stumble and your hand slip." Clyde leaned in, clapped a calloused hand on Diego's shoulder, and gave it a fraternal shake. His breath was sour, his features alight with gleeful mischief. "That's all I'm saying Padre: You gotta watch your step around here."

"Clyde?" Mrs. Weatherlake stood in the hall. "What are you doing here?"

"Nothing, Ma'am. Just making amends with Father Diego now that he's helping the Missus."

"Right. Well, Mrs. Winchester requests your presence in the blue room, Father."

"Now?"

"Yes."

"I thought our meeting was to be after dark."

"It *is* after dark. You must have lost track of the time."

Clyde stepped aside, and Diego followed Mrs. Weatherlake to the nearest stairs.

CHAPTER FIFTEEN

The room behind the blue door was white with blue trim, mostly empty except for a trio of chairs arranged in a triangle, a low table supporting the phonograph, and an iron cauldron on the floor. Sarah greeted Diego at the door. She was dressed in a white silk robe—the first time he had seen her in anything other than black. Over her shoulder he could see a wardrobe of similar robes in a variety of bright colors hanging from hooks in an open cubby space.

"Thank you for joining me, Father." Sarah waved him into the room. "Please, have a seat. I hope your studies were productive?"

"Too soon to tell, but it's a start. Your library is impressive."

"Did you have any trouble finding your way around the house? I could assign you a guide if need be."

"I did get turned around more than once but I prefer to explore on my own. Sometimes the meandering route takes one to just the right place."

Sarah nodded and swept the silk robe under her legs as she sat. "I suppose there's wisdom in that. But do let me know if you have any questions—about the house *or* the book collection. Personally, I find that browsing a library is not unlike exploring a house. A reference may capture the attention like a turret glimpsed through a window, and one is compelled to follow winding paths in its general direction, hoping to reach that elevated vantage by leafing through a number of connected volumes, much like the halls of a house. Are you familiar with Cicero's *method of loci?*"

"The Mind Palace? Yes. I've always been intrigued by the idea, but my own experiments lacked the consistent effort required to truly benefit from it. Have you built a mental structure modeled on your house? I'm sure you could store an enormous treasure trove of information in such a palace."

The practice, as Diego understood it, involved using a familiar architecture as a mental model to store one's memories in. Something about the nature of spatial visualization made the information easy to recall.

"No," Sarah said. "I'm afraid this house is far too strange to keep track of for such purposes. I think a more static architecture would be better suited to Cicero's practice. But once again, you've revealed that your education runs deeper than the subjects prescribed by the church. Please sit."

Diego settled on the one vacant chair—armless and upholstered in blue velvet. Another Asian servant he hadn't seen before occupied the third seat, a horsehair brush and hand bellows on the table before him. It still struck the priest as miraculous that sound could be inscribed and granted the same immortality as the written word. He supposed the process would soon seem as mundane as photography, but for now it retained a hint of the uncanny. He nodded polite acknowledgement at the recordist, but Sarah acted as if the man wasn't present, leaving Diego to wonder if she had chosen him for the task because he lacked the English fluency needed to understand her conversations with spirits.

"Is this your medium?" Diego asked.

"No. Kai is the recordist. I no longer rely on a human medium. Our medium will be the smoke." As if to demonstrate, she opened a silver snuff box and took a pinch of some dark resinous powder, which she then sprinkled on a charcoal briquette in the bottom of the iron vessel. It must have been already burning because on contact, the powder produced thick wisps of creamy smoke that tumbled lazily up toward the ceiling. The scent was musky, almost repulsive. It had an undertone that reminded him of cat urine.

"Pardon the smell," she said, wiping her hands on a damp handkerchief. "I've found that floral scents do little to support embodiment. It seems the spirits prefer a medium with an animal aspect. I suppose it should come as no surprise that they would feel more at home there."

The room was located somewhere in the middle of the house, with no windows to the outside. The only light came from candles flickering dimly in stained glass sconces mounted on the walls. The burning wax and thickening smoke soon made the atmosphere thick and oppressive. The recordist didn't seem to mind. He waited patiently, with head bowed until Sarah signaled him to engage the phonograph, which had been cranked in advance. When he released the catch, the drum turned, making a droning mechanical noise, augmented by the rhythmic squeak and puff of the hand bellows, which the man used to blow the little twists of wax away from the stylus and onto the floor.

Sarah sat up straight, cleared her throat, and addressed the spirit realm. A white lace veil covered her eyes, leaving Diego to wonder at the significance of it. He'd attended initiation rituals in which the candidate was blindfolded to keep the identities of the ritual officers secret, and having been on both sides of that equation, he also knew that a blindfold served to heighten the other senses—including the sixth sense, the third eye or inner vision of the seeker.

There were men of science and psychology who might argue that all mystical practices were designed to promote hallucination and misperception. Fasting and breathing exercises, starving the air of oxygen by burning herbs in an enclosed space, and depriving the eyes of light so that they might misinterpret shadows...these could all be viewed as tools of the charlatan's trade. But was it not also possible that the human instrument might perceive a different reality if the external senses were attenuated and an inner sense awakened?

"Come unto us, any spirits who wish to speak," Sarah intoned in a voice more strident than the husky timbre he'd become accustomed to. "This is a safe place for you to reveal yourselves, a sanctum for those who walk the paths between this world and the next. Here, you may take nourishment from scent, and clothe yourselves in smoke. Appear to us now. For you are welcome here."

Silence followed the invitation. The fumes rising from the cauldron curled and twisted on the currents of air set in motion by the bellows, but as mesmerizing as the languid display was, Diego detected no coherence in its shifting shapes.

A clock ticked somewhere down the hall, and in time, another sound joined it. A distant metal clanging, like the ringing of a bell, or a misaligned gear in an engine—steady and monotonous. He wondered if it came from the plumbing. The others ignored it. Perhaps it was a familiar symptom of the workings of the house.

He wondered how often Sarah made these attempts in vain, with no response from the spirit world. The line of her mouth below the lace veil revealed no hint of disappointment or impatience. Her chest rose and fell in a slow rhythm that had synchronized with the recordist's bellows.

The clanging rose in volume, and now Diego could hear other sounds nestled within it: a ratcheting sound followed by a faint chime, like the cocking of a rifle and the ejection of a spent brass casing.

The ticking of the clock had grown in volume as well, leading him to wonder if it wasn't a clock but perhaps the loudest part of the same machine moving closer or working harder. He imagined Clyde rolling some strange contraption down the hall. Some additional piece of equipment Mrs. Winchester used for spirit communication? Given the number of modern innovations she'd incorporated into the house, it was easy to imagine that she might have built such a machine, though he couldn't fathom what it might look like or what its function could be.

The clanging shook the walls, made the table shudder and the candle flames waver in their stained glass bowls. But Mrs. Winchester and her servant resolutely ignored the racket. Diego stared at the white veil, pleading with his eyes for acknowledgment of the sound, but reluctant to speak.

Wax shavings vibrated across the floor like worms.

And then, just when it seemed the machine would break through the door and reveal itself, the din went silent, replaced with a snuffling sound from the gap at the threshold. Diego imagined a beast taking stock of the room's occupants by scent alone. A notion that felt entirely plausible despite the heavy fumes clouding the air. He couldn't speak for his companions, but he felt certain the perspiration in his own armpits and the trickle of sweat down his spine must be a pungent beacon of fear.

The creature stomped a hoof, shaking the floor, and issued a plaintive bellow. Diego's arms prickled. He held his breath, waiting for the door to burst open, but then the mechanical symphony started up again and continued down the hall, fading like a train leaving a station.

He tucked his hands in his lap under the table to hide their trembling. His gaze remained fixed on the gap beneath the door, watching for some sign of the roving beast's return, even as the sound faded. Then a gout of flame leapt from the cauldron, splashing phosphorous red light around the room and fixing his attention once again on the thick, white cloud just as it resolved into the shape of a girl.

He stared at the image, afraid to breathe too heavily for fear that stirring the air would cause it to dissipate. But the longer he looked at the figure, the more solid it appeared. And its reality was shocking. It was one thing to believe in the stories of the Bible and to have seen people animated by demons, but this was something else: a body manifesting in smoke until it defied the properties of the medium, appearing to take on weight and solidity.

The girl did not look well. With sunken eyes, cracked lips, and thinning hair laid flat against her skull, she in fact looked dead. Her arms and legs, descending from a simple cotton smock, were stained with dark smudges.

"Is it her?" he whispered to Sarah. "Is it Annie?"

"No. Annie is older, healthier."

Diego swallowed and found his throat parched. He wondered if the dark smudges were dried blood. His view of the girl cast her mostly in profile, but he saw no obvious wound like what he imagined would be left by a gunshot. The prospect that this visitation was a Winchester rifle victim seemed remote.

"What is your name?" Sarah asked.

The girl shook her head in a bewildered way. It was impossible to tell if this meant she didn't understand the question or didn't know the answer. Did the dead forget who they were? He had considered that Sarah's education of Annie was in part an effort to ensure the girl would retain her identity and build on that foundation against the forces of erosion that accompanied death.

There was something familiar in the gesture, though. His heart beat faster, and he felt an overwhelming urge to flee the room before the girl could take notice of him and turn her face in his direction, even if that meant confronting whatever mechanical monster he'd heard stalking the corridor.

"Quel est votre nom?" Sarah asked.

The girl shook her head again, and Diego thought he saw a disfiguration of her face as it tilted briefly toward him. A ripple in the smoke?

"Wie heissen sie?"

The girl continued shaking her head slowly, and Diego felt a chill at the thought that Sarah was toying with him, leading the girl through a series of stabs at languages she didn't speak just to prolong the moment. Teasing him with the revelation gradually growing in the pit of his stomach like a musician playing a sequence of descending cadences, circling in on the inevitable tonic note until finally she arrived at the right key.

"Cómo te llamas?"

"Estella." The voice cracked with damage and disuse, and Diego could smell smoke now, not the musky scent of the incense blend, but the unmistakable char of wood smoke on salted air.

The girl turned her burned face toward him, the scars of melted flesh on the far side coming into view like the topography of a planet rotating toward the sun. The dark smudges on her arms were ash, not blood, and he could see now the places where her fingers and toes had been fused together when the flesh melted. Where the blackened bones were exposed. He couldn't say if the damage was progressing before his eyes or if the girl's turning toward the light was simply revealing what had been there all along, but it was horrifying either way. The place where her skull shone through the burned skin, where her hair had retreated from the flames in a nest of singed curls. Where her left eye had run from its socket and dried on her cheekbone like a broken egg frying as it slid across the skillet.

The rotating drum of the Victrola and the rasping of the bellows droned on in their relentless rhythm, the recordist keeping his eyes fixed on the work of his hands. Sarah, however, drank in the horror with ravenous curiosity before mirroring the ghost and turning her gaze on the priest seated to her left. Beads of sweat ran from his temples as if a raging inferno, not a charcoal briquette, burned at his feet.

"Diego," the girl whispered.

"You're not her," he said. "You're not Estella. You can't be."

"But I am," she said in Spanish.

"Estella is in heaven. She was baptized. She was *innocent*," he continued in the language of their childhood home.

"But you're not. Are you? Did you ever confess it? The sin that cost my life?"

"Yes."

"Was it worth it? Spilling your seed in a whore's mouth while my blood boiled?"

"Stop."

"While my skin blistered and sizzled?"

"Stop it," he said in English. "Hold your tongue, demon, or the archangel Michael will silence you with a stroke of his sword!" He rose to his feet, growing in stature and confidence as the authority of his office returned to him and he took on the mantle of exorcist.

"It is no demon that sends me, but an angel. Metatron, messenger of the Lord."

"Do not profane that holy name with lies!"

"It's true, Diego. You deny it at your peril and the peril of future generations. Shush now, and hear the angel's warning: There *is* a demon in this house. It feeds on the souls of murdered children and worships the Devil's steel rod. And you, brother, risk casting it from its prison to wreak havoc on a naive nation. If the beast escapes Lady Winchester's web, its thirst will never be sated. This is the word of the Lord."

Diego backed away from the table, pointing a trembling finger at the apparition. "You're not my sister. And you're no messenger of God." He knocked over his chair, moving around the table, unsure if he intended to kick the cauldron over or flee the room.

"But I am," she said. "I have the scars to prove it. Do you want to see the rest of them?" She plucked at the hem of her gown where it ended at the knee.

Diego backed up to the door. Something pounded against it from the hallway, and it shuddered in the frame. The snuffling sound started up again in the gap where the blue door met the frame, accompanied by a groaning squeal, like hinges in need of oil.

"I'm like a candle, brother. All melted. Don't you want to see what you did to me?" The ghost revolved above the cauldron as it taunted him. He moved away from the door, edging around the room, his back to the wall. There was a cabinet against the wall opposite the door. Sarah nodded toward it. "It's a secret passage. If you really must go."

Diego pulled the cabinet doors open to reveal an adjacent room atop a short step. The chamber was empty, with bare wood slats for walls. It offered three additional exits. He picked one at random, but the girl's voice trailed after him as he hurried through to the nearest corridor. "You should leave this house and never come back," she called, "or it will only lead to suffering."

CHAPTER SIXTEEN

Diego was confronted with a disorienting set of choices: directly ahead lay the humid open space of one of the conservatories, a steep staircase ascended to the third floor, and at the end of a short corridor another staircase descended to the first floor. He had no plan except to be away from the seance room, and yet some instinct told him he should find a hiding place, or at least take an odd and contradictory path to throw off pursuit. He considered that passing among the plants of the conservatory might confound the beast's senses, but quickly rejected the idea. Predators scented prey among growing things all the time in the wild, and the trail of musky fumes he would leave in his wake after marinating in the smoke was bound to leave a trace. Better to simply run and put as much zig-zagging distance between himself and his pursuer as possible.

He didn't know what the creature was, which made the impulse to flee or hide even more unnerving. All he had to go on were the sounds it had made at the door of the seance room. Snuffling and scratching. Was it the dog? No. Something bigger. There had been the thud of what sounded like a hoof. And the din of machinery. Had the heiress invested her capital not only in the erection of this byzantine labyrinth of a house but also in the construction of a deadly automaton to enforce her will upon guests, servants, and intruders? The notion was bizarre, but he'd seen more than enough to feel that nothing was outside the realm of possibilities.

The house was growing dusky as the last vestiges of daylight drained from the windows, and he made a series of blind choices—careening down corridors, cutting through rooms to adjacent passages, and lunging up stairs until he found himself stumbling out onto a veranda overlooking the sprawling estate. A smudge of dirty orange limned the horizon, the scaffolding of the carpenters silhouetted black against it like a gallows.

His flight instinct had driven him to higher ground, a vantage point from which he could get his bearings on the rambling construction. He had a vague notion that the séance room was located somewhere near the center of the house on the second floor. Now he found himself on the fourth floor, the highest after the earthquake. He had migrated westward and could see the carefully landscaped gardens laid out in a courtyard below. The sound of water trickling in fountains mingled with birdcalls reaching the crescendo that signaled nightfall.

He looked back at the last staircase he'd climbed and cocked an ear for any hint of pursuit. Nothing. Leaning against the railing, he caught his breath and contemplated his next move.

Had he overreacted in fleeing the chamber and running pell-mell through the house like a man on fire seeking water?

It was shameful. Was he not an agent of God? An exorcist with the authority to cast out evil spirits? His face burned at the thought of what Sarah must think of him now. How could he possibly repair her damaged faith in his ability to stand against the threat to her daughter?

He'd been caught off guard by the thing masquerading as his sister. He should have fortified his mind against such tricks, preparing for the session with prayer and meditation. Instead, he had walked into the situation disarmed, trusting that Sarah would exercise some control over what she invited. He had assumed she would be continuing an ongoing conversation with Annie, not blindsiding him with a ghost from his own past. And there he was again, falling into its trap and thinking of it as his sister. It wasn't. It couldn't be. There were stories about demons and spirits pilfering information from those who confronted them and using it as raw material to weave their lies, like birds building nests from scraps of cotton and straw.

Of course it would be his most painful memories that were most easily accessible to a creature made of suffering. It was a novice mistake to go unguarded against such tactics. Perhaps the house had lulled him into a state of complacency with its charms and comforts. He'd worried that he wouldn't have enough time to earn Sarah's confidence before the impending eclipse, but now he wondered if he had trusted *her* too soon. Was she still testing him? If so, he'd failed spectacularly. And if not, she'd learned his greatest weakness, his deepest regret—the wound that had led him to the crossroads of his life, where he'd chosen a path of service and supplication.

He didn't know if Sarah had heard more than one side of the exchange he'd engaged in with the entity in the smoke. It seemed likely that she'd not only heard it all but recorded it—a fact that left him feeling naked and vulnerable. Only now did he appreciate her reaction to learning that he'd listened to one of her sessions with her daughter.

If tonight had been an attempt by Sarah Winchester to put her guest on level ground with her, he had to admit she'd succeeded.

His brooding was interrupted by a shimmering motion in the garden below. It looked like moonlight reflected off the surface of a birdbath, but the waxing moon was shrouded by clouds. He leaned over the railing and followed the progress of the light, his apprehension growing with the recognition that it was a ghost, a spectral body, faint and female. He gripped the railing tighter and fought the urge to duck out of view, determined to hold his ground this time, to not be frightened away by the thing disguised as his sister. But the terror passed as he realized it wasn't the same spirit he'd encountered in the seance room. That had been a girl, though it spoke like a woman. This was a young woman, dressed not in an ash-stained nightgown, but a simple contemporary dress, her hair not singed but tied in a long braid down her back. She was made not of smoke but of a weak blue luminescence, barely visible in the shadow of a foliage draped trellis beside a crescent shaped hedge. There was something pensive in her posture, as if she were hesitating on the threshold of decision.

It had to be Annie. A nightbird took flight and the ghost tilted her head upward toward the roofline. Did she see him? It was impossible to tell—her eyes were black holes—but when she turned away and slipped into the shadows of a hedge-lined path, Diego had the impression that she did so with a reluctance meant to encourage pursuit.

Did she want to speak with him in confidence, as she had with Joe Colton?

The possibility offered some hope of redeeming himself. A chance to learn firsthand how Annie felt about her captivity in her mother's maze. A chance to speak with her outside the confines of Sarah's supervision. But if he was going to seize the moment, he needed to act fast and find a direct route to the garden from his current perch. That alone was daunting, but he sprang into action, putting his trust in instinct to guide him. From the overlook it seemed simple: knowing that the courtyard was toward the west end of the house, he determined to keep that direction firm in his mind as he descended to ground level.

But the plan began to unravel as soon as he descended the first staircase and discovered that he had no notion of which path might take him to the next stair, nor how many rambling rooms he might need to traverse in the search. He should be methodical, he told himself, and not act rashly. A series of impulsive decisions could scramble his internal compass in a matter of minutes. It was hard, though, to not be compelled by the sense of time slipping away, and Annie with it. If he hesitated, if he lingered too long to ponder his options at every juncture, she would be gone before he set foot in the garden.

Unless she waits for you there.

He'd just set off down what felt like a promising passage—though without windows, he couldn't be sure—when a huffing sound reached his ears, freezing him in his tracks, a chill tickling the nape of his neck beneath his collar.

He stood near an end table upon which a framed photo of Sarah's relatives was perched beside an unlit candlestick. Both objects rattled as the floorboards beneath the balding carpet runner shook with heavy footfalls. Or were they hooves?

The beast.

It would round the corner at any second. He knew he should flee before it did, but part of him was eager for the revelation, desperate to reconcile the ambiguity: was the huffing a mechanical sound driven by an engine? Or was it breathing? Were the hooves he imagined striking the floor made of keratin or bronze?

A low growl buzzed in the walls.

Fear overcame fascination, and he broke into a run. As soon as he did, the sounds of lumbering machinery ratcheted up. Though he did not dare risk looking over his shoulder, he could hear the thing closing in, bearing down on him, its gears churning, pistons pumping and bolts slotting into place. With proximity came an overpowering smell—a mixture of iron, sulfur, and smoke.

Diego careened down the corridor, sensing the thing at his heels, the faint sensation of hot gusts of steam hissing at his back. He pushed harder, ran faster, and was overcome with superstition against looking back—as if to do so would turn him to a pillar of salt. In reality, it was more likely that turning to look would freeze his muscles with terror and confusion, cause him to stumble and fall.

The creature moved quickly but without finesse, knocking furniture aside and pictures from the walls as it rounded corners and closed in on him.

Diego took every turn the house offered him, with no rhyme or reason, no strategy. Up one flight of stairs, down another. Through any doorway that wasn't shut: bathrooms that connected to bedrooms that gave way to sitting rooms. He encountered servants in none of these, as if the house were deserted.

The longer he careened through the labyrinth, the more he felt that this must be a nightmare. But when would it have begun? Before the seance? Was he still in the ballroom, slumbering in an armchair beside the fireplace with a book in his lap?

If only that were true. It was the unreal nature of the house that lent itself to such comforting delusions, he knew. It felt impossible that such tortuous architecture could be real and not the product of a deranged mind. But it *was* the product of a deranged mind, only not his own. It was Sarah Winchester's dream, and her nightmare as well that he had stepped into. Any demons that pursued him here would be hers, not his own.

That, in itself, was a reassuring thought. But a voice whispered from the back of his mind to refute it: *Estella is your ghost, not hers. You might outrun a mechanical bull, but you'll never outrun her.*

Something caught on his clothing – a hook or claw, snagging and ripping. He was pulled off balance, almost tripped, but regained his footing by sheer momentum, and landed his next footfall without spraining his ankle.

A minor miracle, though he knew his luck wouldn't hold if he continued to test it. His luck was a frayed rope.

All thoughts of reaching the garden had left him. The only imperative now was to escape his pursuer. And the only way to do that was to put an obstacle in its path. There was no outrunning it. He needed a solid door he could lock behind him. And he saw such a door now, like an answered prayer, growing in size at the end of the hall.

Doubt flashed in his mind: had the house itself been driving him toward this all along, presenting bad options and narrowing his choices? Channeling him to this last door like a cow to the slaughter chute?

If so, it was irrelevant now. He'd been dealt one card. He had to play it. He reached for the heavy brass knob, felt his sweaty palm close around the braided ornamentation, and turned it with a flick of the wrist as his shoulder struck the wood. The door swung open on a void. But it was too late to slow his momentum, and he fell through into blackness, the floor vanishing beneath him as he pedaled and clawed at the empty air.

CHAPTER SEVENTEEN

Dim patterns swam before his eyes: fleur-de-lis and lace. Shadows bloomed like ink in water, threatening to pull him back under into dank, dripping passages where the Minotaur chased him, breathing hot plumes of noxious air at the back of his neck. His skull pounded with the crashing of pistons and gears, and he focused on a distant square of pale light, willing himself toward it, a swimmer kicking for the surface—toward the light. A burning house. A pyre.

No. A window. And beyond it, a gray sky.

The dream faded, but the hammering continued. The perpetual labor of the carpenters driving nails into the house. *Crucifying it night and day,* he thought. A nonsensical notion. But that was the nature of dreams, and he'd had a long one. A dream of visiting the Winchester House, where clearly he'd never been. He'd never left his room at the mission, of course, because there was Peter, sitting beside him, looking down at him with worry melting into relief on his boyish face.

But the mission didn't have fleur-de-lis wallpaper and lace curtains, or richly upholstered chairs. And the bed he found himself in was a far cry from the narrow bunk he called his own at Saint Claire.

Peter rose and patted at the air. "Don't try to sit up," he said. "You've hurt your head. Moving too much could make you nauseous. There's a bucket beside the bed. I'll fetch the doctor."

And with that, he ducked out of the room, calling for a Doctor

Neville, with an urgency in his voice that might have made more sense if Diego were bleeding out on the bed. It struck him as odd that the young scholastic should be so easily rattled after all he'd witnessed in the aftermath of the earthquake. And why was he even here? How had he known to come?

Diego propped himself up on his elbows. When the nausea didn't come, he lifted the bedsheet and took a quick inventory of his injuries. His head and right leg were wrapped in bandages, but there was no bloodstain on the leg wrap, and he found he could bend the knee as far as the bandage allowed without pain. A good sign. His ankle, on the same side, was another matter. It, too, was bandaged, and any attempt to test the range of motion of his foot sent a hot bolt of pain up his leg. By the time Peter reappeared with the doctor, Diego's vision was spotting. He lay back on the thick pillow and blinked, watching the black spots drift like moths across the ceiling.

The doctor was older than Peter, but too young for more than a hint of gray in his sideburns. The rest of his hair was black, as were the eyebrows that telegraphed a look of stern reprimand over sapphire eyes as the man moved around the bed, checking the priest's pulse and pupils.

"It's good to have you back, Father. Mrs. Winchester will be pleased."

"Back?" Diego croaked, surprised by the roughness of his own voice. "Where did I go?"

"Now that's a question I would very much like an answer to. You priests are quite sure of where we go after death, but medical science is still working out where we go after a good head trauma. Suffice it to say you've been unconscious. What's the last thing you remember?"

Diego searched his memory for the last thing that might not be a dream. "Did I fall down the stairs?"

"You fell from the side of the house," Sarah Winchester said from the doorway. "You stepped through a door that leads to nowhere, I'm afraid. And you have my apologies for not locking it. The carpenters have made some temporary choices while repairing the damage from the tremor, and that was one of them. Though I can't say I understand why you were running through the house and crashing through doorways like the Devil himself was on your heels. Are you a drinker, Father Diego?"

He clenched a fistful of bedsheet, but stopped short of responding that her cruel parlor tricks were what had sent him racing through the house with a head full of smoke and bad memories. He focused instead on Peter, who stood beside the doctor, looking out of place and unsure of what to do or say. "Why are you here, Peter?"

"You've been gone for most of a week. Father Xavier hasn't heard from you…"

"A *week?* That's nonsense. I've only been here a day. I told Father Xavier that I was providing spiritual counseling to Mrs. Winchester."

"Yes, but that was days ago," Peter said. "They sent me to check on you. I was shocked to find you unconscious. You suffered apoplexy when you hit your head."

"Is this true?" Diego asked the doctor.

"The proper term is coma. You were out for five days. Today is Wednesday, August first."

Diego tried to sit up again. Dizziness washed over him, though he didn't know if it was from the head injury or the information he'd just been given. If today was the first, that meant the eclipse was just three days hence at dawn. He'd lost days of preparation and investigation.

The doctor put a gentle hand on his chest and eased him back to the pillow. "Easy. You're not ready to leave this bed, Father. You've only just come back to us. You'll need rest before you're up and about."

"It sounds like I've had more than enough rest."

"You need to regain your strength," Sarah said. Then to someone in the hall: "Have the kitchen prepare a light soup. More than broth this time. Noodles, carrots."

"Yes, ma'am."

Diego's stomach groaned at the image, and he realized how weak and hungry he was. They were right, of course, he would need strength, and there was no time to waste in rebuilding it. Nor was there time to waste on Mrs. Winchester's games. If he was expected to help her, he would demand her full cooperation. She would need to provide truthful answers to his questions and whatever books she'd held in reserve. The lady knew far more than she'd confided so far. Of that much he was certain. But the time for withholding was over, and he would tell her so just as soon he could clear the room.

"Peter, I appreciate you coming to check on me, but I won't be returning to the mission with you just yet. Doctor Neville is right. I need to recover first. Please inform Father Xavier that I'll be staying a few more days. My work was interrupted and I hope to complete it as soon as I'm back on my feet."

"But that's what I'm here for, Father. To assist you. I have a letter from Father Xavier assigning me to the job. But he wrote it before we knew of your accident, and if I can speak candidly, I don't think it would be wise for you to attempt anything taxing in your present condition. You should return home as soon as you're able. Father Bruno could take over the work. It's an exorcism of the house itself, is it?"

"No, Peter. I won't hear of it. Father Bruno wouldn't know where to begin. And Mrs. Winchester will trust no one but me with the task."

"It's true," she said. "Only Father Diego can do this. He has unique insight into the situation that I would not share with another."

"Well then," Peter said, digging in his satchel, "here is the letter. I have my orders to assist you, and I won't defy them. You'll just have to find a use for me when you're out of bed."

Diego took the envelope. He liked Peter. The young man was capable and sincere. But he loathed the idea of trying to explain the complexities of the task he'd taken on. Protecting the house from a full demonic manifestation and persuading Sarah to release her daughter's spirit would both require extraordinary measures. It might well call for heresy.

He sighed. "I'll consider it," he said, laying the letter on the nightstand unread.

"You can fill me in while you convalesce."

"After lunch," Sarah said. "Come, Peter, let Father Diego rest. We'll have the kitchen prepare something for you as well."

When they'd left the room, the doctor completed his examination and gave Diego an inventory of his injuries: "Now that you've regained consciousness, I can call you lucky. You have a sprained ankle and a good laceration on your head. We'll need to keep the bandages fresh, but I'm not too worried about infection of the head wound. You will, however, need to guard against a second blow to the head for some time. Taking a tumble because of the bad ankle presents a risk of exactly that, so if you absolutely must get out of this bed, you'll need to take great care. I'd lean on young Peter as much as possible, if I were you, and use a cane or crutch until it mends."

"I can do that. Thank you, Doctor."

A servant entered with a lunch tray, and Doctor Neville took his leave. Diego read the letter while he waited for the steaming broth to cool.

Dear Father Diego,

I have just read the note that you sent by courier, and while I understand that your recent actions are motivated by a desire to help our neighbor Mrs. Winchester in her time of need, I am greatly displeased with the manner in which you have undertaken this task on your own authority without my approval or consultation. A note informing me of your errand after you had already visited the estate and made promises to the lady is not the way to obtain permission for something so serious as an exorcism, if that is even the proper classification for the work you described. Even in cases of demonic infestation of a property, there are protocols that require Church approval, as well you know.

You made mention of the need for privacy, given Mrs. Winchester's high station in the community and the virulent rumors to which she has been subject in recent months. I do respect her concerns in this area, though it would have been far more proper for her to have consulted with me directly. Nor do I blame her for the breach of protocol, as it is abundantly clear that you have positioned yourself as her most essential contact with the Church, circumventing any effort I might have made to assess the nature of her troubles for myself.

Though you have not asked for my advice, I shall give it. I would remind you, Father, that not all spiritual afflictions are the result of demonic forces.

I would have warned you, had you granted me the opportunity, that it is unseemly to encourage the superstitious fears of an elderly widow. As I am sure you know, there is no shortage of charlatans who have made a second gold rush of such opportunities.

You also mentioned in your message the prospect that the rifle heiress might express her gratitude for your consultations through a donation to the mission in support of our charitable work…

Be careful what you wish for, my dear friend. The Church does not trade salvation for recompense, and I will not be beholden to the whims of wealthy patrons because a priest sought to make Faustian bargains without leave. Hinting at such advantages does not have the persuasive effect on me that you might have imagined.

Of course, it is now impossible for me to rescind the offer you made on our behalf. And all this without regard for the other duties assigned to you which I will now have to burden your brothers with.

In an attempt to mitigate further harm to the mission's reputation, and to keep your spiritual adventurism in check, I have assigned young Peter to assist you in this project. Make no mistake: he is my eyes and ears. Should I receive word that you have strayed from Church doctrine in so much as the choice of prayers to recite, the consequences will be profound.

Yours in Christ Jesus,
Father Xavier Garzero S.J.

Diego folded the letter and returned it to the envelope. Xavier had needed to rattle his saber and assert his authority, but as judgments went, it could have been worse. For all his moral pearl clutching on the written page, the old man stopped short of calling Diego off and jeopardizing Mrs. Winchester's patronage. As for Peter, Diego was sure he could keep the younger man from interfering if he played his cards close to the vest.

He mused on the political dimensions of his current predicament only briefly while eating his soup and bread. The rich broth awakened his hunger, and he wished for something more substantial, but the doctor had warned him he would need to treat his stomach with care at first. Hopefully not for long. Regaining strength would be his most urgent priority with the eclipse fast approaching.

The priest turned his mind to the preparations required, but before he could reach for a notebook and pen, he found his mental acuity fading, his eyelids drooping. Had the doctor put a sedative in the soup to enforce additional rest? It would be absurd to knock him out again when he'd only just regained consciousness. But no sooner had the thought formed than he found himself pulled back down into the murk like a sinking boat.

CHAPTER EIGHTEEN

Someone was in the bed with him. The comforting weight of her head resting in the hollow of his shoulder, warm breath on his bare chest, dark hair splayed over his biceps. A hand on his hip, sliding down the slope of his groin, caressing his thigh, then pausing. He drew a deep breath. He should stop her. He parted his lips to speak, and petite fingers curled around his member—already stiff and eager—silencing him.

He knew her touch. Julia. The only female touch he'd ever known. She was still seventeen. She would always be seventeen. The smell of her hair was intoxicating.

He wanted her to look up at him. He wanted to see her eyes one more time. Wanted it even more than her touch. And he also did not want it. More than anything. Because as warm and real as she was, he knew, deep down, that her eyes would tell the truth.

The rhythm of her hand was slow and steady, her touch gentle but firm. He arched his back, pushing his pelvis up to meet the downward stroke. Wetness spread around the base of his shaft, thick and warm. Had he lost control? Had she oiled her palm? An icy dread climbed his spine, and he went soft, as her hand went cold.

He touched the puddle at his groin and brought his fingers to his upper lip, smelled iron: blood. Julia released her grip and ran the gash in her wrist down the length of his shriveling cock. He recoiled, bolted upright, and pulled the bloodstained sheet aside.

The room was dark, lit only by the faint glow of distant gas lamps through the frosted interior windows. Enough illumination to see that the knife wound on his forearm had opened and wept a sluggish smear of blood. He lay back, staring at the pale glass while consciousness and its implications gradually dawned on him.

He'd had a nightmare.

It was night.

He'd been drugged again, forced to pass precious hours unconscious.

No more. He swung his feet to the floor, and suffered the dizzying rush that came with sitting upright for the first time in days. He waited for his vision to clear, his eyes to adjust to the darkness. The soup bowl had been removed from the nightstand. He searched the shadows for a silhouette, half expecting Peter or some other guard to be watching him from the chair in the corner. Someone was there. No. Just the shape of his cassock draped from a coat hook.

Diego stood and gently applied weight to the foot with the bad ankle, then tested it with a few tentative steps. A lance of pain shot up his leg, but he persisted, biting his lip and moving to the window. The grounds below were frosted in moonlight, the carpenters' tools and sawhorses abandoned for the evening. Palm trees swayed in the night breeze. His gaze lingered at the tree line, searching for a sign of the spirit that had beckoned to him from the courtyard on the night of his fall.

Nothing stirred but the palm fronds. Both the house and grounds were shrouded in silence, leading him to surmise that the hour must be somewhere in the deepest reaches of night.

He paced the room, restless, unsure of what to do, but certain that the last thing he wanted was more sleep. He found fresh gauze on the bedside table and awkwardly replaced the bandage on his arm where the wound had reopened. There was a small desk in the corner, furnished with writing instruments and stationery, a Winchester repeater mounted on the wall above it as a decorative touch. He considered lighting a candle and writing in his journal, but what did he have to record? The dream? He couldn't bring himself to document it. It was too personal, too painful. Julia had taken her own life on the night when Diego's father had visited her parents in a drunken delirium, blaming her for the loss of his home and daughter on the first anniversary of the fire. Upon hearing the news, Diego had packed a small rucksack and set out on the long trek to Santa Rosalía to join the priesthood. He hadn't even woken his father, sleeping off the drink, to say goodbye. And he'd never looked back.

He believed that sometimes the Lord made his will known to men of the cloth in dreams, but he could recall no such dreams from the days he had spent in the coma. Nothing of value. No wisdom to direct his actions. And the dream that had just woken him came from anywhere but heaven. Possibly Hell. More likely the murky depths of his own guilty mind. He took a drink of water and tried to shake it off. If it *had* come from a demonic influence present in the house, he could not allow it to distract him from his purpose.

Writing his thoughts down might help to clarify them, to reconnect him with his deliberations prior to the accident. He felt a great sense of agitated urgency, that he should be taking action, even at this hour when the entire house slept—maybe even more so at such a lonely hour, when no one would interfere with his explorations. He remembered that he had been agonizing over the best course of action after searching Sarah's library in the grand ballroom and finding an Arabian treatise on demonology. Images of newspaper clippings flashed in his mind, and pieces of the puzzle returned to him in a chilling sequence of nightmarish fragments: the horns of a bull, hooves made of iron shaking the floor, blood dripping from a bearded muzzle, red embers burning in a bronze furnace where the bones of children lay on a bed of white ash.

Even in the dark, the room seemed to spin. His stomach lurched, and he touched his bandaged head, probing the folds of gauze and eliciting a dull, throbbing pain.

A shadow moved in his peripheral vision, a body gliding past the frosted windows of his room, moving soundlessly down the hall toward the bedroom door. He waited for a knock, staring at the ornate brass knob and expecting it to turn. Something about the silhouette had seemed feminine. Was it Mrs. Weatherlake? A servant? It seemed too tall and swift to be Mrs. Winchester, but that could be a trick of perspective, the light that cast the shadow angling it upward.

He approached the door with the feeling that whoever was on the other side was listening for his movement as carefully as he was listening for theirs. And now, all his aches and pains retreated, drowned out by the cold flush of fear.

The knob turned before he could touch it and the door swung open with a creak.

The young woman he'd seen in the garden stood at the end of the hall, beckoning to him, too far away to have opened the door. She wore the same simple dress as before, her pale limbs shining in the lamplight in a way that her eyes did not. Glimpsed through a curtain of loose curls that reminded Diego of her mother's black veil, Annie's eyes seemed to absorb the scant light, like pieces of coal. She was barefoot, but her feet were lily-white, showing no sign of having traipsed through the dirt of garden paths. But of course, dirt would not cling to a phantom.

Diego took a step toward her, his heart racing and ankle throbbing. The ghost smiled and vanished around a corner, down an adjacent corridor to the left. He searched the bedroom for a cane or crutch, but he'd been left with no such thing. In desperation, he limped to the desk and took the rifle from the wall. Was it loaded? He didn't know how to check, but thought it unlikely and assumed that as long as he didn't cock the lever, it would remain inert.

Wrapping his hand around the wooden stock, he placed the barrel against the floor and used the gun as a makeshift crutch. A few cautious steps proved the pain was bearable. Confident his leg wouldn't buckle, he hobbled down the hall, as barefoot as the ghost he pursued and almost as white as his cotton nightshirt.

He feared there would be no sign of her when he reached the juncture and rounded the corner where he'd last seen her, but there she was, waiting at the next archway. It felt like a child's game. And why shouldn't it? Her height and shape were that of a young woman, but he suspected her mental development had been stunted by growing up dead.

What a strange notion. This house had turned every assumption he had about the workings of the universe upside down.

He followed Annie through the maze, struggling to keep up, never losing sight of her, but at each new turn finding her farther away until he was sweating and huffing, his ankle screaming.

He wondered if it was the speed of her flight that increased, or the length of the corridors that stretched away from him exponentially, the architecture elastic—carrying her farther away each time. It was a mad notion, but this deep in the night anything seemed possible. If the ghost of an infant could grow up, why couldn't a house stretch its limbs?

The number of windows and doorways diminished as the chase wore on, the corridors growing darker as a consequence, until he could barely discern the form he pursued. Now he slowed his step and used his hands to feel for the next corner, afraid of stumbling down a staircase in the dark.

Had he ever been to this wing of the house before? He doubted it. An unsettling awe swept over him as he wondered at the scale of the place. He'd known that Winchester House was vast, but no house could contain these distances.

At length he came to a turn beyond which light spilled across the wallpaper, but when he rounded the corner, Annie was nowhere in sight. The hallway ended at a closed door inset with a stained glass window. A milky glow that could have been moonlight filtered through the panes, painting a mirror image of the design in pools of color on the varnished floor: a star-shaped purple flower with white inner petals and a spray of yellow at the center.

Beyond the most common types of flowers, Diego couldn't tell one from another, but the name of this one was written in black calligraphy at the bottom of the pane: *Columbine.*

He opened the door and stepped through. At first, he thought he had entered one of the conservatories—the windows in the room were so abundant, running in rows to his left and right. But there were no plants, and no humidity in the air. Annie stood in the center of the space, gazing placidly at the windows like a woman perusing an art gallery. And a gallery was exactly what the room was—a hall of stained glass, lit from without by the waxing moon.

Diego stepped gingerly into the room, afraid that Annie would flee at his approach before he had a chance to examine the artistry in the glass. But she remained where she was, inviting him with a look. Though her eyes still seemed lightless, a curious expression played in her features, as if she harbored some secret she was considering sharing.

He took a moment to catch his breath and rest his leg.

Each window was a variation on the same design: a brick building rising from a bright red pool, a long-horned demon rising from the roof of the building, its downturned crescent mouth open to reveal tongues of flame. Each building was slightly different, but beside each was an American flag at half-mast, and below each pool of blood was a name inked in the same blackletter calligraphy that had identified the flower in the door.

Diego limped down the gallery, reading the names as he went. Tears of blood fell like rain from the sky in each image. He noticed that the number of ruby droplets varied.

Red Lake
Blacksburg
Oakland
Newtown
Roseburg
Rancho Tehama
Parkland
Santa Fe
Oxford Township
Uvalde

The names continued out of sight.

"What are these?" he asked, his voice rough with disuse.

Annie studied him with her lightless eyes. The effect was unsettling. "Massacres."

"Do you mean battles in a war? Are these fortresses?"

The ghost stared at him. It was uncomfortable. At last, she said, "Schools."

"I don't understand."

"You won't be the last."

"Is the horned figure in the sky Satan?"

"Moloch. Eater of children. You hold his magic rod in your hand."

Diego looked down at the rifle that supported him. He'd almost forgotten what it was.

"When did these massacres happen?"

"Not yet. They happen if the beast escapes the maze. They are the price of Mother's pact."

"Tell me about this pact."

Annie studied the window in front of her. "Mother is a learned woman. Very wise, she is."

"Indeed she is."

"A cunning woman."

"Yes."

"*Too* cunning. Father was a businessman like his father before him. Do you know what they made?"

"This gun..." Diego said, putting his weight on his good foot and turning the stock of the rifle in his hand, as if to show it to her. As if she'd never seen one, growing up in a house where they decorated the arches and fireplaces. "And others like it."

"Did you know the Winchester company made shirts? Before the rifles, that's what they made. Men's shirts."

"I didn't know that."

"It's hard to reinvent a shirt, Mother says. But they remade the rifle, so you could shoot a whole party of Indians without reloading. But it wasn't the guns they made that the fortune come from, it was the *deals*. That's what a businessman makes, no matter what he sells. He makes deals."

"I suppose that's true."

"It is. Mother taught me and she knows. She knows how to make deals even better than Father's father. Because a businessman..." Annie's face looked troubled, as if she were searching her memory for the exact words. "A businessman's most powerful deals are with the leaders of countries and armies. But a cunning woman's most powerful deals are with gods and devils. Powers that rule men even if they don't know it. Do you know about that?"

"I think I do."

"But deals with those powers are strange. They are not normal contracts. You have to use the right ingredients to bind them and make a pact. The right combination." Annie smiled. It looked wrong on her dead face. It made Diego's flesh crawl.

"What's funny?" he whispered.

"Words are funny. I said *combination* because there are ingredients you combine to make a spell. But mother also keeps the spell locked up with a combination. And I know what it is. I can be invisible sometimes. Did you know that?"

"No."

"I can be. Even to her. But I can't always control it. There's times when the house lines up right and makes me solid. And times when I'm thin as morning mist. The solid times like now are the best times, mostly. But the thin times have benefits. Like sneaking. Also, there's other things that get solid when I do. And them's not good at all, them things that eat souls."

"Moloch…is he one of them?"

Annie nodded. "The king," she whispered. "And kings demand a tithe. Do you know about that?

"I do."

"Mother knows it well."

"And what does she pay to the king you speak of?"

Annie's coy playfulness was gone, her mouth a severe slash across her pale face.

"You can see for yourself," she said. "Mother made a pact. Signed in blood but not her own."

"Whose blood?" His dry lips crackled with the question.

"The victims. A portion of the victims."

"The victims of what?"

She looked confused, as if it should be obvious. "The victims of Moloch's rod. A portion of the suffering that makes our fortune. The blood soaked soil the money tree is rooted in."

"Is that how your mother describes it?"

"She doesn't talk to me about it. About the trick she played to hide me from Jehovah. But I know more than I let on. I watch her when she thinks I'm away in the darkness of the moon. I look over her shoulder and I hold my breath, and she hasn't an inkling I'm there. That's how I learned the numbers. Numbers are important."

"Do you mean like the number thirteen? It's everywhere in this house."

"Mother is very fond of thirteen. It's the number of Death in the tarot.

But there's a whole language of numbers in this house. The number that feeds the monster is in the heart of the house—the innermost chamber."

Diego's mouth had gone dry. His voice was husky when he asked, "Where is that?"

"The safe in the grand ballroom."

"Is that the combination you learned by looking over her shoulder?"

Annie nodded. "My birthday."

A crash like thunder echoed throughout the house causing the glass panes to tremble in their frames.

Annie's eyes flared—a red line of light, smeared like a sunrise. "It's coming," she said.

"Moloch?"

Annie stared past him at the door with the flower window. A rumble, like a boulder rolling beneath the floor, rattled every nail and plank.

"Go!" she said.

Diego braced the rifle against the shuddering floor and took a step toward the door they had entered through. Annie touched his arm, a subtle sensation that tingled and then numbed his muscle like a shot of Novocain.

"Not that way."

There was only one other direction available to him, but he had no idea where it led to. Either way, he would be hopelessly lost in the sprawling house.

"Come with me," he said. "Show me the way back to my room."

She shook her head. Her hair, when it moved, seemed to do so with a delay, as if the air around her was thicker than the stuff he was breathing. As if her body moved differently through time.

"I can hold it here while you go. It senses you're a threat, but it's easily distracted in this gallery. It likes to look through the windows to the future, to savor the offerings people will make to it."

"Offerings?"

"Blood sacrifices. No cult in history will spill more blood than Moloch's worshippers."

The doorknob rattled, turned, and clicked. The door swung open on a rectangle of blackness.

"Go! Before it sees you. Before it changes the house around you."

"It can do that?"

Annie stared at the black gap.

Diego didn't wait for an answer. He lurched down the hall, using the rifle as a cane again. Could he brandish it as a weapon, if it came to that? Would it even work? The beast was more physical than any fiend he'd ever faced. It sounded mechanical, a thing constructed of steel and bronze, like an automaton. A demon that needn't take up residence in human flesh because it somehow manifested in its own shell.

He was tempted to wait and watch it emerge from the darkness, to satisfy his curiosity about what he was up against. But the stronger urge to flee prevailed, and soon he was shambling through twisting passages again. He threw doors open at random, almost hoping to disturb some sleeping person who might take pity on him and guide him back to his room. But he found no one. The sounds of pursuit receded with his random progress, until he started to hope the monster might have lost his scent.

The rooms he traversed now were increasingly empty of furniture and marred with dust and cobwebs, as if he'd entered a wing long abandoned. No lamp or candlelight penetrated these desolate chambers with the promise of a return to inhabited realms. Only moonlight, distorted through thick glass, fractured in stained mosaics.

He slowed to examine these, his previous pace impossible to sustain, and saw that they were crude pieces, lacking the craft and composition of the panels he'd seen in the gallery. These looked executed by a child or a lunatic, if such could work in stained glass. The subjects chilled him.

They were scenes from his own life: A burning house viewed from the bow of a rowboat across an expanse of dark water; a rose entwined about a cross, dripping tears of blood from its thorns; a clawed hand reaching through the rubble of broken bricks for absolution; a ghost formed in smoke, rising from a cauldron beside a phonograph horn with accusation in its twisted features.

He stood in a bedroom, empty of all but a bed, unable to walk anymore, weary to the marrow. Aching and sore. He dropped the rifle, collapsed on the dusty mattress, and surrendered to sleep.

CHAPTER NINETEEN

On Friday, August 3rd, the day before the pre-dawn lunar eclipse, Father Diego Montero woke in a familiar bed. His black cassock hung from a coat hook beside the door. The rifle he'd used as a cane was returned to its mounting above the humble desk in the corner, and an actual cane leaned against the bed. A glass of orange juice on the nightstand caught summer sunlight through plain windows beyond which the sound of hammers and saws heralded the break of day.

Peter sat in a chair by the door, reading a book. He glanced up when Diego stirred.

"Good morning, Father."

"Good morning, Peter. Where is Mrs. Winchester?"

"Down the hall, meeting with your doctor. She's worried you won't be able to...*perform your duties* was how she put it. Dr. Neville was in earlier to check your ankle while you slept. It doesn't look good. How bad is the pain?"

"Not too bad. I'll be fine with the cane. They should have provided one sooner."

Diego sat up and took a sip of juice. His throat was parched, and he coughed into his fist after swallowing, but the sugar gave a boost to his brain right away.

Peter lowered his voice. "May I ask, while we have a moment alone, what exactly your duties are? In your letter, you spoke of an exorcism, but I've been here for three days and seen no signs of anyone possessed. Is the victim locked away in some remote room? Forgive me, but Mrs. Winchester refuses to tell me anything."

"It's not a person that's possessed; it's the house itself."

"Do you mean to say it's haunted?"

"That might put it too simply."

"You seem reluctant to confide in me, Father. But I can't help you if you don't. I've gathered that tonight is important."

"Yes."

"Because of an eclipse? I do have ears, you know."

"The house is more than a house, Peter. It's an occult engine, built on precise celestial alignments. Everything about it—the numerology of the measurements, the geographical orientation, even the designs in the windows—is meant to position it just slightly askew to the material plane."

Diego thought the younger man might laugh, but the expression on his face was one of horror. "Is that why I feel nauseous ever since I set foot here? My body rejects the place."

"It might, if you're sensitive to it."

"But what was her purpose in building such a thing? Is she insane?"

"No. Only desperate to preserve her daughter's ghost. The girl died in infancy, and Winchester House has enabled her to endure." Diego spoke in little more than a whisper, expecting Sarah to appear in the doorway at any moment. "It has provided her with a refuge between worlds."

Peter looked pale. They had confronted evil together before, but this was different. The young scholastic was processing the ramifications. Defiance of the rule of heaven.

"I believe she did it out of love," Diego said. "The baby was unbaptized."

"*She hid a soul from God?*"

"Keep your voice down. I'd hoped to persuade Sarah to let the girl go. But after my accident… I've lost precious time. I fear I've lost control."

"Did you ever have it?"

"No. I suppose it's fair to say I didn't. I worked to earn her trust, but she's still keeping things from me."

"And what is it she expects you to do?"

"The architecture of the house has done more than allow her a place to hide her daughter. Or, I should say, while it has enabled the girl to exist in a *between* place, it *hasn't* kept her entirely hidden. Not from the forces of evil, in any case. The oddness of the place—the *wrongness* of it—is a beacon to creatures of the abyss. One in particular is attracted to the house. It's a predator, a devourer of children. I believe that even though Annie's ghost has grown into something like a young woman, the monster wants its meal."

"What is it? This monster you speak of?"

"Its name is Moloch. It grows strongest when the house's defenses are at their lowest ebb."

"What defenses?"

"Wards. Occult barriers. Sarah crafted their designs into the ornamentation of the house. But the eclipse is a window of opportunity for the beast. While the moon is black, Moloch can fully manifest. It has already started. It's growing stronger by the hour."

"And you believe you can banish it?"

Diego thought of Annie's words to him in his dream, in the hall of colored windows. Her warning against the consequences of casting the demon out into the world, into the future.

"It might be wiser to bind it than to banish it. To capture it in a spirit trap, where it can do no harm."

"Like a genie in a bottle?"

Diego scratched his arm where the knife scab itched. "Something like that."

"How would you even do such a thing?"

"There are methods. She has a lesser spirit trapped in a music box. It might be possible to trade one for the other. I wish I'd had more time for research, but her occult library is extensive. And there is no time to waste."

Diego struggled to get up, but Peter made no move to assist him.

"You're mad," Peter said. "Planning to use magic to trap a demon?

Trading spirits like poker chips? I won't be involved. I won't let you do it. I'll send word to the mission."

Diego gripped the head of the cane in his clawed hand and hoisted himself to his feet, grimacing. Looking down at the younger man, he said, "Peter…you must trust me. We want the same thing. To defang the evil that inhabits this house. But I promise you the usual rules do not apply here. It will call for desperate measures."

"So the end justifies the means. Is that what you're saying?"

Diego hobbled to the doorway. At the threshold, he looked back. "Let us pray that I can *find* the means."

Diego found Sarah waiting for him in the dining room. His entrance was apparently expected—a servant pulled out a chair for him, while another brought covered trays from the chef's cabinet.

"I'm glad to see you up and about, Father. How is the pain?"

"Manageable, thank you."

"For a man who slept most of the week, I have to say you don't look it."

"To be honest, I've not slept much since waking from the coma."

"We have time for nothing less than honesty. What disturbed your sleep?"

"Annie visited my room last night."

"Do tell."

"She led me through the house."

"And you were able to walk?"

"Not well, but she was patient. She showed me a gallery of stained glass windows."

"A gallery?"

"An entire corridor lined with them, illuminated by moonlight. She said they depicted future massacres."

Sarah scoffed. "I've commissioned many Tiffany glass windows for my house, but none that portray massacres."

"When I left the place in search of my own room, I encountered other windows. One of these showed a burning house."

"You must have been dreaming. There is no such window in this house." She gestured at the plates. "Eat. You must regain your strength."

"Perhaps I *was* dreaming. Has Annie ever visited you in dreams? Has she ever led you to parts of the house that don't exist?"

Sarah held his gaze. He could sense the deliberation behind her eyes. At last, he looked down at the steaming food and stabbed a sausage with his fork.

"Yes," she said. "She has led me to parts of the house that did not exist *yet.* Rooms she wished for me to build. And so I have. But that's different from what you're describing. She and I have collaborated in the creation of our home. What visited you was likely a meddlesome spirit masquerading as my daughter."

Diego chewed his food. The meat was flavorful, with enough spice to enliven him. "This girl, or woman...she looked exactly as Joe Colton described her."

Sarah sliced a deviled egg with a spoon. "Are you sure it wasn't the same spirit that had words with you when we conducted our seance on the night of your accident? That was also a young woman, I believe. She seemed to have dire unfinished business with you."

"It wasn't the same. That was my sister who died when we were young. Though I'm far from convinced it was truly her, just as I seem unable to convince you that my guide of last night was your Annie. I suppose we will have to live with uncertainty."

"An all too common state of affairs, I'm afraid. I would caution you against taking *anything* you see in this house at face value. It exists outside the bounds of the ordinary world. As such, it acts as a beacon to all manner of lost souls and spirits. And one thing you may have learned about spirits is that they are loath to reveal their true identities, yes?"

"True. Demons resist giving their names until compelled to do so under a divine authority they are powerless to resist. But the demon that pursues Annie...I believe you *know* its name."

Sarah nodded, ever so slightly.

"Say it."

"Moloch," she whispered, as if the name alone would summon it to join their breakfast.

"From browsing your library, I gather you also know it was worshipped in antiquity as a pagan god?"

Did he sense her posture stiffening? If she didn't want him snooping in her books, she should have kept them from him. But there was one she had withheld, wasn't there?

"You've been reading *The Black Flame of Canaan.*"

"The first volume, yes. I couldn't find the second."

"I keep it under lock and key. The first volume is devoted to theory, the second to practice. In the wrong hands, it could be quite dangerous."

"Whose hands? Clyde's? I doubt he could read the Arabic."

"It's the sigils that tend to stir things up. You know what they say about how a picture is worth a thousand words. I wouldn't want to be responsible for the dreams that might come from gazing too long at one of those glyphs."

"Some of the pictures I saw in the first volume were woodcut prints of Moloch receiving sacrifices." He omitted mention of the newspaper clippings he'd found nestled between the pages like dried flowers, but surely she knew he would have seen them.

"The beast feeds on the souls of innocents. That's why it hunts my baby girl."

"She's not a baby anymore."

"No. I've raised her to the extent that I can. But despite the education, she is an innocent. Tainted only by the original sin of Eve."

"And that's why you've kept her here, hidden from the eyes of heaven. You fear that unbaptized she would be condemned to purgatory…or worse. So you've confined her to this in-between place. Neither living nor dead."

"And there it is," she said. "The other shoe drops. You present yourself as an ally, a fellow traveler, an open-minded seeker, all the while waiting for the moment to pronounce your judgment."

"I can't help you if I don't understand the powers you've employed, the pacts you've made, and the terms of the bargain."

Sarah sat up straight. A fire kindled in her eyes. "I make no *bargains*, Father. What I have achieved here, I have done by my *own* power. You may think you understand the cost, but you do not."

"The cost, at the very least, is Annie's spiritual progress. Trapped in a half-life, she will never reach the gates of the Kingdom. It's against nature. And it has made her vulnerable to the appetites of the abyss. You may believe she's safe here, but she's not. You've admitted to yourself that you almost lost her at the last eclipse, and the next is upon us."

"So you're helpless to protect her. You finally admit it."

"That's not what I'm saying."

"Then say what you mean!"

"I am trying to tell you that there may be more than one way to save her. Holding the predator at bay while the shadow crosses the moon is only one of them, and a poor one at that because the next eclipse will come. And another after that."

"What else would you propose?"

Diego hesitated. He'd lost his appetite, but he looked at the table as he spoke, his eyes focused on his own blurred reflection in a polished silver teapot. "If I were only a Jesuit priest, you would never have welcomed me into your house. Priests and ministers are the ones who told you your infant was damned for not living long enough to be anointed. It's my other education, my other affiliation that led you to trust me. And on that path I have found hidden wisdom, even in the Bible. Wisdom known in other times and places. Lost wisdom."

"Speak plainly."

"Other lives. Reincarnation."

"Only a moment ago you spoke of the kingdom of heaven. Pick a side, Diego. Which do you believe in?"

It was the first time she had used his name. A sign she was dismissing his authority? Or that she was willing to see him as more than a priest?

"Both," he said. "Of John the Baptist, Jesus said to his followers 'If ye will receive it, this is Elias, which was for to come.' What could that mean but that he recognized John as the reincarnation of the prophet Elias? I believe we are given more than one chance to purify our souls here on Earth before God calls us to the Kingdom. You might give your daughter another chance. Another life."

Sarah scoffed. "You expect me to risk her soul based on how one priest reads a single line of the Bible?"

It was hard to argue that she should, but he could see a conflict stirring within her. She waved a hand in frustration, looked away, and dabbed at the corner of her eye with a napkin.

"You speak of John the Baptist," she said, looking out the nearest window. Then meeting his eyes, "While we're speculating… What would you think of baptizing a ghost?"

The witch's cap at the top of the house looked very different from the last time Diego had set foot in it. A large ceramic bowl filled with clear water rested atop a marble pedestal in a corner of the room beside the door. The floor had been swept and mopped and now glistened with a sheen of fragrant oil, lending the space an air of purification.

Five Tiffany glass panes hung from wires suspended from the bare rafters, forming a pentagon around the center of the room. Each featured colorful alchemical and astrological symbols within intricate black spider webs. Diego recognized some, but not all, of the glyphs.

"What are these windows?" he asked.

"The house is designed to channel energy to the cone that comprises the roof of this room," Sarah said. "When the moon reaches its nadir, and the power of the demon surges, it will be inexorably drawn to this place. The webs and wards of these windows will constrain it for a time. Then it will be your job to force it into the box."

"By the power of Jesus."

"If that's what it takes."

The silver music box was set atop a second pedestal, situated diagonally across the room from the one supporting the water basin. He approached it, examining the filigree designs that ornamented the outer walls without touching it.

"I imagine this will make a suitable cell for the demon. The mechanical nature of the box should make it feel at home. This demon has an affinity for machinery, does it not?"

Sarah nodded, her lips pressed in a severe line.

"I've heard it roaming the halls of the house," Diego said. "It creaks and groans like a suit of armor, or a mechanical man."

"The grimoires depict it as a titanic bronze statue, a crucible of sacrifice," Sarah said.

"Do you believe it was only drawn to the Winchester House because of the strange architecture? Or might it also have felt an affinity for the machine that built your palace...the repeating rifle?"

"I've heard the rumors about how wracked with guilt I am over the source of my fortunes. There's no truth to them."

"I wasn't asking about your feelings toward the rifle but the feelings it might inspire in a demon. After all, it's an extraordinary gun, an innovation. The repeater can fire how many rounds without reloading?"

"Thirteen rounds at .44 and .45 caliber."

"There's that number again. That's a lot of bodies before the smoke clears. A sacrifice befitting a king."

"It's the rifle that won the West," Sarah said. "And the War of the States. Perhaps it was God's will that my father-in-law should have put such a weapon into the hands of worthy men in such desperate times."

"I don't claim to know the will of God. But don't you fear what will happen when devils take up the weapons men of God have left lying around?"

"I seldom leave my house, Father. My concern is for my daughter's soul. I have no fear to spare for the course of history. I've given my life to my Annie, and there isn't much left of it to give. But with your help, she could be protected even after I'm gone. That's why you're here."

"You want me to bless the water. To baptize her."

"Will you do it?" For the first time since he'd met her, Sarah's voice betrayed a nervous tremor.

Leaning on his cane, he turned away from the music box to face the woman and the basin of water behind her. He scratched his beard. "I don't know if it's even possible. No one has ever done it before."

"She isn't merely a ghost, Father. She's nearly alive."

"Baptism is a purification of the flesh. She has no flesh to speak of. The droplets would fall to the dust."

"I polished this floor on my own hands and knees." She fused with the folds of her black dress, and for a fleeting moment, he feared she might be preparing to get down on her knees right now in front of him to beg for the boon that only he could provide. But no. She was fishing in a pocket for something. Her arthritic hand emerged holding a fat stick of chalk. She held it up to show him, then opened a door in a low cabinet and removed a leather-bound book.

"Is that..."

"Yes," she said. "*The Black Flame of Canaan, Volume 2.*" She opened the book to a page marked by a silk ribbon and laid it on top of the cabinet. "Draw this magic circle on the floor. You will find that it has much in common with the Circle of Solomon, but with some powerful modifications. Complete my work and make this room a sanctuary between worlds. Then bless the water. We will meet her between life and death, where your blessing can reach her. Just as the eclipse will allow Moloch to approach the physical, so it will for Annie as well. In that moment when she is most vulnerable to attack, she will also be better able to receive the blessing."

She had thought of everything, it seemed. Who was he to argue with the architect of a celestial scheme when he was but a cog in the machine? Or was he the spark of God in an otherwise infernal contraption? The only one who could make it holy. If so, it gave him bargaining power, but only if he took a firm hand.

"Annie wouldn't need the blessing to protect her unless she left this house," he said. "If I do this, if I baptize her, you'll have no need of an elaborate demon trap. You can let her go. Let her pass on and be reborn."

Sarah's face contorted at the suggestion. "No. I would never willingly cast her out into darkness. It's a precaution, a last defense, in case we fail and the house comes down around us."

"The last quake terrified you. You had a glimpse of your defenses failing."

"We can leave nothing to chance this time. Please, Father." She took his hand, pressed the stick of chalk into his palm, and closed his fist around it.

CHAPTER TWENTY

Sarah retired to her chambers to rest while Diego applied himself to the work of inscribing the magic circle on the floor of the witch's cap. The heat of the day had gathered in the cone, making the sweat that fell from his brow the greatest obstacle to the completion of the design. Several times he had to retrace lines where a salty droplet striking the floor had broken them.

The day passed by in a blur, his mind drifting into a trance state, mesmerized by sustained focus on the sigils and Hebrew letters. He was surprised to notice the light fading from the windows at dusk. He set down the chalk, took up his cane, and struggled to stand without tipping over. His joints popped and his cramped muscles flared with pins and needles, but he managed to regain his feet without overtaxing his bad ankle. Breathing in ragged gasps, he leaned on the cane, contemplating the chalk dust on his black clothes, and the clear water in the basin. He considered blessing the water before taking up the chalk again, but decided it could wait. There would be time to make holy water later, after he was refreshed. *One job at a time*, he told himself.

"Is it for me?" a voice whispered in his ear like the rustling of leaves on an autumn wind. He froze and turned his head slowly. Annie stood beside him, her spectral hair tickling his neck, her black eyes like obsidian marbles, absorbing any light that reached them. A rush of fear electrified his skin.

"Yes," he said. "To protect you outside of the house and grounds. But it's a last resort. Your mother doesn't want you to leave."

"No," Annie said. "She would never allow it, never break the spell."

"What spell?" His gaze flicked around the room like a restless bird, touching on each of the webbed windows in turn. "Are you trapped in webs like these?"

"No. A spell. Go to the ballroom and see. Do it while Mother is sleeping."

"But the safe is locked. You haven't told me the combination."

A gust of cold air brushed the priest's face, scattering the apparition. He turned toward it and looked down at the design he'd drawn on the floor, nearly complete, the stick of chalk spinning and rolling under the influence of the agitated air. There was a string of numbers he had no recollection of writing among the names of protection running along the border of the magic circle: 6-15-66. Annie's birthday? It had to be.

Diego smudged out the numbers with the sole of his shoe, then braced his weight against the cane and set off for the nearest staircase. His sense of direction when navigating the house by daylight had improved, much to his own surprise. Just when he'd begun to doubt his intuition, he rounded a corner and saw the red wallpaper and crystal chandelier of the ballroom. A few more steps brought the pipe organ into view, and he let out an exhausted sigh.

The room was empty, but he hesitated at the threshold. As soon as he committed to raiding the safe there would be no turning back. He would have to act quickly, trusting in Annie's assurance that Sarah truly was taking a nap to gather her strength for the night ahead.

Would the ghost warn him if Sarah rose and came looking for him? And what of the other members of the staff, such as Clyde and Ms. Weatherlake? If any of them caught him with his hands in the safe, there would be no excuse for the transgression.

The sound of the cane on the polished floor seemed impossibly loud as he cut across the room and opened the wood and metal doors that concealed the cast iron safe with its brass combination dials.

He spun both dials to clear them, then set the right side dial to 66, spun the left to 6, then reversed direction and stopped on 15. The bolts retracted with a *thunk*. The door swung smoothly open when he tried the handle.

Only splinters of light from the chandelier reached into the iron cavity. An odor spilled out, ancient and earthy, the scent of a root cellar. There was no time to gather a candle and matches from the mantle. He reached into the murk and felt for the contents. He touched paper first, a sheaf of thick, brittle pages. Then a rough tangle of some coarse material—roots or hair? He withdrew the object and discovered it was both: a mandrake root, in the shape of a fetus, with a lock of black hair pinned to the part that resembled the top of the head.

Diego was familiar with the shape. The mandrake was famous in folklore for its association to witchcraft and the primitive belief that the plant screamed when pulled from the ground. As with most superstitions, he suspected there was a principle of sympathetic magic at work behind the belief. The simplest of symbolic inferences: the plant resembled a human infant, therefore it must possess other characteristics of an infant.

Turning the root over in his hands, he realized that his disdain for such simplistic folk magic was misplaced. He liked to believe that the mystic formulas of Rosicrucian magic were of a higher pedigree, more rarefied and philosophical. But at their heart, these doctrines functioned on the same core principle: We use *this* to symbolize *that*, and thereby influence *that* by the manipulation of *this*.

When the code was composed of divine names and their numerical values, it seemed scientific. When it was a grubby root pulled from the earth and embellished with the trappings of a voodoo doll, the process lost some of its luster, but none of its essential power. Magic, at its heart, was the empowerment and manipulation of symbols. The cross itself was a symbol—the vertical intercession of the divine in the horizontal plane of human life. So too was the rose, symbol of the blood of Christ. Their juxtaposition encoded another layer of meaning: the phallus and vulva, key and keyhole on the door of life. And the fruit of their conjunction could be represented by the root in his hand.

This meditation passed through his mind in the space of seconds as he examined the object in the fractured light, searching for any engravings on the root that might reveal its purpose. But there were none. If the mandrake had been dedicated to a particular human child, the operation had not been accomplished with a name but with a more potent link: the lock of hair pinned to the apparent head. These hairs had to have been taken from baby Annie. He wondered if they'd been trimmed while the child was still alive, or after she'd died? Either way, the spell had clearly worked. It had given the child's soul a material basis of support, an anchor at the heart of Winchester House. Annie's spirit was quite literally rooted here. It had grown from this nexus just as the house had grown toward all points of the compass from this steel box. This covenant.

But it was not a covenant made with the Lord. Sarah had admitted as much already. And what had the demon required in return? Diego put the root back inside the safe, then removed the documents and unfolded them.

The first page of the sheaf was a contract, signed by Sarah Winchester in a rust-hued sepia ink. Or had the quill been dipped in blood?

> I, Sarah Lockwood Winchester, do hereby dedicate 777 shares of the Winchester Repeating Arms Company to Moloch, Prince of the Valley of Tears that is Topeth in Hinnom. May this portion of the fortunes of the kingdom of Earth suffice in trade for a sanctuary totaling six acres of the astral plane, upon which my house shall stand.

Diego tilted the paper to the light and scanned through the remaining passages. He doubted that an attorney had been consulted, but the terms were clear. The demon king was awarded the spiritual substance of the revenue generated by Mrs. Winchester's stock holdings. More precisely, a measure of the suffering inflicted upon innocent souls by the use of Winchester arms. An infernal tax on a mortal sin. In exchange for such sustenance, the beast was constrained to the boundaries of the house in which the covenant was sealed, and by his presence would sustain a piece of purgatory on Earth. A sphere within which Annie's ghost could live, in a sense, and even flourish.

"Put it back."

Mrs. Winchester spoke from over his shoulder. She'd crept up as silently as a ghost. Her bottom lip and extended hand trembled, but not from any medical condition. She was enraged, barely able to constrain the emotion, or to speak beyond the simple command. When Diego didn't move, she pointed at the safe and repeated the words, "Put it *back*."

Diego glanced down at the contract in his hand. "All this time you've acted as if the demon were a threat. To the house, to Annie… But you made a pact with it."

"You have no idea what we are dealing with, Father. No notion of the powers at work. If you harmed so much as a single hair upon her head…"

"*Whose* head?" He squinted. "The mandrake doll? The poppet you bound to the house in your blood covenant with Moloch?"

"You, Father, know just enough to do irreparable harm. I could have used you to constrain this evil, but you couldn't abide serving under a woman, could you? You had to go poking and prodding and sneaking around my house. Defying my rules. Violating my privacy. Defiling my inner sanctum. You're no better than that carpenter—a liar and a thief!" Her face twisted with puzzlement. "But how did you know the combination?"

"Annie told me."

"She would never betray me, never risk her own existence. You lie."

Diego set the papers down inside the safe. "Don't worry. Your dark treasures are just as I found them. But how dare you accuse *me* of dishonesty? You're the one who lied. You never wanted to expel the demon from this house. You *built* this house as a trap for it. You've kept it like a pet, feeding it on the blood of innocents. And all to keep your daughter from God. If I have it wrong, then tell me how. Go ahead and tell me."

"I have done what your Church has failed to do. I *have* made evil my prisoner. I baited it with blood and trapped it. And I have kept it from running amok."

"You've fed it on the souls of innocents." Diego stabbed the papers with his finger. "That's what you promised it. A share of the suffering of Winchester rifle victims."

"What would you have me do then? Release the child-eater on my neighbors? Unleash it on the world?"

"As if you didn't summon it in the first place."

"And you have no notion of how many lives I have saved in doing so! How many have been *spared* from the rifle. You have no notion of what's at stake if we fail to constrain the beast at the critical hour."

"All you care about is keeping Annie for yourself. But she wants to be free."

Beneath her veil, Sarah's mouth contorted in a grimace of grief. She knew the truth of his words too well to argue. "So does Moloch," she said.

"I could Christen her," he coaxed. "I could grant her the protection to leave this place."

"You said yourself it might fail. I could only allow it as a last resort. You want the truth, Father Diego? I would never gamble on letting her go with only your blessing to protect her."

"Please, Sarah. You must trust me. I beg you."

Her eyes softened. "I have made mistakes. I know that better than anyone. But I also know the cost of trying to undo them now. And on that score, Father, you must trust *me*."

CHAPTER TWENTY-ONE

When Diego and Sarah reached the witch's cap, they found Peter standing in the candle-lit room, staring at the magic circle chalked on the floor. A broom and a rifle leaned against the rough beams of the wall behind him.

"What is this?" Peter asked. "Are these incantations in the Devil's tongue?"

"These are names of God and his angels, to protect us from demons." Diego eased himself down onto one knee, and taking up the chalk he'd left behind, inscribed the final names around a triangle he'd drawn outside of the circle: ANEXHEXATON, PRIMEUMATON, TETRAGRAMMATON, MI-CHA-EL.

"You can call it what you like, but it's witchcraft, isn't it? It's black magic."

"No, Peter, it's white magic, just as we've always done."

"Then why aren't the normal rites of exorcism enough? Why do you need all this?" he waved his hand around to take in the stained glass windowpanes. The candle flames wavered as the air in the room, already thick and sweet with burning wax, was agitated by the gesture. Sarah must have lit a dozen of them in sets of candelabra before confronting Diego in the ballroom. Most were positioned behind the colored glass panes. The curtains had been drawn aside on the windows, allowing the light of the full moon in, a pale contrast to the dancing yellow flames.

With the work completed, Diego leaned on the cane to hoist himself upright. He looked Peter squarely in the eye and answered, "Because we are to constrain it, not cast it out of the house. It *wants* to escape the house, to wreak havoc on the world. The moment of greatest peril will come at the fullness of the eclipse, just before the dawn. If we can hold the defenses until the sun rises, we will have prevailed."

Peter had been a brave companion in their previous ordeals, but then they had always been grounded in church doctrine. Now he looked sweaty, twitchy, like a man perched on a precipitous ledge above a mist shrouded abyss. He worked his jaw, as if groping for a rebuttal, then closed his mouth and swallowed.

Sarah had moved around the perimeter of the room while the two priests faced off. Now she stepped forward and placed the silver music box in the center of the triangle. She laid the rifle in front of it, along the base of the chalk diagram, then took a small, shiny object from a pocket of her dress and held it up to catch the moonlight.

"What is it?" Diego asked.

"A shotgun shell from a local accident, filled with grave dirt from the victim. It will attract the demon to the triangle."

Peter let out a moan of despair.

"A local accident?" Diego said. "Are you referring to the little girl who was shot by the neighbor boy in Modesto? I found the news clipping in your library."

"Yes. It's the freshest kill I know of."

Diego grimaced. "And is that the rifle that fired it?"

"It is."

"How did you acquire these things?"

"Clyde obtained them for me. These sorts of errands are part of his job. The families are well compensated and my name kept out of it."

Peter was shaking his head. "No," he said. "It's witchcraft. I can't believe you're endorsing it. We *must* leave this place, Father."

Diego laid a placating hand on Peter's arm. "You don't have to witness this, but I can't abandon her now. I've pledged my help. Her daughter's soul is at stake."

Peter contemplated the crossroads they'd reached, his eyes fixed on the triangle. At last, with shaky resolve, he said, "I will not abandon you to face devils alone."

Diego nodded and took a pouch of sea salt from the pocket of his cassock. He handed it to Peter and gestured at the basin of water in the corner. "Prepare the salt for the holy water."

"You truly intend to christen a ghost with it?"

"Just proceed as usual. We may need it in any event."

Peter took the pouch and retreated to the corner. In a moment, Diego heard his muttered prayer: *O salt, creature of God, I exorcise you by the living God, by the true God, by the holy God, by the God who ordered you to be poured into the water by Eliseo the Prophet so that its life-giving powers might be restored. I exorcise you so that you may become a means of salvation for believers, that you may bring health of soul and body to all who make use of you, that you may put to flight and drive away from the places where you are sprinkled like every apparition, villainy, and turn of devilish deceit, and every unclean spirit, adjured by Him who will come to judge the living and the dead and the world by fire. Amen.*

A servant entered bearing the iron cauldron from the seance room. He set it down in the center of the circle and left without a word. Sarah took herbs and charcoal from a box of drawers and set them burning in the cauldron. Plumes of fragrant smoke wafted up into the cone above their heads.

"Explain the process you envision," Diego said.

Sarah moved around the room while answering, her hands busy with final preparations and paraphernalia. He saw that she was careful to avoid stepping on the elaborate names and symbols he'd chalked on the floor.

"The house itself will not be an adequate prison to contain the demon in the hour of shadow. We must lure it into a trap within a trap. The outer layer of constraint is the triangle of the art. The other is the Arabic box within the triangle, which was designed to imprison rebellious spirits. The circle will protect us while you constrain the demon to the triangle by your authority. The shell casing and grave dirt will serve as bait to lure it into the box."

"And the cauldron?" he asked, though he thought he knew the answer.

"It will grant Annie's spirit substance in the circle with us, so that she, too, will be protected."

Peter, with his back turned, was surely listening to every word. He moved on to sprinkling the salt into the water basin with the words of exorcism: *O water, creature of God, I exorcise you in the name of God the Father Almighty, and in the name of Jesus Christ His Son, our Lord, and in the power of the Holy Spirit. I exorcise you so that you may put to flight all the power of the Enemy, and be able to root out and supplant that Enemy with his apostate angels: through the power of our Lord Jesus Christ, Who will come to judge the living and the dead and the world by fire. Amen.*

"What about the djinn trapped in the music box?" Diego asked. "Won't it escape when you open it?"

Sarah produced a black glass bottle and a small scroll of parchment tied with black ribbon. Holding the scroll up, she said, "On this is written the djinn's name in blood." She dropped the scroll into the bottle and stoppered it with a cork. "When we open the music box, I will inhale the spirit from one vessel and exhale it into the other, then seal it with wax."

"Will that be enough to hold it?"

"For a time. Perhaps I'll cast the bottle into the sea, as Solomon did with the demons that built his temple."

"And what of Moloch?"

"Do not yet speak that name!"

"What will you do with the child-eater when the crisis has passed? Will you set him loose again to roam your house, feeding on tragedy and powering your sanctuary until the next eclipse?"

"I won't risk another breach. The music box will go into the safe with the rest of the covenant. It's what I should have done in the first place."

Silence spread between them as Diego considered the cracks in Sarah's plan, the desperation underlying it. Peter, who had paused to listen, now sprinkled the salt into the water in the pattern of a cross and completed the blessing.

Blessed are you, Lord, Almighty God, who deigned to bless us in Christ, the living water of our salvation, and to reform us interiorly.

Grant that we who are fortified by the sprinkling of or use of this water, the youth of the spirit being renewed by the power of the Holy Spirit, may walk always in newness of life.

As he spoke the final lines, the house began to shake. The glass panes and floorboards rattled, bottles clinked, and dust rained down from the rafters, crackling in the shuddering candle flames.

Peter looked around, his eyes wide with alarm. "Another earthquake?"

"No," Diego said. "It's the demon. Step inside the circle, but be careful not to harm the writing."

Peter lifted the hem of his garment and stepped over the chalk lines. The circle encompassed almost the entire breadth of the room. The triangle containing the music box and the basin of holy water were both within reach from within its protective borders.

The house trembled again, and the cries of the servants could be heard from other parts of the house, muffled and distant, as if reaching Diego's ears from underwater. Sarah bent and blew on the charcoal in the cauldron, her breath energizing the burning of the herbs. "Come to mother," she said. "Join us in the circle, Annie. Appear among us now."

There seemed to be no response to the command. The smoke continued flowing in a wavering stream, gathering in the peak of the room. But just when Diego felt sure that Annie was defying her mother's wishes, the fumes twisted, looped in on themselves, and took on the shape of a young woman in a nightgown. Within a moment, she looked almost as solid as her mother, though she wore white and her mother black, which, if anything, made her appear even more present in the moonlight. Diego was tempted to reach out and touch her, to see if the strands of smoke would unravel, but he resisted. When he had seen his sister manifest from this same cauldron in the seance room, she had been nowhere near as solid. He didn't know if Annie's solidity was owed to the celestial conditions of the night, or the years her mother had invested in reinforcing her presence on the material plane. He supposed it didn't matter. She was here, safe in the circle, and he felt certain that if he were to anoint her head with holy water from the basin, the droplets would bead on her forehead and hair.

But though the girl's physical form was so plainly present, her mind seemed somewhere else. She made no acknowledgment of her mother or the priests. Her gaze focused on the door of the room as if she could see through it. Perhaps she could see through every wall and beam of the house and every other solid object to the end of the Earth. Diego had never encountered anything quite like her. He reminded himself that he was ignorant of her true nature and powers. But he didn't think her gaze was focused on the ends of the earth—he thought it was focused on the approaching demon.

Another crash resounded through the floor. The house shuddered as if struck like a drum, and cries of distress from below flared up again like sparks from a bonfire. Then another crash, and another, until the impression was of approaching footsteps, and now a cacophony of mechanical sounds arose: gears turning, bolts ratcheting, brass and steel slotting into oiled grooves.

Something was climbing the stairs outside the door. When it reached the landing, it stopped, sniffed, and snorted. A dank cloud of foul air wafted through the gap beneath the door. Peter took a step back and almost tripped over Diego, then clutched the older priest's cassock in his white-knuckled grip.

How long they waited in silence, staring at the door, Diego couldn't say. Time seemed to have lost all relevance in the circle. Through his clothes, he touched the amulet that rested on his chest and felt his heart thumping through the metal disk.

The room had grown darker, as if a cloud had passed over the moon with the exhalation of the beast. Coming back to himself, Diego looked around at the candles. None had guttered out. Was it the beginning of the eclipse that cast a shadow over the house? Could the hour before dawn have crept up on them already? It seemed impossible, but so did everything about the situation, and he felt—not for the first time—that he was woefully unprepared for what was to come.

The door exploded inward, the wood splintering and scattering, leaving only ragged fragments still clinging to the hinges. The trio of the living shielded their faces reflexively as the shrapnel crossed the circle. Only Annie remained impassive as the debris passed through her glowing visage, rippling her flesh, but only for a moment, like stones cast in a pond.

Diego expected to see a towering creature of metal filling the doorframe. Instead, a roiling cloud of black smoke rushed in and swept around the circle like the plume from a locomotive. Its form was protean, but shapes emerged from the chaos as it traveled, lending it the identity he expected: Long horns extending from a bullish snout, pistons driving the cloven hooved feet of a beast, human hands tipped with talons, and below the thickly muscled chest, an oily fire burning in a vortex at its belly.

The fragrances of burning wax and herb were overwhelmed by those of gun powder and spilled blood. The cloud gathered in the peak of the cone and the orange fire at its core leapt up to kindle a pair of flaming eyes beneath its crown of horns. Annie tracked its motion with a graceful pirouette, staring up at it with an expression Diego was hesitant to interpret. Did she feel some sympathy for the caged beast? Did she understand the ways in which her fate was bound to it? Whatever she felt, it didn't look like fear. Peter, on the other hand, cowered on the floor, a silver crucifix clenched in his fist.

Sarah uncorked the bottle and handed it to Diego. She held the shotgun shell aloft. Moloch's flaming eyes flashed as the furnace in his belly coughed up a plume of fire. Once the creature's attention was fixed upon the shining fetish, Sarah knelt and raised the lid of the music box. The lilting melody chimed out as she placed the shotgun shell inside the box, the grave dirt spilling onto the blue velvet interior, the air rippling around her.

Diego raised his hands and intoned, "By the Lord Adonai and in the name of the archangel Michael, I constrain thee, Moloch, and bind thee to the triangle of art. In the name of Yeheshua, the living God made flesh, I command thee!"

He pointed the mouth of the bottle toward the music box to capture the djinn, but the distortion of the air hovered around Sarah's contorted face. It condensed into a forked tongue of white mist fighting to penetrate her nostrils. She resisted it, but he felt helpless to aid her in the struggle. If the blood-written name was insufficient bait to draw the djinn into the bottle, the dirt-packed shell insufficient to lure Moloch down into the music box, then they were in for a battle with two loose, vengeful spirits at once. Sarah had been so confident of her plan, but it was fatally flawed. The powers they sought to control were too great.

Sarah's face twisted in pain, and Diego saw the moment when her resistance to the invading spirit broke, her features transforming as the djinn surged through her nostrils and into her lungs. Her temples grew steep and arched, as if the very bone structure had been altered. Her jaw unhinged and her mouth dropped open. Even her teeth appeared to have grown sharper when she hissed at him, her eyes glazed with pale blue cataracts. Her breath smelled like rotten meat.

Peter recited the Lord's prayer, though it had no apparent effect on either of the hostile forces in the room. Diego reached past him and dipped his fingers into the holy water, then lunged forward and flicked droplets at Sarah's face. The water sizzled on her skin. Her eyes flashed with rage and her hand lashed out and raked across his face, her nails gouging his cheek. He winced at the pain but remained steadfast. He pressed the black bottle to her lips.

Maybe the pain inflicted by the holy water gave her an opening to momentarily seize control of her body, or maybe she seized the reins by force of will. In any event, Diego nearly cried out in triumph when Sarah exhaled, emptying her lungs into the bottle.

With the outpouring of breath, the djinn drained from her features. Diego corked the bottle with trembling hands, then spun around and seized a dripping taper from the nearest branch of a candelabra. He sealed the cork with wax, then rolled the bottle across the floor, away from the circle.

The chiming melody of the music box continued, discordant against the mechanical symphony issuing from the black cloud gathered above the triangle.

Diego gasped for breath in the smoke filled room, the taste of iron, char, and feces lining his throat and sinuses. He'd never fought in a war, but knew this must be the stink of the battlefield. And yet, it was also familiar—the smell of a burning house and a roasting child.

Above Winchester House, the moon waned to a thin crescent of cold fire, then vanished, a dark disc in a field of stars. The fearful voices of the servants and the dire barking of the dog fell silent. In the witch's cap, the black cloud unfurled vast wings that billowed from the cone, extinguishing the candles until the only points of light were the orange embers of the demon's eyes and the filthy fire at its core. Diego saw tormented souls writhing in agony in that furnace, a winding river of them, stretching into infinity.

Beside him, Sarah looked frail, unsteady on her feet. She had taken up the broom he'd seen leaning against the wall and now held it poised to slam the lid of the music box shut. But first they needed to draw the demon down into it. The bait had attracted it, but the hour of its greatest strength had also arrived. Did it sense the trap? Diego had no concept of the workings of its alien mind. Was it cunning? Or did it operate on mechanical impulse and animal instinct? Would its appetite for the residual suffering of the murdered girl draw it down into the box with the artifacts of her slaughter? Or having attracted it like fishermen with a bucket of chum in the water, would they now need to constrain it with hooks and nets?

As if in answer to the question, Sarah whispered an incantation, and the spiderweb patterns in the Tiffany glass panes lit up around them, a lattice of cerulean lines.

"By the Father, the Son, and the Holy Ghost, I constrain you to this triangle," Diego intoned. "By the flaming sword of the archangel Michael, I command you to obey."

Sarah continued her chant, a droning stream of barbarous words.

Diego was vaguely aware of Peter, kneeling on the floor with his hands over his ears, moaning at the blasphemy.

The roiling cloud flashed defiance as it descended into the triangle, burnishing the silver box with orange fire.

Peter tugged at the hem of Diego's garment and shouted in his face. "Stop it, Father! Cast it out! You can't let her keep feeding it. The souls of the dead are *not* yours to give!"

Diego met Peter's desperate, pleading eyes. It was an impossible conundrum and there was no time for argument. "We cannot let it loose!" he shouted. Then turning back to the plume of oily smoke hovering over the triangle, he traced a cross in the air and said, "In the name of the Father..."

The face in the cloud became that of his father, twisted with grief and drunken rage. The priest recoiled at the sight.

"You think the Almighty listens to *you?*" his father said. "A filthy sinner?"

"And the Son..."

"Your jism boils on your sister's charred flesh in Hell!"

"And the Holy Ghost..."

"You came while she burned."

Diego pulled the amulet from under his shirt, brandished it at the demon, and cried, "By all the powers of Heaven, I bind you to this box!"

The form of his father's face blurred in a whirlwind. The black smoke formed a funnel above the music box, the melody accelerating, as if the energy of the demon were driving the mechanism harder. Sarah raised the bristled end of the broom, prepared to bring it down on the lid, but at that moment, Annie, who until now had stood as still as a garden statue at the center of the circle, reached out and shoved Peter by the shoulders toward her mother.

The young priest grappled with the broom handle, yanking it back before the descending arc of the bristles could reach the box and slam the lid shut. The broom raked across the floor, smearing the chalk lines and breaking the triangle. Sarah fell to the floor and let go of the shaft. Moloch erupted from the silver box, sending it skittering across the floor to ricochet off the nearest wall, the melody winding down feebly to silence.

Red light spread like a bloodstain through the cloud, forming horns, wings, and outstretched arms. The webs of light from the Tiffany glass panes burned blue in defiance against it.

Diego stared transfixed at the demon thrashing in its cage. They may have failed for the moment to trap it in the box, but it was trapped in the room nonetheless. Amid the din of machinery, he heard the sound of a rifle bolt, close to his ear.

Peter had taken the gun from the floor at the base of the triangle.

He braced the stock against his shoulder and fired, shattering one of the webbed panes and the clear window in the wall beyond it.

The web of light encircling the room flickered out.

Through the south window, dawn seeped into the sky. The moon hung low over the horizon, its face still veiled in shadow. The demon condensed and whirled around the room one last time before streaming out through the broken window and vanishing over the treetops, leaving the candle flames extinguished in its wake.

Sarah, on her knees, stared up at her daughter's ghost, already fading. Annie held her hands out to touch her mother's upturned palms, but her fingertips looked like wisps of smudged paint trailing in the air, an effect that was spreading throughout the rest of her form. She was coming undone, the details of her features blurring.

"You did this," Sarah said to Peter. Her voice was threadbare. Where Diego had expected rage, there was only regret. "Get out of my house."

Peter made no argument. His eyes fell on the place where the music box lay on its side near the wall. The brass shell casing had spilled a trail of grave dirt. Without a word in his defense, he laid the rifle on the floor and backed out of the room. Diego heard his footsteps echoing down the stairs, picking up pace as they receded.

"Annie. Don't go," Sarah said. "*Please*, darling. Stay with me."

But the ghost made no reply. Diego didn't know if the silence was a choice or a constraint of her deteriorating condition. The covenant had been broken. The demon had fled. The bubble that had sustained the girl's spirit for decades had burst. Whatever Winchester House might be in the future, it would not be a safe harbor for the departed.

Diego scooped a cupped handful of holy water from the basin and poured it over Annie's dissolving head. "In the name of the Father, the Son, and the Holy Ghost," he said.

The droplets pattered on the chalk-dusted floorboards like a mother's tears.

CHAPTER TWENTY-TWO

Father Diego's confessional hour was almost over. He had sent the last boy on his way with a penance of one rosary to atone for cheating on an exam—which *was* a kind of theft if a minor one—and before leaving the booth, the boy had told the priest that he was the last in line. Muscles aching from the hard bench, Diego checked his watch and decided he would leave if no latecomers arrived in the next three minutes. It was almost lunch hour at the college, and past experience told him that the Lord had yet to make a young man who would skip a meal to unburden his soul of petty sins. In his estimation, they *were* petty, all of them, no matter how large they loomed in the minds of those too young for any sense of proportion. At least, if the students of Santa Clara were guilty of stronger sins, they had no intention of confessing them to him.

He was pondering this when the sound of familiar shuffling footsteps approached the curtained booth from the last row of pews, stopping his breath in his chest.

It couldn't be...

Whoever it was had apparently waited some time for the line of boys to thin out. Diego imagined a diminutive figure, clad in black, her face hidden beneath a widow's lace veil. His heart sped up as the shuffling footsteps drew near. Sarah Winchester had driven him from her house, her man Clyde pushing him out the door as roughly as he'd been pulled in when he'd first arrived uninvited. She'd been in a state of shock, bereft, and beyond all reason. As if anything they'd done together had been within the bounds of reason. He'd been certain he would never see her again. And now, after a month of working to put the monumental failure behind him, here she was on *his* doorstep, their roles reversed.

He wondered if she had crossed paths with Peter on her way to the chapel. Diego had not spoken to the young scholastic about their final moments at the Winchester House in the weeks that had passed since their return, and the tension of things unsaid still hung in the air between them when they were required to work and pray together. The hour would come when Diego would need to confront Peter, but the words required to make him see what he had done remained elusive. At least, as far as Diego could tell, Peter had refrained from telling Father Xavier all that had transpired at the house. For that, he was grateful.

He wondered, with some alarm, if Mrs. Winchester had visited Father Xavier's office on her way to the chapel. Had she made her promised donation to the mission in person? She was the sort of lady who would be unlikely to forgo such a formality. Diego shuddered at the thought of a conversation between the two about what services he had performed for her. On the other hand, she did have her own privacy to protect.

The thick red curtain swished, the bench creaked, and having settled, the lady cleared her throat. Through the partition screen, a familiar voice reached his ears. "Father forgive me for I have sinned. This is my first confession."

"Are you Catholic?"

"No, Father. Baptist."

"Protestants don't recognize the sacrament of confession."

"Be that as it may, I wish to confess to you. Will you hear my confession?"

He hesitated. "I will. And so will the Lord."

"I have made sacrifices to strange gods, Father."

He let the statement hang in the air without comment. After a pause, she continued. "I coveted the soul of my infant daughter when the Lord tried to take her from me. I concealed her from the Lord so that she might grow in the darkness like a moon flower, watered with the blood of innocents. I fed the demon Moloch on a portion of that bloodshed reaped from the machinery of murder, and I confined the demon to my house—a prison and a temple beyond the jurisdiction of heaven and hell. I confess these sins, though I do not regret them, for I believe they were the lesser evil."

"There is no atonement without remorse. You must repent your si–"

"I have many regrets, Father. But I do not repent. Let me speak my piece."

"Continue."

"I treated you poorly, and for that I am sorry. I believe that your concern for my daughter's soul was sincere. When I embarked on the construction of my house and sealed my covenant, I did so for selfish reasons. But as I came to understand the consequences of my work, I found myself confronted with greater evils than those I had wrought. That my daughter should be condemned if ever she escaped the labyrinth was a horror I could not abide. That a drop of water should be all that stood between her and everlasting life is the cruel joke of a perverse god. I stand by that judgment."

"This is no confession. You sin more with every word! This is a house of God. You speak through me to *Him*."

"Then let me remind the Almighty of why I bargained with the lowest of his creations. It was to amend his monstrous laws. But hear me, Father. Hear the cost of *our* failure, yours and mine. Hear the price of the righteous judgment of young Peter."

Diego took a deep breath and expelled it. He wiped his clammy hands across his knees and waited for the lady to continue.

"I won't lie and tell you that I regretted a single hour of my time with Annie. But I soon realized I'd caught a tiger by the tail. The longer I held the demon, the more ravenous it became. Surviving on blood squeezed from rags...unable to prowl the larger world, to possess men and inspire violence. But despite the meager nourishment provided by the terms of the pact, the beast grew strong in captivity. The house... the way it focused celestial rays, granted the beast power that waxed like the moon. An irony then, to discover that the bonds which constrained it were weakest when the moon was eclipsed.

"Three years ago, on April 11th, 1903, there was a near total lunar eclipse at dusk, and the demon tested its growing strength against my web. The house shook, but my neighbors were spared the effects of the quake. The damage to Winchester House was minor.

"When the hour passed, and the violence settled. I believed the wards had held, that Moloch had never breached the wall of the maze.

"Some months later, I learned I was mistaken. The news reached me from a small town in Kansas. Winfield, it was called. A place I'd never heard of. But the tragedy of August 13 was so great that it was carried by newspapers across the country. The eclipse shook my house in the spring, but the repercussions followed that summer. You may rightly wonder how I knew these events were connected. How I knew the beast had escaped the labyrinth, however briefly. It was the date that convinced me. The thirteenth. My mystic number, like a signature on the wretched event. But I also believe that was how long it took for the poison seed the demon had planted in the mind of a madman to germinate, take root, and flourish. Four lunar cycles.

"What happened on August thirteenth?"

"A mass murder by rifle. The worst ever in America outside of war. I've collected every newspaper that covered it, from across the entire country. Read them until the ink smeared beyond comprehension. I can see it so vividly in my mind. Like a moving picture from a kinetograph."

The rifle heiress smoothed her skirts, drew a deep breath, and told the tale.

When she'd finished, the priest sat in stunned silence.

"Are you still there, Father?"

"Yes." A husky whisper. He cleared his throat. "Yes, I'm still here."

"It will happen again," she said. "I'm sure of it. Now that the beast is free, it will happen again. And again. That is the price of our failure to constrain it." Her voice trembled. "If I seek God's forgiveness for anything, it is that."

"Annie knew," Diego said. "I don't know if she spoke to me in a dream or while I wandered your house awake at night, but she showed me windows, like tarot cards, places where tragedy would strike if Moloch escaped."

Silence settled on the confessional while Sarah absorbed this.

"How many were there?" she asked at last. "How many windows?" He had never heard her sound so weak.

"Sarah... It has always been God's work for us to confront evil where we find it in the world. It was never his intention that you should trap it by your own designs."

"How many?" she asked again.

"Too many," he replied, and made the sign of the cross.

"Father?"

"Yes?"

"Do you believe it worked?"

"I'm sorry?"

"The baptism. Do you believe it worked? Do you believe it will save Annie from damnation?"

Now it was his turn to struggle in silence. He ran his thumb over the contours of the scar tissue that marred his wrist. "I pray that it will, Sarah. I pray that it will."

EPILOGUE

There was no forerunner, no inspiration among men. He was the first. He would not be the last.

Gilbert Twigg had been planning for weeks, but the dark thing whispering in his mind had been growing for months. They had called him sick in the Philippines. That army doctor had conspired against him and said he was a monster. But that wasn't fair. They'd had it out for him. He'd only been doing his job that he'd been trained to do, and suffering like any soldier would in a jungle blood bath.

What would those pricks say if they could see him now? Bowdish and Woods. If they thought he was a monster back then, what would they say now? Sure, he had his fair share of rage back then, but he didn't have the shadow in him, not yet. The war blew holes in people. A lot of fine young men. A lot of gooks, too. Women. Children. Twigg had made a lot of those holes himself. That was the job. And the war had left a big old whistling one in him, too, only it wasn't in his flesh; it was in his soul. The soul that first got a tear in it when that slut bitch Jessie Hamilton called off their engagement. And then, one night last April on the full moon, a horned thing that smelled like iron and char had burrowed into that hole while he slept and made a nest inside him. Laid a black egg in it.

He'd gotten down on one knee for Jessie, he had. And she'd said yes. You didn't go back on a thing like that. Not after a man knelt like a beggar before you and offered you his life. And that wasn't even the worst of it, breaking off their engagement. No, she'd conspired against him, too. Made it so he couldn't even get a job in this town when he finally came back after the war and his time in Montana.

He had good skills. He'd worked as a telephone operator in the Army. But they turned him down for a job as a lineman back in Winfield. Turned him down at the Water Works, too. And he knew it was because that cocksucker Ernest Cramer still knew people there. He'd run off with Jessie to Wichita and married her, but he still had friends in Winfield who saw to it that Crazy Twigg couldn't even get a job.

Well, that was fine and dandy. He'd hardly been treated any better out west. Like people could smell something on him. Smell the stink of rejection. He'd served with honor and had the papers to prove it, but was there a wife waiting for him back in Kansas? A job? No. All he had was a shitty little room in the Thompson block that smelled like mold.

Well, he'd given himself *a job just two weeks ago when he walked into Winfield & Miller General Goods and Hardware and bought a twelve gauge double-barrel shotgun and a hundred shells, each loaded with twelve bullets.*

Mr. Winfield himself had stuck his nose into the transaction, wanting to know what he was going to do with all that ammo. Twigg answered him honest, said he hadn't decided yet. Because he hadn't at the time. All he knew was that he was going to give himself a new job. Or maybe it was the thing coiled in his chest with the horns that was giving him a job. It was getting harder to tell which ideas were his and which came from that other thing. It was all a bit murky, which voice was his own. But the job itself was crystal clear. More clear than anything since Jessie said yes to him before she said no. He was going to be a teacher. He was going to teach people a lesson.

He didn't know which people would be his first students when he purchased the shotgun and the five dollar .32 caliber pistol at the hardware store. The answer came later, and it was also crystal clear: he was going to give his first lesson at the most crowded place in town—the weekly brass band concert on Thursday night. That was one fine band, even if their leader, W.H. Caman was a backstabbing son-of-a-bitch who'd worked to keep Twigg from getting hired at the phone company. They played all the hits, they did. Damned near the whole town turned out to listen on Thursday nights.

Looked like a few thousand people easy, milling around the bandstand in the dark after dusk, waiting for the musicians to strike up a tune. Electric street lamps had yet to come to Winfield, Kansas, and Twigg thanked the shadow coiled in his chest for that. The darkness made it easy to pull his cart up into the alley behind Milligan's shoe store without anyone noticing.

Beneath a canvas tarp draped over the cart was the shotgun and shells, along with enough black powder and nitroglycerine to blow up the whole bandstand. He hadn't decided yet if he'd set the wagon off, but it was good to have options. It looked too crowded to wheel it any closer while the band tuned up, and he decided not to risk drawing attention. No one had given his buckskin hunting jacket a second look, even in the August heat, but he did have a reputation for a few loose screws, and he thought it best not to forfeit the element of surprise.

Twigg reached under the canvas and took out the rifle. When he turned around, there was a boy standing in the mouth of the alley, just staring at him with a loose jaw, the crowd shifting around behind him to make way for the musicians taking their places on the gazebo. Did the kid recognize him? Did the boy's parents tell stories about Crazy Twigg at the dinner table? Hard to tell.

"What are you gonna do with that gun, Mister?"

"I am going to do some tall shooting, son. And you had better run."

The boy froze.

Twigg loaded the firearm. "I wonder if I can get Caman," he said.

The boy blinked, and then scampered away around the corner of the shoe shop. Twigg emerged from the alley near the corner of West Ninth and Main as the band was passing their sheet music around.

"I'll kill every one of you!" Twigg shouted. He dropped to his left knee—just like he'd done for Jessie Hamilton—and aimed the long gun.

The first shot missed Caman and grazed the back of a horse. The animal reared up with a whinny and bolted away. Twigg adjusted for the recoil, taking a step back with each subsequent shot and dropping low, just as he'd been trained to do when picking off gooks. The second shot sent pellets through the drummer's shoulder and gut, and the man slumped over like a rag doll, bleeding out onto his snare. It looked like a plate of tomato sauce. The third shot shattered the horn of a tuba, sending brass shrapnel into the face of the player cradling the instrument in his lap.

The band scattered, wide-eyed cowards tripping over music stands, instruments, and each other. A woman screamed, and the shrill sound uncorked the assembled crowd like a shaken bottle of champaign. After that, it was mayhem.

The dark thing uncoiled from the cavity in Twigg's chest and stretched up and over him like the cobra sheltering the Buddha on that statue he'd seen abroad. The long horns of a steer grew from the top of his shadow, cast on the street by the light from a shop window.

He raised his Winchester.

Six bullets shattered the head and chest of a man standing on the steps of the National Bank, peppering the stonework behind him. His brains slid out of his broken skull and hit the concrete before the rest of his body landed on them with a splat.

Twigg dropped again and put three bullets through the back of a running man, one into the head of another.

He recognized Dawson Billiter, the local barber standing frozen in shock in front of Craig's Bookshop, and put slugs through his neck and bowels before reloading and dropping another three men who'd just spilled out the stairwell of the Odd Fellows Hall.

Sixteen-year-old Roy Davis took the next bullet to the gut. The boy fell to his knees trying to keep his insides inside while a muddy pool of blood and shit spread around him in the street.

Twigg's aim was good. He'd been decorated for it before they turned on him. Those center mass shots were the most reliable killers, but he also got in plenty of less lethal hits: knees and shoulders, two women in their necks, a third in the thigh. A man who stepped in to help them got two of his fingers blown clean off for his trouble and waved the spraying stumps around screaming.

Twigg laughed at the sight. It was like watching clowns at the circus.

His laughter dried up though, when he saw that negro cop, George Nichols, approaching from the end of the alley he'd been drawing back into with each retreating step. Nichols, on night watch patrol, was armed with both a rifle and a .44 sidearm. Worst of all, the man didn't look scared.

Twigg turned and ran to his wagon. There was no time to wheel it out and light it up. He could hear the cop's footsteps getting closer, pounding the bricks over the din of the panicked crowd. Twigg drew the .32, held it to his temple, and pulled the trigger. The last thing he saw, behind the approaching lawman, was a flaming man made of bronze with the head of a bull, down on all fours licking blood and brains off the street. It faded to black as the void claimed him.

BLEW OFF HIS HEAD

Used a Winchester Rifle to Accomplish the Ghastly Act.

Special by Herald leased wire.

RENO, Nev., December 28.—Lieutenant Gordon Freeman, late of the First Nevada cavalry that did service in the Philippines, committed suicide last night by blowing the top of his head off with a Winchester rifle.

Lieutenant Freeman was subject to fits of despondency, accompanied by suicidal mania. He was the soul of honor and greatly respected and loved by every one of the ninety-two who composed his company and was very popular. Lieutenant Freeman was a native of Missouri, aged 30 years.

The Rosy Cross in Tibet.

Any of the British officers now on the road to Lhasa who may happen to be Freemasons have, perhaps, just an outside chance of solving an interesting question. For there are those who believe that the high Rosicrucian adepts, having emigrated to the east about the beginning o' the seventeenth century, still inhabit the Tibetan plateaus today, and some of the mysteries of Freemasonry have been supposed to have been acquired from the Rosicrucians. If they ever existed, the Rosicrucians were a secret society possessing the art of turning baser metals into gold, and vowed themselves to gratuitous healing of the sick. Skeptics, however, maintain that there never was such a society, but that it was invented as a ponderous joke by a learned seventeenth century treatise writer.—London Chronicle.

Killed by a Stray Bullet.

MODESTO, January 5.—The mystery surrounding the death of Lafayette Steele at his ranch while plowing Tuesday afternoon has probably been cleared up. At the inquest Fred Reynolds, a neighboring farmer, testified that he, at about the time of the killing, had fired at a hawk in a tree distant over half a mile, with a Winchester rifle, and missed the mark. The bullet was found in Steele's heart and one from the rifle corresponds in every particular. No arrest has been made.

Deed of a Coward.

PLACERVILLE, Nov. 13.—This evening near Shingle Springs in this county, Jack Nickle shot and killed both his wife and mother-in-law with a Winchester rifle. Afterwards he removed the shoe from his right foot and with his toes discharged the rifle at his own breast causing death almost instantly.

SENT TO HAPPY HUNTING GROUNDS BY SHOT FROM A WINCHESTER RIFLE.

Bill Kirk, an Indian living on the Julian sheep camp near Fruto, was sent to the happy hunting grounds yesterday by a shot from a Winchester rifle in the hands of his 12-year-old stepson, Carol Cook, and was not even arrested for the crime, because he acted in self defense and was exonerated by the coroner's jury.

They tell us that the only "good Indian" is a "dead Indian" and Bill Kirk is now a "good Indian" all right enough.

According to the story, as brought to Willows, Bill Kirk was in the habit of beating his wife (just for exercise) and Carol Cook, his stepson, objects to that relaxation of his make believe father.—Willows Journal.

Moloch Wins at Los Angeles.

LOS ANGELES, June 25.—In the coursing at Agricultural Park to-day, the card being a thirty-two dog open stake, Moloch won first money, Nashville second, Stella B third, Perseus fourth. The rest divided. There were several surprises, and the short-enders fared well, notably in the Kitty Scott-Belle of Frisco course, an 8 to 1 shot. The courses were, as a rule, long ones, and staying qualities counted for almost as much as speed. The attendance was only fair.

Little Girl Kills Brother.

TACOMA, July 31.—A very sad tragedy is reported from Addy, a small town in Stevens County, near Colville. George Derringer, aged 14 years, died last night from the effects of a gunshot wound received two nights previously. His sister, aged 8 years, picked up the boy's Winchester rifle, which George had stood in a corner, and playfully pointed it at his head. He sprang toward her to take the rifle away, but before he succeeeded she had pulled the trigger and discharged the gun. The bullet entered the boy's forehead above the left eye and passed entirely through his head.

TRAGEDY IN MISSISSIPPI.

Two Farmers Fight a Duel With Winchester Rifles.

COFFEEVILLE (Miss.), Sept. 9.—W. J. Johnson and John Wilbourn, two prominent farmers, fought a duel with Winchester rifles at fifty yards near here to-day, which resulted in Johnson's death.

A feud has existed between the men for some time. They owned adjoining farms, and when they met to-day a quarrel arose. There was only one witness to the affair. Wilbourn and the witness, Sam Lewis, had been hunting squirrels, and while returning home they met Johnson armed with a Winchester rifle. A dispute arose, and Johnson opened fire on Wilbourn without warning. Wilbourn returned the fire, and a regular fusillade was kept up between them, which resulted in Johnson being pierced with four balls, Wilbourn escaping without injury.

Wilbourn has been placed in jail. He claims that it was a case of self-defense.

RECLUSE HEIRESS WILL ENTER COURT

Mrs. Sarah L. Winchester, Millionairess, Sues Contractor E. W. McLellan

Woman Whose Pastime Is Building Fantastical Homes Is Stanch Spiritualist

REDWOOD CITY, Jan. 9.—Sarah L. Winchester, heiress to the vast wealth of the Winchester arms company, has at last decided to throw her cloak of mystery aside.

Mrs. Winchester has stasted an action through her attorneys against E. W. McClellan of Burlingame, the contractor, for the purpose of securing 98 acres of land now held by McClellan and other defendants near Burlingame. The complaint alleges that the defendants' lease expired on the first of the year, but claims that they still hold possession of the property in question and refuse to give it up. Mrs. Winchester further avers in her complaint that the property was damaged by the removal of a quantity of gravel from the land and by the custom of allowing a herd of cows to graze upon it. She asks for rent amounting to $33 and damages in the sum of $900.

The present contention has arisen over a large tract of what was formerly marsh land near the polo field of Francis J. Carolan, the Burlingame clubman, and which was bought by Mrs. Winchester a number of years ago with the idea of erecting the finest country home in the west.

An immense concrete seawall was constructed to keep out the encroaching tides of the bay, the man who is now being sued by Mrs. Winchester carrying out the work. Throughout the entire tract of land a costly system of canals with proper floodgates was constructed through which the Winchester private fleet of launches and yachts were to wend their way.

An avowed spiritualist, Mrs. Winchester soon became tired of her costly toy and after constructing a boathouse and erecting a huge mountain of earth upon which the mansion was to be erected where it could overlook the entire canal system of the estate and the bay, work was stopped. San Mateo, Fair Oaks and San Jose then came to know of Mrs. Winchester, although her existence was skeptically regarded, so seldom was Mrs. Winchester seen.

Through all the years that she has been a resident of California, Mrs. Winchester has retained her property acquiring mania, ever being on the verge of completing elaborate country cottages or fantastical palaces. San Jose has known her longest, where Mrs. Winchester remains today secluded in her mansion on the Los Gatos road, surrounded by trusty oriental servants, the grounds being further guarded by a pack of bloodhounds. Believing that if she ever completes the construction of the home in which she lives her death will shortly follow, the lonely heiress to millions has found her sole pleasure during the last seven years in directing the efforts of workmen who are called upon to construct one month what they destroy the next.

NEGRO TAYLOR FOUND GUILTY.

KANSAS CITY (Mo.), October 5.—Bud Taylor, who last March shot and killed Miss Ruth Malard, a former sweetheart, was tonight found guilty of murder in the first degree. The jury was out only fifty-five minutes. The defense made a strong plea of insanity. Taylor had secured a Winchester rifle and lay in wait for her. He secured a position in a second story window on West Ninth street in a busy part of the city and waited. Finally she started across the street with her sister. Taylor rested his rifle on the window sill and took deliberate aim. He fired twice and both shots took effect, Miss Millard falling dead while her sister was untouched.

OUR NEIGHBORING COUNTIES.

CALAVERAS.

From Our Exchanges.

On Thursday afternoon Geo. Cox went to Sheep Ranch and gave himself up to the authorities, stating that he had killed his son-in, law, H. G. Cook. Cox, when taken into custody had a Winchester rifle, a Winchester revolver, a dirk knife with a ten inch blade, and a coat of armor, the latter is made of steel wire, and weighs about 25 lbs. From the evidence of Mrs Cox, before the coroner's inquest it appears that Cox, Cook and one of the children were eating dinner. Cox got up from the table and went through a hall into a bedroom and taking his Winchester rifle, he stepped to the door leading from the hall to the dining room, and fired a shot at Cook, who was seated at the dinner table. The bullet struck Cook in the left breast, and passed through his body. Cook stood up and then fell to the floor, Cox firing another shot as Cook fell, which struck the table in front of the little boy. Mrs Cox and Mrs Cook were in the room when the second shot was fired and before Cox had reloaded his rifle the third time Mrs Cook sprang across the room and caught hold of the gun and pushed Cox into the hall. During the struggle Cox kicked his daughter and struck her on the head with the rifle, which knocked her down, but she got up and pushed Cox out of the house and locked the door. Cox went to a window and pointed his rifle at Mrs Cook, and swore he was prepared for any of them. In all probability Cox would have killed his wife and daughter had not the latter caught the assassin and put him out of the house by main strength. There appears to have been no cause whatever for committing the murder. There had not been an angry word spoken that day, or on any previous occasion by either of the men to one another. The coroner's jury charged Cox with having committed a cold-blooded murder.

A VOICE FROM THE GRAVE.

How a Young Woman Heard Her Father's Speech in a Phonograph.

A pathetic story is that told in connection with the phonograph. A judge in a southern state came to Cincinnati not long ago, says a writer in the Commercial. He had never heard the phonograph. When he visited an office he spoke into the funnel, and was amazed and amused to hear his own voice repeated afterward through the tubes of the machine.

Two days after he returned home he died suddenly. His daughter came to Cincinnati on business, and while here a friend took her to hear a phonograph. It was a curious coincidence that she should have been escorted to the very office her father had visited but a short time before. The young woman, who was in deep mourning, was very much entertained by some of the musical selections the phonograph repeated.

The operator afterward picked up a cylinder from a pile, placed it in the phonograph, and said: "Listen to this." The young woman placed the tubes again to her ear, the bar was pulled out and the cylinder began to revolve. Before a dozen words had been repeated the woman in black swooned. Not until she recovered was the cause of her fainting known.

The voice that had come to her ears from the phonograph was that of her dead father. It was as a voice from the grave. She afterward purchased a phonograph, and the cylinder containing her father's speech was given to her. It is carefully cherished in her southern home.

WORSTED IN A FIGHT, HE USES A RIFLE

FORT BRAGG, July 25.—Caleb Greenwood, a young man, was killed by "Gyp" Young at the Hollow Tree wood settlement, about fifty miles north of this place, yesterday. After a fight, in which Young was worsted, he procured a Winchester rifle and shot Greenwood to death.

A Terrible Crime.

By the Associated Press.

PLACERVILLE, Cal., Nov. 12.—This evening near Shingle Springs in this county, Jack Nickle shot and killed both his wife and mother-in-law with a Winchester rifle. Afterwards he removed the shoe from his right foot and with his toes discharged the rifle at his own breast, killing himself almost instantly.

Carefully Plans His Death.

ANGELS CAMP, April 25.—Joseph Navis of Murphys left his home yesterday morning and went to his blacksmith shop. There he took off his coat and vest and cut a hole in his shirt over the heart. He then tied a cord around an anvil, fastening the other end to the trigger of a Winchester rifle. Placing the muzzle of the rifle to his left breast he pulled the string. The ball passed through his body and came out of the right shoulder, lodging in the shirt sleeve. Navis was not found until last night by his son. He was still grasping the barrel of the rifle. The suicide was 30 years of age.

Shakespeare a Mason.

Dr. Orville W. Owen of Detroit has sent out a little book addressed to the Masonic fraternity, in which he says: "In deciphering the Shakespearian plays (1623 folio edition) and other works of Bacon, for the preparation of 'Sir Francis Bacon's Cipher Story,' I have found unmistakable evidence that the author of them was not only a Mason of high degree, but that he placed in the plays a large portion of the Masonic ritual. Believing this to be of the greatest interest and importance to the brotherhood the following parts of the plays, with the places from which they come, are now given to the order. Understanding fully the obligations under which I rest as a Mason (of the seventh degree), I have taken pains to hide the work that none but the brethren will understand. Francis Bacon, the author of the plays, was a Master Mason, and claims to have been grand master of the Orient and a Rosicrucian knight, and hidden within his works are directions by which it is not difficult to travel into Illyria."

BLEW HER HEAD OFF.

The Desperate Deed of a Jealous Lover Near Cairo.

CAIRO, Ill., Oct. 30.—A sensational murder and suicide took place at Belknap, near here yesterday. A man named Hevotline, having become jealous of his sweetheart, Miss Thurman, met her on the road last evening and taxed her with having other admirers. She remonstrated with him, when he placed a Winchester rifle to her ear and blew her head off. He then turned the rifle to his own head, fired and fell dead beside his victim.

A Skull from Wooden Valley.

"A skull has been found near Wooden Valley, Napa county, and has been left at this office," says the Woodland Mail, "together with some badly-corroded empty brass shells belonging to a 44-calibre Winchester rifle. The finder states that in his opinion the skull is a portion of the skeleton of Pete Olsen, the Wooden Valley murderer. He says that a 44-calibre Winchester rifle was found within fifty feet of where the skull lay, over a year ago. For some time past the finder of the skull had noticed bones lying around in a little hollow near a large boulder, but did not think they were portions of a human body until he happened to see a hog nosing a portion of a femur, or thigh-bone of a man. Then he instituted a search and found the skull, which is now on exhibition at this office."

ACKNOWLEDGMENTS

Special thanks to Joe Morey and Cyrus Wraith Walker at Weird House Press for making this book a reality, to Nick Nafpliotis for valuable editorial notes and story suggestions, and to my family for providing a bright counterpoint to these dark dreams

ABOUT THE AUTHOR

DOUGLAS WYNNE is the author of numerous critically acclaimed horror, thriller, and suspense novels, including *The Devil of Echo Lake* and The SPECTRA Files series. His short fiction was recently collected in *Something in the Water and Other Stories* from Weird House Press. He lives in Massachusetts with his wife and son and a houseful of animals. You can find him on the web at www.douglaswynne.com

WEIRD
HOUSE

www.ingramcontent.com/pod-product-compliance
Lightning Source LLC
Chambersburg PA
CBHW030320020726
47493CB00004B/1101

* 9 7 8 1 9 5 7 1 2 1 4 4 4 *